The *Journey*

To
GAIL
Enjoy

The Joining

The Ainsworth Chronicles Book One

By Frank Talaber

Photo By SueB Photography
Digital ISBNs
Kindle: 9781696461078
Copyright © 2018 by Frank Talaber
Cover art by
Miblart

Also by Frank Talaber

Ainsworth Chronicles
The Joining
The Mystery Of Ms. Teak

Seeds of Ascension
Spirits Awakening
Book Two: Gateways

Short Story Anthology Book:
What I'd Say To Buddha If I Met Him In The Pub
What I'd Say To Einstein If I Met Him On The Dance Floor

Stillwaters Runs Deep: Book
Raven's Lament
The Lure
The Awakening

Standalone
Shuttered Seductions

Watch for more at https://franktalaberpublishedauthor.wordpress.com.

Dedication

To my son, Rory, whose move to Victoria, and our subsequent annual holidays to visit him, introduced me to Victoria and its ghostly goings-on. To my wife Jenny, for aiding and abetting me with her analytical crime solving skills. To the many ghosts of Victoria, thanks for sticking around.

This book wouldn't be possible without you.

To my mom, Judy.

The muse in my life, the determination in my heart, the laugh in my soul. Who raised us, all seven of us, by herself, when she had nothing to give except her heart and soul. But she had us and for her that meant everything.

And to Jean L.

For everything you went through growing up.

May the Blue Fairy always be within.

Dedication

To my son, Rory, whose move to Victoria, and our subsequent annual holidays to visit him, introduced me to Victoria and its ghostly goings-on. To my wife Jenny, for aiding and abetting me with her analytical crime solving skills. To the many ghosts of Victoria, thanks for sticking around.

This book wouldn't be possible without you.

To my mom, Judy.
The muse in my life, the determination in my heart, the laugh in my soul. Who raised us, all seven of us, by herself, when she had nothing to give except her heart and soul. But she had us and for her that meant everything.
And to Jean L.

For everything you went through growing up.

May the Blue Fairy always be within.

Frank Talaber, Writer by Soul.

A natural storyteller, whose compelling thoughts are freed from the depths of the heart and the subconscious before being poured onto the page.

Literature written beyond the realms of genre he is known to grab readers; kicking, screaming, laughing or crying and drag them into his novels.

Enter the literary world of Frank Talaber.

Foreword

For those of you who are new to my books, welcome! What kept you? No, seriously, thank you for buying, or obtaining somehow, my latest muse. I hope you enjoy meeting these characters as much as I did. Some are old friends of mine you've met before, but some are brand new. I'll tell you a bit about their earlier adventures in the *Stillwater Runs Deep* series in the Afterword. But for now, let's get this new party started, shall we?

Prologue

Somewhere in the darkness the coarse flax fibers of the Hangman's

noose sing,
Its hollow voice swinging to the hangman's beckoning. Waiting for the answers
buried into the gurgle of time and the finality
of voices ending.

F*rom the stillness comes a subtle calling. Echoing reminders of what*

remains, Disturbed and unsettled.

~Frank Talaber~

Chapter One

F

ront deskman Samuel Desmond's eyes opened in horror as the wet, naked man thumped towards him bearing only a bath towel, a watch and the look of a man stepping into a warzone. The splodge of soapy footsteps echoed behind him as he thumped down the ornate front staircase of Victoria's Fairmont Empress Hotel.

"Sir, do you realize you are naked in our lobby, dripping soap and water all over our new and *very* expensive Isfahan rugs?"

The man thumped his hand on the counter. Water splattered. "I'm wet, pissed, cold and locked out of my room. Jake Holden, Blanshard suite."

Samuel looked down, bowing to the sheer anger seething in Jake's eyes, and clacked away on his booking computer. He hesitated a moment, pressed the button for the day manager and, summoning up his courage, turned back to Jake while water continued dripping onto the counter.

"It would appear you are not a registered guest. I would need ID to let you back into any suite."

Jake stepped back and opened his towel. "Does it look like I've got any ID on me?"

Samuel's eyes widened in shock. "But I'm not allowed to let anyone in without ID."

Jake re-wrapped the towel, leaned over and grabbed the clerk by the scruff of his neck, effortlessly pulling him over the counter, until all Samuel could see was the man's watch. Mickey Mouse's left hand stood at ten, his right at two.

"The only ID I got are these fingerprints and if you don't let me back in my room your face is about to become an ink blotter. *Kapish?*"

Her private cellphone rang as Carol Ainsworth, ostensibly Day Manager, actually undercover cop on assignment, was about to bolt from her office in response to Samuel's panic button. She wasn't sure what she'd expected to find but a naked six-foot giant of a man yelling into Samuel's face and half dragging him across the counter wasn't on her list of possibilities, not in a world-class hotel.

Forgot to turn off my phone. Carol glanced at the text from her sister and the first word was

Urgent. She paused, her sister wasn't a person to send idle chat. "Urgent! Nathan has vanished."

As she quickly texted back Samuel struggled to reach the buzzer.

"Will call ASAP."

Carol turned off her phone and quickly marched over to the front desk. Her and her sister, Barbara, didn't talk much but Barb was never one to overreact. Whatever happened to her nephew must be serious.

So much for a quiet first day on the job. Okay, calm down. One thing at a time.

"Yes, sir, how may I help you?" She dropped her hand to gain comfort in the holster she didn't have on this assignment. *Damn it! Shouldn't have listened to the morons telling me not to carry!* Her cop instinct took over, mentally noting every detail of any possible importance. *White Caucasian, six two, light tan, light brown hair, Mickey Mouse watch on left wrist, ripped to the max. Probable weightlifter strung out on steroids. Jeez, I might as well be back on the skid rows of Vancouver! What the hell would a real hotel manager be doing right now?*

She tried to think of something, anything, she'd learned in the week of intense hotel management training they'd put her through in preparation for this assignment that might be of any possible use to her in this situation. As a street cop she'd just chop him across the back of the knees and slap the cuffs on him as he fell. Somehow that didn't seem like the way to treat a guest of this grand establishment. *Plan B's definitely lock him up and then ask questions, though.*

"I asked for the hotel manager," he growled.

Carol glanced around the newly refurbished lobby, with its gold balustrades and pastel shaded panels. Fortunately, no other guests were milling around this time of the afternoon so hopefully this wouldn't turn into a full-blown media fiasco. That was the *last* thing she needed, considering the guests who'd be arriving in the next little while.

"What seems to be the problem here?" She folded her arms in front of her.

"I said I asked for the—"

"And I, sir, *am* the hotel manager, and before I discuss anything with you, you will let go of my desk clerk." She caught the nearly imperceptible rise of his eyebrows. "And gently. The Fairmont Victoria Empress Hotel does not take kindly to hotel guests strolling naked in public areas, nor do we care to have them accosting our front desk staff." His eyebrow raised higher as he glared at her.

Carol had certainly handled bigger men. She stood her ground and glared back. If she hadn't been on assignment, she'd have told him to drop the desk clerk before she shoved his eyebrows so far up his ass it'd take a laser scope to get them out, but since she was, she didn't.

The glare-down continued as Samuel's face turned redder. Finally, Jake broke eye-contact and glanced down at her name tag. Carol had established control. She allowed herself to breathe.

Time to press her advantage home.

"I *said* Let. Him. Go. And I'm not telling you a third time."

Jake lowered Samuel to the ground. "Sorry, didn't expect a skirt. I mean a female manager." And he certainly hadn't expected a gorgeous brunette. She even looked good in her standard designed-for-all-shapes-and-sizes corporate uniform. She wasn't intimidated in the least, not by his size or his state of undress. In fact, she was absolutely in control of the situation. Something very sexy in that. He liked his women assertive. Her eyes, though. Something in her eyes grabbed him right in the gut. Too much knowledge of the world and how bad it could be, that was it. He'd learned long ago to read people's faces in his career, it'd saved his life many times when undercover.

Something about this woman he knew almost nothing about stirred his blood and wearing just a bath towel probably wasn't such a good idea. Especially in light of what he *did* know about her. She was undoubtedly Canadian undercover detective on duty Carol Ainsworth. *Our file reports don't do her justice.*

"Jake Holden, and you have my apology. I've been overstressed at work recently and decided to take a relaxing trip here." He extended his hand. It was partly the truth, he'd taken this assignment to get away from LA, a place where you always had to watch your back and no man was a friend. *Especially the crazy ones strung out on drugs.*

She made sure Samuel was breathing well on his own before she shook hands. The touch sent an erotic jolt through him. He glanced down and smiled. *No ring. Possibilities.*

"Apology accepted. Carol Moore, Day Manager of the Fairmount Empress Hotel." Carol studied Jake. She liked what she saw. And then again, she didn't. Those dark eyes of his — they reminded her of places she hadn't been and feelings she hadn't felt in a long time. Not since Alan, her fiancé, with the same dark, dangerous eyes she fell in love with was shot dead on duty six years ago. *It's been too long. Too damn long. So get a grip, get over it, and get on with it.*

I've got possibly even more urgent matters to deal with my nephew.

"So why don't you tell me the problems leading up to this little *au naturel* trip into my lobby, Jake Holden?"

"Two things. One, I was taking a — quote — luxurious bubble bath — unquote — as stated in your hotel's brochure and after using over half the bottle found it didn't even make enough suds to coat the tub. Two, seeing as how my bubble bath was a no-go, I stupidly stepped out to grab some ice for my whiskey, leaving my key inside and locked myself out of my room. And since I didn't think the hotel would appreciate me breaking the door down, I came downstairs so someone could let me back in. That's when this employee of yours informed me while I'm standing here cold, wet and naked, he's not going to let me back in my room without proper ID."

"I can verify that indeed he does not possess any identification." Samuel straightened his tie and blushed. Of course, he took the precaution of backing as far away from the counter as possible. "Sir, the hotel's policy is quite clear on allowing the use of an extra key. We must have ID. We have high profile clients attending and high security standards at this hotel. However, I was about to call the manager when you put my neck in a vice, rendering me unable."

Carol caught Jake twitch one hand and decided to take over before Samuel got himself killed. "Okay, Samuel. I've got this." Carol turned to Jake. "I'll take you up and you can show me your ID then, is that acceptable?"

"Yes. And what about the bubble bath?"

"Well, I can assure you if the hotel's brochure states we provide luxurious bubble baths, we'll provide you with a luxurious bubble bath and I personally will make sure this matter is handled." She passed him a business card, even though he had no place to put it. He glanced at the card and handed it back.

"Good. I'm starting to get just a tad cold, standing here in nothing but my birthday suit. Things are beginning to shrivel up into my throat."

Jake stepped backwards. A cool rush of air reminded him he was naked except for the undersized bath towel and his proximity to Carol was making continued coverage by that undersized bath towel precarious. The scar below his left ear twinged in response to the memory of what happened the last time he'd responded to a woman. *Crazy bitch. And she was better left forgotten.*

Jake maintained as much dignity as possible as he walked toward the elevator. He had to admit the situation was totally ludicrous. He hoped to hell there weren't any witnesses and no videos of the past ten minutes captured on any unseen guest's phone. He could read the local headlines now. *Naked Man Roams Lobby of Five Star Hotel.* So much for being discreet in this assignment.

One thing he knew. By the time he'd gotten what he'd come here for, he'd also know a lot more about Carol than her name. *Maybe one hell of a long, cold shower is more in order than a hot soapy bath.*

———

SANDY TIED THE RUBBER tube around her arm and flicked at her skin a couple of times. The stink of the sewers they were in, didn't seem to effect either. "Oh man, everybody says this

White Lady skank is good shit."

"Yeah, Wildflower said it was the best, like mixed with enough fentanyl to put you away. I saw angels, girlfriend. Lights, the light. You, like, brought me back from the light."

"Cool. Yo-yoing is so freaking trippy." Cindy sat on her haunches, unable to stand. Coming back from the dead had that effect on a girl. She held the free government Naloxone needle with both hands because she shook all over. Her skinny frame was pocked with jab wounds and scabs where she'd scratched herself over and over, something she did every time she came down.

Sandy found a vein undamaged enough to take the needle and plunged it into her own arm. "You know the deal. After I go limp, count to ten and bring me back. Don't get any better high than flat-lining and coming back." Her needle-scarred arm shook, and she slumped backwards.

Her eyes rolled into the heavens. The needle clinked to the concrete floor.

Cindy raised the needle. "One, two..."

Blue light flooded the chamber, coming up from the sewer tunnels leading in and out of the room.

"Three, four... *what the fuc—*"
Blue flames tore up through her, the Naloxone vial exploded.
"Sandy's gonna die without the ..."

She screamed as flames tore through her, taking her over until she became the flames and the flames became her.

You and she shall join us instead. Another mass of blue flames descended on the drugged-up woman on the ground and lifted her body up, then slammed it to the ground. Cinders sparked upward before Cindy's eyes exploded in embers and her body burned from the inside out. A haze of blue sparks skittered over the ground.

Both blue flame elementals stared at the two piles of ashes left behind and at the countless needles stuck into the Chambers wall, some leaking their contents onto the cold cement floor.

Neither was the one we seek.
He is coming.
Yes, he disturbs us, the undead and those seeking deliverance.
We are restless and the one we dread is coming with a vengeance.

They scratched at each other with long angry fingers. Flames and sparks exploded. They swept down the cold tunnels and left the chamber, needle tubes clinking in the dark.

He comes.

In the blue glow a pair of eyes stared waiting before he moved to get up watching the blue sparks slowly going out one after another.

⚬⚬⚬

CAROL FOLLOWED JAKE into the elevator, tapping the plastic key on her other hand as the elevator rose, catching the scents of the fragrant bubble bath and his natural sweat. *Gotta admit, if a naked man had to roam around in the lobby, at least it was a good-looking one.* That was the problem, he reminded her a lot of Alan, muscular and hard. *You could bend chisels on those biceps. Crap, focus on work lady, I've got other serious matters to attend to.*

Jake reached down to snug the towel tighter. "You know, it's the hotel manager's job to keep the guests happy. If you wanted to help make all this up to me, you could have dinner with me. You're not married, are you? I don't see a ring."

"No. I was engaged but my fiancé passed away a few years ago."

"Sorry to hear that. A few years ago? Dating anyone seriously now or are you open to dinner? I was joking about it being part of your job description and really, I'd like to say thank you for the way you handled things back there."

Man, so much for being sincerely remorseful. He doesn't take long to dive in when the opportunity presents itself. "I'm afraid not."

"Meaning no you're not going out with anyone or meaning no you won't go out for dinner?" He glanced her over.

Christ, the way he's looking I think he just peeled my clothes off with his eyes, son of a bitch. God, I hate men like him. Sometimes. "Why don't we do this? You leave me a message on my cell phone. It's on my card. I don't discuss personal business while on duty."

"The one I handed back to you since I didn't have anywhere to put it?"

"I'll give it back to you when we get to your room. I might consider going out for dinner later." Carol wasn't an idiot. Both of them liked what they saw in the other, but she had more important things to deal with first. She was working and her first group of Mafia were about to arrive. That took top priority.

The doors opened, and they trundled down the carpeted corridor. Carol gave the key reader a quick swipe and pushed the door open.

"Here you go. And as promised, here's my card again."

"I'm free tomorrow at eight. Like seafood? Heard of a place that has great reviews just down the street, Nautical Nellies."

"I'll think about it. But only if you wear more than a towel. I don't think the fish would blush, but the women might get flustered."

Jake walked over to his jacket and pulled out his wallet, handing her his ID. "Lady, I think the scallops would turn red seeing you naked. And I think

I might just too." He grinned as Carol took the proffered document, ignoring his blatant come-on as she glanced at his driver's license.

American.

"Seeing me naked isn't going to happen and I'd watch your tongue and manners in this establishment. Any other reports of rude, vulgar or disrespectful behaviour to guests or staff and

I will have you evicted."
He scowled at her. "My apologies."

"Now, this appears to be in order. I apologize for the confusion." She committed his driver's license number to memory. For some reason alarm bells were going off in her head.

He escorted Carol to the doorway, admiring her rear view.
"And what makes you think you're going to see me naked?"
"A guy can always hope, can't he?"
"I think blood's rushing to the wrong part of your body."
"I don't suppose you'd care to stick around for a drink or three?"

"Don't push your luck, Mr. Holden, I haven't even agreed to have dinner with you yet. In public. Let alone have drinks with you alone in your room. That goes beyond our employee guidelines, even for management."

Oh, yes. She was definitely his type. Guts, fire and willpower. "My apologies for being rude and presumptuous, and thanks again for letting me into my room. Please apologize to your clerk for me. I'm known for my short-fuse back home."

"I will, but I really think you should apologize to him yourself too, if your ego can take it. I'll let you know about dinner." Carol walked out before he could respond. The entire episode had certainly given her a new respect for hotel staff. *Do they really have to deal with things like this?* And her naked guest was American. A fluke, or was he there because of the expected guests? Dinner was definitely on the cards because she seriously needed to check this guy out, and not just for his physique, although it helped, he was easy on the eyes. Something didn't smell right. One background check coming up, but first things first, she rounded the corner at the far end of the hotel and rang her sister.

"Carol, thank God you called. Nathan's missing. I found his window open and he's gone." The voice of her sister trembled. Carol knew how much she loved her son and her two daughters.

They were her whole world. "Wow! Okay I'll be there tonight."
"Tonight?" Barb's voice shook.

"I'm in Victoria. So I'll head over when I can, but I really can't leave my post right away.

Understand? I'll explain more when I get there. Later in late afternoon."

She could hear Barb begin to sob on the phone. "You're here? In Victoria?"

"Yes, can't say anything more, working undercover. I'll be over as soon as I can. Where did you see him last?"

"I woke up in this morning and... he wasn't there." She stopped, allowing herself to think about what Carol had just asked. "The bedroom, I tucked him in. He's gone, and his bedroom window was open."

"Okay, I know this is hard, but you got to hold it together, for him, for yourself and for me. I'll be over and you show me what you know. Now have you called the police?"

"Yes. They left a couple of hours ago."

"Good. I'm really sorry I can't leave right now but you're in good hands."

"Thanks Carol. I wouldn't know what to do if you weren't in my life."
"We'll find him."
"But what if he's ..."

"He ain't. You gotta trust yourself and think positive. I *will* find him no matter what."

"Yes, yes, think positive. See you tonight."
The phone went dead cutting off the sound of Barb bawling freely.

Not having children Carol couldn't really feel the depths of Barb's anguish. But she knew

Nathan, he was a good kid, raised by a loving, caring mother. *And here I thought I'd have a couple weeks of a somewhat sedate undercover operation babysitting pretentious rich people and the mob in stuffy Victoria. Not the pinkies extended and pass the tea and crumpets day she expected.*

⚜   ⚜

A SIX-YEAR-OLD BOY stands on the corner of Shelbourne Street and Hillside Avenue and stares at the sky as his hands tingle. The blue begins to splinter into shades of purple and orange, even though it's only midday. Houses vanish, concrete dissipates. His skateboard melts beneath him until his feet touched gravel road, not asphalt.

"Mommy?"
Only fields of waving grass answer his plea.

Behind him an older woman emerges from the swirl of dust, stepping out of the past into the present. She stares at the boy and gestures for him to approach. She holds two chocolate bars in her hands. She seems nice enough as she offers him one. He reaches up to take it but hesitates.

"My mom said don't talk to strangers."

"Of course not. But I'm just a sweet old lady, what do you have to fear from me? I think you'd make a wonderful playmate for my son."

He takes the chocolate bar and begins to unwrap it.

"Come with me, I'll introduce you to him."

The boy follows. His skateboard reforms in his hands. Concrete coalesces back into reality, replacing gravel with asphalt, and houses grow anew. The chocolate wrapper lies crumpled on the deserted sidewalk.

Carol closed her office door behind her and dialed Big Dan McKinney, her superior. A bulky six-foot two that didn't take shit from anyone. Carol had the greatest respect for the man that some called tough as nails. Others, but never to his face, called him an outright asshole. One thing he was, was honest and up front. "What's up, lady. Didn't expect to be hearing from you already. Have the mob arrived yet?

"No sir. I've got a problem. Just got a text from my sister, who lives in Victoria. Her son, my only nephew, appears to have been abducted. I want —"

"That ain't happening. We just put you on the case and slammed you through intense upper hotel management." He hesitated. "Is your sister's last name Pendray?"

"What? No? Why ask?"

"Have you read the morning papers yet like I told you to, so that you keep up to the latest in town?"

"No, I just dealt with a crazy naked man in the lobby and was about to call the IT guys when

I got a text from my sister. She asked for my help."

"Look at the damn first page of the paper."

Carol grabbed the daily paper that was on her desk and read the newspaper's lead story.

Pendray Heir Missing! The young son of one of Victoria's elite families is missing. The pioneer Pendray family discovered their six-year-old son Robert was not in his bedroom this morning. Police believe he was abducted from his second storey bedroom during the night and are asking for any information.

"Shit. That's not her, his name is Nathan."

"Crap. Okay, I get that this is important to you, but I need you to stay on this case. I'll make some calls and try to get someone to step in or sub as much as possible. I'll contact Victoria, appraise them of the situation, get hold of their files and tell them we want you to join in that investigation as well. I'm double dutying you, so don't let me down. Once the journos hear of this the shit is going to be spread all over the place. So, low profile, but the focus is on the mob, got it?"

"Yes, sir, and thank you."

"You owe me a favor, I'll get hell for this, but I get it, its family. Hope none of this is linked to the mob showing up, but I don't believe in coincidences or Chinese lucky draws. If there's a connection here. Find it." He was about to hang up. "Oh, I've just been informed the Americans have an operative there in the hotel as well."

"Are we supposed to be working together on this case then?"

"They haven't said as much, but that's the Americans. What I hear you'll hear." "I think I may have already met him." She told him of Jake in the hallway.

"So much for keeping a very low profile. Could be the guy, call IT and check him out. I'll pull some strings. Damn Americans. Thought they were our friendly next-door neighbors."

"Not after that crack Trump made about us burning down the White House."

"Well, we did, way back in history, and kicked their butts twice in a war, otherwise we'd be singing the Star-Spangled Banner and drinking that watered-down piss water they call beer.

Keep me abreast of either case." Dan hung up the phone.

Yup, never a man to mince his words.

Carol called the Crime Lab's best IT guy, Louie Degraff next. She pulled up her secure email as she waited for an answer. "Hey, Louie, can you run a check on a Jake Holden for me? I'm e-mailing his fingerprints right now."

"No problem, that's why I'm here. You use the business card trick?"

"Yeah, that thing comes in handy. Got a still of him off the lobby security camera as well, so you can run a facial recognition search and see who we see who we really come up with."

"*Ahh,* you did that just for little old me? You spoil me. 'Kay, I'll get back to you *ASAP.*"

"Don't suppose yesterday's a possibility?"

"Not unless somebody invented time travel and didn't tell me. Patience is a virtue. Hit you back soon as I can."

"Thanks. Text me on my private line, I've got other business to attend to."

Carol leaned back in her chair. She couldn't wait to hear back from Louie. Her gut told her Jake Holden was either mob or American law enforcement who might, or might not, be on or off duty. And if he was on duty, he'd be butting into her operation. But whoever he was and whatever his reason for being here, one thing she was sure of. With those looks he was definitely trouble of one kind or another.

She called her sister on her private line. "See you later today, I've joined

the case will talk more when I get there."

She checked incoming emails, but nothing on Barb's file had arrived yet.

Chapter Two

B

arely an hour after dealing with Jake, Samuel buzzed Carol, this time hopefully in response to her instructions to alert her to a particular wedding party's arrival and not because of another naked

emergency at the front desk. She strode out of her office, her eyes sweeping across the newly redecorated lobby in admiration. The Fairmont Victoria was definitely five-star, all the way from the deep green Berber carpet on its lobby floor up to the multi-tiered chandelier and its quarter of a million crystals in the middle of the grey, gold and marine blue ceiling. *Amazing what sixty million bucks can do.*

Carol went behind the front desk and stood beside Samuel as the first guests arrived for the wedding between Maria Rizzuto and Alexandro Belletti, two prominent New York Mafia families. Her cop's eye recorded details on Antonio Rizzuto while he walked towards Reception. Per the police files she'd consigned to memory, he was fast approaching sixty, but was still a handsome man whose appearance announced his Italian heritage as completely as did his name. As expected, he traveled with an entourage of hard-as-nails men even an inexperienced eye would peg as personal protection. She recognized a few faces from the police pictures, including one of Rizzuto's sons, Lorenzo, who smiled as she caught his eye. *The photos don't do him justice. Didn't catch the bad boy in his eyes. Oh, yeah, the ladies love him. Until they piss him off, anyway. Not a good guy.*

The others were the men who did the real dirty work for the Rizzuto family, and judging by what she'd read about Antonio and his sons, there was a lot of it. The Mafia was a well-oiled machine with a strict chain of command

and they never missed a chance to mix business with pleasure. Antonio might be here for the impending wedding, but there's no way he and the Belletti family weren't scoping out expansion possibilities in Victoria, which extended down into the Strait of Juan de Fuca and was virtually surrounded by the Olympic peninsula of Washington state. It was likely Victoria was a route into America, but for exactly what, only God knew at this point. For sure, the Victoria Police didn't. Some low-level intel reports indicated they might be trying to strike up associations with the Asian gangs or, even worse, trying to make headway into the lucrative Asian drug trades which could start a possible gang war on the island. The VPD had been in touch with all the different agencies, including the Americans, to trade information but nothing firm had been forthcoming, whether because the Americans didn't know anything either or because they just didn't choose to share it. *Damn Americans.*

A blonde draped herself over Antonio's arm, hugging tighter than a well-tailored suit. She was maybe in her twenties, with lots of curves and over-sized breasts that couldn't get within two feet of a microwave tower without melting. She smiled at Carol with that patented gold-digger look, the look that swept over other women and dismissed them as no threat. *Wait until you've popped a kid or two and he'll have ten on the side looking just like you, younger and with bigger breasts.* Carol smiled back. *Probably already has.*

Antonio Rizzuto stopped and nodded to one of the men. The underling stepped forward. "The Rizzuto party will check in now." *Glad there's not a check-in line. I'd have some pissed off guests to calm down 'cause these boys damn sure would have cut to the front.*

Judging by the bulges under their armpits, some were carrying guns that never would have made it past customs. *Note to self—they have some good buddies on the Canadian side of the border.* She put on the best *I-am-just-the-hotel-manager* face she could muster. One thing about being undercover — she had to bite her tongue. *A lot.*

She checked them in personally and called over all the on-duty porters she'd had waiting on standby to take their luggage up. Between the two families and all the guests, the entire top floor of the hotel was booked for the week. The bride and groom would be in later, no doubt they were still on some very expensive bachelor and bachelorette weeks, one night, or even a weekend, no longer being acceptable.

As the group turned to leave, Lorenzo Rizzuto turned back to her. "We heard there's a ghost tour, not our thing, but the Bellettis would like it. Set it up to collect them at the front door and leave us a message about the details." Dismissing her, the arrogant bastard turned away.

"I'll look into the tour times," Carol called to his back. She vaguely recalled being told about ghost tours during her induction to hotel management and Victoria in general. Ghost tours and hauntings were big for many tourists since Victoria had the title of the most haunted city in

Canada. She hadn't thought any of this crowd would be interested.

He said something to one of his men. The subordinate turned to stare at her, eyeing her up and down, smiling with a lewd look.

Smug bastard. Enjoy it. You won't be so smug when we're through with you.

<hr />

"HOLY SHIT, THAT'S NEVER happened before." Brad Handley rose from the corner of the Wall of Wonder chamber in the sewers. He kicked at the smoldering blue ashes. "Not much left to try and retrieve and add to this collection." He stared at the liquid filled vials that he had seen the first time he came down looking for his drug addicted father, jammed into the mortar, many of them were frothing, partly from the heat, but more from fear. All of the vials he'd pulled from the dead or nearly dead bodies contained something, something alive. *Their tortured souls?* He wasn't sure, nor how this could be happening, except something to do with the vortex located near them. Or something to do with the *Lekwungen* feeding off of them. "I haven't found anything to explain how this is happening." Some of the vials slowed their movements. "It's funny, I don't do drugs and the *Lekwungen* aren't interested in me. I guess I haven't got anything they want." He patted the medallion around his neck. "Or this First Nation's protection amulet I bought off that old native man keeps me safe from other native spirits. In any case there's nothing here to do but sweep up this mess and head home."

He stared intently at the one vial that meant the most to him. "Sorry, Dad". He closed his eyes. "I know, they ain't happy and I don't know what's pissing them off. Something is disturbing this area and I need to find out what that is before all hell breaks loose down here."

Brad turned to leave the room. In the darkness left behind several sparks smoldered, throbbing. Instead of going out they lingered on, somehow feeding impossibly off the juices leaking from the cracked vials dripping their contents.

⚬⚬⚬

MOMENTS LATER, ON THE corner of Shelbourne Street and Hillside Avenue, the blue sky begins to splinter into shades of purple and orange, even though it's midday. Houses vanish, concrete dissipates. A cat stares, confused, as all around fields of waving grass replace the concrete and cement.

Behind it a woman emerges from a swirl of dust and the past begins to bleed into the present. She stares at the cat and the crumpled chocolate bar wrapper, lifts her large, brimmed hat, swipes at the sweat beading her brow, sets the heavy wrapped package on the ground and checks the time on her watch.

She stares hard at the buildings, at the cards in her hands and without uttering a word, walks beyond the borders of yesterday into today. "I'm back. It's time to begin settling matters."

⚬⚬⚬

CAROL'S CELL PHONE signaled an incoming text just as she finished up the ghost tour arrangements. A quick surveillance update on the operation.

Belletti party delayed at airport.

Carol sighed. Now that things were in motion, she'd much prefer for all parties to be checked in. Although if the delay was overnight, then she could duck out and visit Barb. She texted back.

Why and for how long?

Problem with baggage. Guess the bazookas and AK47s didn't sit well with Customs.

Carol didn't laugh out loud, but it was a near thing. She missed Bob Hanson and his whacked sense of humour.

"*Urumph.*" Samuel cleared his throat in a tone clearly indicating his disapproval of her concentration on her personal phone rather than the lobby.

She pocketed it quickly. "I've just gotten word the Bellettis will be delayed. You should get some lozenges for that irritated throat, Samuel."

"Ms. Moore, may I present Mrs. Agnes Van Lunt, one of our most esteemed guests. She's checking in and would like to have a word with you."

Carol looked up, her bright public relations smile firmly in place. Mrs. Van Lunt looked exactly the way a normal guest on a normal day should look in the Fairmont Victoria — elderly, rich, well-bred and classy. With her fur trimmed collar and wide-brimmed hat, she could have stepped right out of a 1940's *Harper's Bazaar* fashion layout. Three carousels of luggage trailed behind her. *Crap, some people take their whole damn house with them on holidays.*

Mrs. Van Lunt smiled as if she knew exactly what Carol was thinking. "I asked for the manager on duty. I presume by your attire you work here. You'd think they'd give the staff a better budget for clothing." In that one haughty comment and glare the theory of wealthy entitlement and the fact that Carol rated well down on the scale of civility swiped like a tiger's claws at Carol's pasted smile. *What a bag. I don't know how Samuel does it.* Carol kept her submissive smile pasted on her face.

The old gal flashed a diamond ring on her finger that gleamed with nearly the same dazzle as the new chandelier installed in the front foyer as she fussed with her hat. "I do say it is a might drafty in here. Does the hotel not pay for heating or is everything set on dry air conditioning mode?

Which would require me to request a humidifier for my room."

"I'm the manager on duty." *Some damn, the diamonds in that ring are probably worth more than some third world countries' GNP.*

Agnes Van Lunt smiled at her again. "I had a few special requests I'd like to check on before I go to my room. I asked for a larger-than-normal safe in my room, one large enough for my closest and most valuable, unreplaceable traveling possessions. Your clerk seems to think they may be better in the hotel safe, but I do like to have them on hand."

Ah! Not just rich, but a nut job to boot with the list of requirements.

Carol reached into the drawer where she'd made sure to stash this guest's list of required needs. "I can assure you; the security protocols of this hotel are of the highest standards. And yes, the larger safe you requested has been installed in your room, it's the most secure model of its size. Samuel was just pointing out the main hotel safe may still be more secure. All your other special requests have been fulfilled, including..." She glanced down at the weird items on her list and continued. "Two twelve-inch candles of pure beeswax, the lights in the suite have all been changed to incandescent bulbs, and we've supplied the ten sticks of Nag Champa incense, one of which was lit about ten minutes ago to facilitate the calm entering of your spirit. And of course, I've made sure the room's been smudged to encourage the exit of previous occupants' energies." She read the words from the email they received at the time of booking. *Yes, a complete over-the-frigging-top whack job.* But one the hotel charged double the going rate for her rather radical requests, so definitely a welcome whack job.

"Then I see no need to talk further here in the drafts of this lobby and you may escort me to my suite now to make sure I'm entirely satisfied."

"Me?"

"Yes, certainly you, dear. If anything's wrong, you'll be the one to make sure it's corrected, after all. Why would I bother to go through a second party? I do hope you've arranged the maid service I requested. You seem to have left it off your little list. I need a maid to unpack. I'll supervise, of course, I wouldn't trust the staff to handle my *haute couture* or other priceless possessions without my observation. If there's anything damaged or out of place, I expect the management to be fully accountable."

"Of course. The maid will come up with the porters and the luggage." Carol breathed deeply. Between the naked man in the lobby, the Italian Mafia family and society's upper elite, she'd definitely earned a stiff drink tonight. And to think Samuel did this every day. *I'd have slit someone's throat by now.* "Yes, Mrs. Van Lunt."

"Agnes. You may call me Agnes." She smiled slightly at Carol and pulled her fox headed fur stole more closely around her neck. Then she ran a single finger back along her throat, watching Carol's eyes as she made the subtle gesture.

Carol blinked and subserviently followed the old lady towards the elevators. *Christ, that move across her throat! Like she'd just read my mind.*

JOHN ANDREWS CURSED as his golf ball dove deep into the blackberry bush behind the sixth green of the Victoria Golf Club. "Son of a bitch! Worst shot of the day." He danced his club across the green as the other two men laughed.

"Hey, thought this was supposed to be relaxing," Jim Low howled, smug because he had only a two-foot putt to win the hole.

"Not when I've got a fifty on each hole." He cursed as he picked up his nemesis club and used it to part the prickly bushes. No way was he going to retrieve the ball with the club. He sighed and resigned himself to reaching in to get it.

"Hey, leave it there, it's only a ball. Take a penalty drop," David said, as he waited to take his putt.

"It's only a ball? Next you'll be saying 'it's only a game of golf'. I take my game very seriously and that's my lucky Arnold Palmer ball, haven't lost yet when I use it. It's my trusty good luck charm and I ain't going to lose it now." He reached in and one of the sharp pricks of blackberry needles punctured his flesh. Blood oozed, but John could open his mouth to swear the terrifying scream of a woman broke the serenity of the golf course. The bloody figure of Doris Gravlin ran by, her husband in full pursuit, his hands drenched in red. He caught up to her and grabbed her by the throat, cutting off her cries of help. Before any of the men could even register what was happening, the Gravlins started fading and vanished into the manicured fairway.

"What in the—?" The three golfers stared wide-eyed. John winced in pain as his hand moved and another prick cut into him. He pulled himself free. "You're right, no ball is worth this. I'm out of here." He made for the buggy. David jumped in beside him and John floored the accelerator.

"Hey, what about the game?" Jim yelled.

Turns out it *is* only a game of golf. You can have my money," John shouted back.

"You gonna just leave Jim back there?" David asked, incredulous.

"This is a case of every man for himself. I ain't going back. You can if you like."

"Not on your life. Some people take their golf way too seriously." David shouted back at Jim. "You can have mine too."

Chapter Three

"I see the renovations were geared to le nouveau chic. Personally, I'm not a fan of the new crystal chandelier, I liked the old one better. But at least everything isn't new or covering some kind of fake façade, like some of the people I meet." Agnes prattled on as they walked to the elevators.

The customer is always right even when they aren't. Carol repeated the hotel staff motto to herself as she followed the elderly woman, pulling one of the luggage carousels behind her.

That mantra had been grilled into her over and over in the intense seven-day training stint she'd undergone to get her ready for today. *And the customer is always the customer.*

"I'm glad you agree," Agnes said as they entered the elevator alone.

"I'm sorry, excuse me? I didn't say anything just then."

"I know. Your job is to go beyond the call whether the customer is right or wrong."

Carol nearly fell over backwards as the elevator rose. *Beyond the call?*

The VPD motto?

"I—excuse me, but how did—?"

"How do I know? Sorry, just showing off. Let's talk in the security of my room. There's a lot of unrest and evilness around here. Quite unsettling and ..." she hesitated before continuing. "More to come, I'm afraid. The spirits are very restless. It happens when the Ley Lines or Earth energy centers cross a region and something enters to disturb that Karmic energy. And oh, just so you know, I'm really not a rude, demanding person, I just pretend to be occasionally. I like to listen to people's internal responses."

Mrs. Van Lunt, I'm afraid I don't understand. What's going on?" Carol had read the known dossiers on the incoming Mafia clan members, but it hadn't occurred to her that any other guest might be worthy of special attention.

"Again, it's Agnes, dear. You may call me Agnes. And I'll certainly explain, but not here, in my suite. We'll be far safer there. You did confirm it's been smudged, didn't you? I don't want any bad spirits listening to our conversation and for your information, no, I'm not part of the wedding party. Or connected in any way to the Mafia families currently in residence under this roof."

Bad spirits? Carol looked over her shoulder. *And how'd she know about the Mafia?*

Carol ushered Agnes into the room and closed the door behind them. They'd be alone until the rest of Agnes' luggage arrived. The smell of the sage from the smudging and the Nag Champa incense lent a calming effect to the air in the large, opulent suite. *Might be something to that smudging thing after all.*

"Simply put, I can sense things." Agnes reached up to her large, wide brimmed hat and tried to unpin it. "Be a doll and help me with this cumbersome device. Keeps the dampness off my head, but such a pain to wear. I trust your maid service will be available to help me dress in the morning? And why don't you pour us both a nice, stiff drink? Like you, I could certainly use one."

"I've assigned two of the staff to be at your every beck and call." Carol struggled with the hat pin. Carol glanced at her watch. "Well, I'm off in about an hour anyway. Why not? Whiskey?"

"Yes, please, straight, it calms me down and relaxes me. My chest gets too tense when I'm in a new city." She scratched at her ample bosom.

"I don't meet many women that like whiskey at all, especially not straight." And after that scene with Jake this morning she could use something to calm her nerves. "Just one small one though."

"Good, I'm glad. I could use someone to chat with. I usually put people off just by being around them."

Probably because you act so damn stuck-up.

No, because I'm psychic and I often, quite unintentionally I promise, read minds. Part of my stage act. I'm here for the annual ghost tours. You know, of course, that Victoria has quite the collection of haunted sites."

Carol's eyes widened in shock. "I'm sorry, I shouldn't have said that! Wait, I didn't say that, did I? So, the other times—none of them were accidents? You seriously can read minds? And you've been reading mine? And you're telling me, you came for the ghosts?"

"It's quite alright, dear. As I told you, I frequently provoke such responses on purpose. I've developed a thick skin and quick tongue over the years." She chucked half her whiskey back in one long swallow and held the glass out for a second. "You must know Victoria is the most haunted city in all of Canada. You do work here, do you not?" Agnes raised her eyebrows as if to suggest she knew differently.

"No. Well yes, but I'm new to Victoria, I'm from Vancouver. I thought Victoria was all British stiff-upper-lip, fish and chips. Very civilized *haute couture* and all that "salute the queen" stuff." Carol broke off as she realized Agnes actually had her flustered. Not many people did that. Agnes pulled a large gleaming object from her suitcase and gently removed the wrappings. It was shaped suspiciously like a human head. "What the hell is that?"

"My crystal skull. I call her Cider."

"A crystal skull? You travel with a crystal skull? Why Cider? And how do you know it's a she? Couldn't it just as easily be a he? A George, a Bob, or a Tom Jones?"

"She's named that aptly because I can see inside her and I like to think of her as a she, my closest girlfriend. Well, my only girlfriend, really. She's my version of a crystal ball. I like the macabre touch it brings to my act and so does my audience. It's my *Woo-woo* version of the internet. Besides, it helps to pretend to be stroking her while I'm reading people's minds, it adds to the effect."

"Say what?" Agnes completely floored her. Not what she would have expected in a dozen lifetimes from an old woman dressed to the nines in jewelry and furs. *Crap, need to shut my sarcastic head up or she'll hate me forever.* "Aren't they very rare, and expensive? Built by some Andean Monks in Tibet or something, using only chopsticks and spit as tools?"

Agnes laughed. "I'm beginning to like you. This one was discovered in Central America, in Belize, 1924 and is believed to be one of the original Mitchell-Hedges skulls made by Mayans nearly four thousand years ago. Mitchell-Hedges' daughter Anna found hers behind an altar. Or so the story goes."

No way that's real. I mean I thought there were only one or two crystal skulls in the whole world. And haven't those turned out to be fake?"

"There're several such *real* crystal skulls in the world, many not reported to the public and regrettably quite a few more that did turn out to be fakes. But Cider isn't fake. I met her prior owner while on a tour through the States. He fell madly in love with me and knew I was a clairvoyant. So, he gave her to me, just before he died, knowing I'd make good use of her. Funny that I never saw his death coming. Cider's been very useful over the years, not just as a prop, but for finding out information. Care to hold her?" Agnes held Cider out to Carol.

Carol thought about it a moment. "Not on your life. I used to hang out with this shaman type nutcase dude and I've learned over the years never to mess with stuff I know nothing about. I leave that up to the experts like you and ..."

"Charlie."
"You're reading my mind again. Cut that out."

"Sorry, bad habit, and the reason I usually travel alone. It's the downside of being psychic. As much as people say they want you to read your mind, they don't. I, on the other hand, am the one hearing what a person truly thinks and it isn't often nice, reading that someone else thinks you're acting stuck up."

"Sorry, but you were quite pretentious."

"I'm teasing, dear. As I said, I did it on purpose to illicit just such a reaction from you." Agnes chugged back the rest of the second glass in one gulp. "I'm rather tired now. I'm in need of an afternoon nap, a by-product of getting older. Can you meet me for High Tea tomorrow afternoon? I would like to chat some more. I get the sense you're not scared of me, like most people, you're curious more than anything else, probably because of the badge underneath."

"The badge? Didn't think I could keep that from you either. Then you probably know I'm undercover."

Agnes smiled back. "I do now."

Carol shook her head, "Damn! Okay, you're on. I'd like to hear more about you and your life, Agnes. You strike me as quite the character and not..."

"A stuck-up old woman."

"I'm sorry about that. As a police officer I'm trained to take in first impressions, and they are often on the mark. But with you, I was sadly mistaken. Mostly because you wanted me to be." She glanced at her watch. "Time to go."

"Come," Agnes called, just before Carol opened the door to find one of the maids about to knock.

"About time too, young lady. Come in, come in, and let me show you where I want everything to go. And be quick about it. It's past my nap time."

Carol left Agnes in her natural element and made a hasty exit, pleased to be off Agnes' radar. Or at least, she was off Agnes' radar until the next time they met.

"My radar has quite a radius you know," Agnes called through the closing door. Before it shut fully Carol saw the small smile on her face and smiled back. She'd definitely enjoy getting to know Agnes better. She glanced down at her buzzing phone. Samuel.

"Yes?"

"The Bellettis have arrived, madam, and they're—"

"Asking for the Duty Manager. Isn't everybody today? I'll be right there."

Damn, they were early. Carol quickened her pace and squirted some breath spray down her throat. She shouldn't have had a drink and her sister would have to wait. The last thing she needed was for a guest to smell whiskey on her breath.

FOOTSTEPS ECHOED EERILY down the corridors of Hatley Castle. The janitor glanced at his watch. It was late, time to go. He glanced down the long dark hall as he grabbed his keys to lock up. There was nothing there, but still the steady thump of feet broke the stillness as the clock struck eleven.

The sound of young girls giggling, and boys whistling joined the thumping footsteps. Still, his eyes saw nothing. There was only the coldness that ran through the darkness when no one was watching.

"Think I'll be grabbing a drink on the way home. Haven't heard that in a long time." He shivered from the sudden chill. "The ghosts are restless this week. Very restless."

CAROL WALKED AROUND Nathan's room; glad she was away from the craziness of the Empress assignment. She gave her sister, who was still in tears, another hug. It was late afternoon, but she'd managed to get Samuel to cover the rest of her shift.

The boy's room looked just like it did since the time she was there three years ago. Younger then, he wanted her to read him a story, like she'd done many times in the past. That and shoot her gun, which of course Carol couldn't allow him to do. Or even hold it. "So, the report says the window was open." Carol glanced through the police report she down-loaded to her cell phone, finally getting it just before she arrived. *Good Ol' Big Dan; hard-nosed bastard, but he lives up to his promises.*

"Yeah, and like I told them I always keep them locked when the kids go to bed. I listen to you on security stuff." Barb's voice began to tremble, threatening to break into another sobbing session. Judging by the puffiness of her eyes, Barb had been crying a lot. *And how could she blame her?*

"Now, pull yourself together. Nathan can't be helped by a blubbering woman. He can be helped by a woman that has it together and starts remembering something that can help him. Or

I'll just have to cuff you and have you roughed up by Big Dan in Vancouver."

Barb cracked a smile and began to giggle. "Depends what kind of roughing up he's going to do on me."

Carol knew Barb had the hots for Dan. They met at some police function Carol had invited Barb to. She thought something about his tough commanding nature turned Barb on. What she saw in Dan, Carol didn't know, but at least it got her mind off the current situation. "Man, you always could make me laugh. Thank you."

Carol walked over to the window and took several pictures. Barb lived in a rancher, so the boy's bedroom was ground level. It would not have been difficult for him to climb out.

"So, could Nathan have unlocked the window? Is the key nearby?"

"Well, yes. We keep it in that pot on the dresser. I have shown him how to unlock it in case there's a fire or something and he needs to get out. But he would never unlock it for anything else. Unless I never locked it. Oh God." Tears began to streak her face again.

"Don't make me slap you, like I did that day in junior high over who got to go out with ..." "Bobby Sanders. God, he was a hunk. Think I heard someone told me they saw him in a gay bar in Vancouver, dancing with another guy."

"Yeah, dammit, why are all the good-looking ones gay?"

Barb smiled. "Yes, he went out with me and I never told you, but I virtually threw myself at him. Any hot-blooded male would have had a stiffy in a heartbeat."

Carol smiled as the talk helped Barb get her mind off Nathan. "So, the only other thought then is that he woke up and opened the window himself."

"Come to think about it. I thought I heard him get up and use the bathroom just after I went to bed. I guess he could have, but why would he have done that?"

"Let's go outside and look closer. I'm thinking that if he did, something got his attention."

They walked outside. Carol searched the ground below the window. Bending closer something caught her eye. It was a small toy figurine of a green guy with a purple mask and beside it lay a toy camera.

"Oh my god! That one is Nathan's! He always had it with him when he was playing detective. Not sure about the green man though." Barb started sobbing again and pulled another

Kleenex from her pocket. "But the police made a thorough search out here so why didn't they find these?"

"Good question." *They would have.* Which meant one thing, as bizarre as it sounded. The boy was alive, and someone was letting her know. *Abducted, possibly.* She pulled out her gloves and an evidence bag. "We'll have these checked for prints and DNA."

Further investigation found a small footprint. Possibly a woman's foot, about a size six. Carol pulled her phone and snapped a picture. *That wasn't in any of the reports either. Must have happened after.* She stared at Barb's feet. *Not her, she's about an eight.* Carol rang the local police asking them to come and take a cast of the footprint. "Okay back inside, you need to get some rest. Stay by the phone in case there's an update and I'll see what the investigation has found so far. Got it?"

Barb nodded as more tears began to flow down her face.

I can't say I blame her. What if this is related to the other boy disappearing?

Chapter Four

The call from Louie came the next day. "Your Jake Holden is really Cole Brady, FBI undercover specialist. His specialty? The Mafia. But I can't find anything that says he's here on anything but vacation."

"Oh, yeah, like he just lives to sightsee in quaint old towns. Trust me, if that Mafia specialist dude is on vacation, he's on a beach somewhere. He's not in Victoria by fluke." Carol clicked off the phone. She'd do a little re-con on her own before she called Big Dan to appraise him, if he didn't already know.

CAROL PACED THE FLOORS housing the Italians the next day, too restless to sit behind a desk. It was late afternoon, the maids all but finished cleaning, so the corridors were virtually empty, as were the rooms. She had only a few moments with Agnes over High Tea as their meeting was cut short by an urgent call to do with the Belletis and their rooms. *How was it possible in a hotel of this prestige that beds could be too stiff? I couldn't deal with snotty rich people every day without losing it.*

Although it was interesting to watch the Rizzutos experiencing the hotel's famous High Tea, and wasn't that quaint? The Godfather sampling tiny sandwiches and strawberry scones.

Carol wrinkled her nose when she caught the scent of staleness, a smell the cleaning staff kept well at bay in this fine establishment. Her nose twitched again, her senses were suddenly on full alert, and she turned swiftly to look behind her. An older, distinguished gentleman was trying Antonio Rizzuto's door. Having no luck with that door, he moved on to the next. *What the...?* When he approached a third, Carol intervened. "Excuse me, may I help you?"

He looked up. His face was bearded, his clothes, though smart and formal, were old, not as in worn and tattered but as in old-fashioned; turn of the century old-fashioned. *Doubly odd.* The man just turned and headed down the corridor. Carol sped up as he disappeared around the end of the hall, walking as though he belonged there. *Damn it.*

She hightailed it and rounded the corner. No one was there except a couple waiting for the elevator.

"Sorry, good afternoon. I was just looking for someone. A bearded man, about five-ten. Just came around this corner?"

The woman looked blankly at her. She checked Carol's name tag and stepped closer to her husband, nudging him to response. "You must be mistaken, Ms. Moore, no one has come around the corner since we've been here, a good couple of minutes." The elevator chimed, announcing its arrival. "Now good day." He picked up his bag and escorted his wife inside the elevator.

"Ah, sorry about that. Didn't mean to startle you. Hope you're enjoying your stay at the hotel." She turned around, glanced down both ends of the corridor, and headed back to her office. *I think I've just seen my first ghost. Time for a smoke, get some nice clothes on, a bit of makeup, meet Mr. Yankee. As for Agnes, we need to chat.*

IN THE DANK DARKNESS of the sewers the blue sparks intensified, throbbing as if alive. Slowly they began to flow to each other and merged. A glow lit the room and when it faded away all that remained was a small oval blue egg-like object. Throbbing with life.

"I'M A SUCKER FOR GOOD seafood chowder and I hear this restaurant makes some of the best on the West Coast," Jake, aka Cole, adjusted his chair closer to the Nautical Nellies' table they sat at. "A great meal with a beautiful woman—what more does a man need to make a night one to remember?"

Still an arrogant bastard. "Well, I'm not really a fan of water, boats or the ocean. Honestly, I'm more a meat and potatoes kind of woman. But what woman in her right mind passes up a dinner invitation from a handsome man?" She smiled and let her eyelashes flutter a bit.

"Exactly. Just two lonely ships in the night. And what are you drinking, Ms. Moore?"

"Whiskey on the rocks, please."

"And here I took you to be a Chianti type of lady. You're full of surprises. I love that about a woman." Jake signaled the hovering waiter over. "Two whiskeys on the rocks, please." He turned back to Carol and gave her a hungry look, the look men assumed women found sexy.

"So why are you in town, Mr. Holden?"

"I'm in sales. Here for a trade show."

"Really? What kind of sales? Where's the show being held? I thought I knew all the trade shows and conventions going on this week."

"High tech security software. We don't advertise it, so I'm not surprised you didn't hear about it."

She smiled at him over the top of the menu. "What a *great* cover story, Cole Brady. Now why don't you tell me why you're really here?"

A genuine grin replaced his on-demand smiles. "I was wondering how long it'd take you, Detective Ainsworth. I told the big boys they were making a mistake, not telling you straight up.

I'd have thought your superiors knew you better than that."

"I'd have thought so, too."

"Well, it was fun while it lasted. And of course, you know my attraction to you wasn't—and isn't—part of the cover. But we're both professionals and since we've now confirmed that, we'll guard each other's backs. Which means sharing our intel whether the brass's authorized it or not.

Agreed?"

"Absolutely. Agreed. So what angle are you covering?"

"Word has it the Bellettis have convinced the Rizzutos to expand their operations into the west coast from their New York center. That's what this wedding's all about, it's setting up a combined new family group here in Canada. The Rizzutto's have been reluctant to have anything to do with the west coast. Most of the Asian trade enters America between Victoria and Vancouver. I don't have to tell you mobsters are basically nothing but forward-thinking businessmen."

"Except they kill their competition. Literally, not figuratively."

"*Touché*. And in this case, there's a small problem of already established American and UN gangs. They don't take lightly to competition."

"So, we've heard. We're worried of the conflict on our side, and you're worried about contraband entering the US from Canada."

"That's the bare bones of it, yes."

"Fair enough, but enough shop talk. Let's order, and then before our food arrives, you can tell me something about yourself."

⚬⟞⟍ ⟍⟝⟞

CAROL WALKED AROUND the large Pendray estate's backyard just off St. James Street. They were one of the original founding families with successful business operations in early Victoria and had done well. She took several pictures on her cell phone. The back window where the boy had his room was broken from the outside in. Marks in the soil indicated a ladder had been used. Forensics was already working on that, along with a couple of shoe imprints. She bent over and looked closer at a flash of color under the shrubbery. A green headed toy figurine, very similar to the one left at Nathan's crime scene except the mask around his head was red. *Something else the police missed, or...*

Carol parted the branches around the figurine. A small footprint. *Yup, I'd say same, size six.*

Okay, that isn't in the report either. So, Louie is someone leaving me clues? And Why? She snapped a couple of shots of the figurine and footprint then, after donning her gloves, she placed the small toy into an evidence bag. She then texted Louie the pictures and requested forensics to take a cast of this footprint too.

⚮ ⚮

"VAON! ZODACANEA, ZODAMERANA! Odo femura Daa: zodareje, lerna madired, Noca Mudu, hoat Saitan!

Appear! Open the grounds beneath! I am the same as you, a believer! I worship you the eternal King of Hell!"

The white-hooded figures chanted over and over as they stood around the pentagram in the basement of Hatley Castle. In the center was a dark seemingly endless opening into the bowels of the earth.

A low deep breath hissed upwards. "Who disturbs me?" Acrid sulphuric vapours filled the chamber.

Several gagged. "We ask for your blessings."

"Bring me sweet morsels to slake my hunger." Whispered up from the darkness.

"He, the Almighty One, has spoken," the leader intoned. "We must act on this in order to get his blessings."

⚮ ⚮

"COME IN." AS WITH THE maid, Agnes called out the invitation before Carol had time to knock. Carol shrugged and complied. A haze of light smoke from the incense sticks layered the room. Carol immediately relaxed as she breathed it in. "I won't even ask! Reception said you needed to see me now, tonight. Is everything okay?"

"I'm sensing something."
"Really? What?"

"I'm not sure I understand it myself. I started in the circus and then vaudeville, billed as Psychic Lucy and later Ms. Teak. At first it was just that—an act. But apparently, I got an awful lot of things right, more than just coincidences, and word got around. A lot of people came to see me and some still pay me big bucks to help them."

"So, you're saying you started out as a fake who became real?"

"You already know I'm real. But you don't know I often see things from people's pasts as well as read minds." Agnes smiled sweetly back at her.

Carol stared blankly. "So—you want to read my past?"
"Give me your hand, darling. You're still a misbeliever."

Carol did. "As you already have guessed, I'm a police officer. I only believe in the facts."

"Interesting. You're not who you say you are, although I already knew that and ... call your dad, tonight, and ask about your older brother George. Meet me for High Tea tomorrow." She let go of Carol's hand. "Now at my age I need a lot of beauty sleep. Thanks for the help."

Perturbed, Carol replied, "I don't have an older brother George. Don't have any brothers, only one sister."

"Call your dad if you don't believe me. Now I'm off to bed. I'm still recovering from that ghastly airplane. Air travel is so tiresome." *I'm overdue a call to check up on my dad anyways.*

Carol walked out the door, images of Agnes in her gypsy get-up playing in her brain. She could see Agnes in her swirly skirt, headscarf and dangly earrings, bamboozling the crowds with her weird crystal skull.

As she entered the lobby, a plaque caught her eye. She'd seen it a dozen times and never really paid attention to it. A picture of a man, the builder of the hotel, Francis Rattenbury. Carol stopped and did a double take. *It's him! The ghost from the corridor earlier.* She'd heard stories the owner's ghost, along with others, haunted the hotel. *No, can't be. That's what I get for hanging out with psych-jobs.*

⚜   ⚜

"AH, YOU'LL MAKE A SPLENDID specimen for the young master of the house," Gladys Townsend said to her unconscious companion. She drove along the street and quickly pulled into the back of the Windsor Hotel parking lot. She made sure the boy was still out and pulled his limp body from the back of her new tan 1987 GMC van. "I'm getting old. It's hard to lift these strapping young lads like I used to, but at least I've another playmate for my Jordon."

She stared at the spray-painted graffiti on the back door. It looked like a being of some sort, hair all askew like he was on fire. "What is this town coming to?"

Gladys unlocked it and walked into the basement. She moved the filing cabinets and boxes aside, revealing a three-foot high doorway. She pulled an old key from around her neck, unlocked the ancient door and turned on the lights. Two dehydrated corpses were arranged either side of a Snakes and Ladders game. Gladys dragged the still body into the room and propped it next to the others. She filled a syringe with fluid and plunged it into the boy's arm.

"Now tomorrow I'll return and see how you three are getting along, shall I? Oh, young boys are such trouble these days, I do hope you'll all play nice. I've always wanted to have some nice sons to entertain. Maybe we'll go to the park and have some fun on the Merry-Go-Round."

Satisfied all was in order, she patted Jordon on the head. "Now, no cheating, and I'll see you lads in the morning. It's getting late and I must return to the vortex." She held the pentagonal pendant that hung around her neck. "I hear my master calling." She turned off the lights and trundled back up the stairs after putting everything back in its place.

THE BLUE EGG-SHAPED object in the sewer throbbed hard and split itself into two. Both halves pulsed several times, absorbing more of the liquids left by the dead girls and the vials on the floor of the room. Then they reached out, reabsorbing each other and doubling in size. The new egg lay still as fluids coursed within it.

Chapter Five

"Hey, Dad, you doing okay? Sorry for calling so late and for not calling

sooner. Work's been crazy, and I haven't had a chance to breathe."

"Quite alright, been busy myself."

"I'm really glad you've finally decided it was okay to enjoy life. Mom would have wanted you to, you know that."

"I know. It just took me a while after she died to be able to." After Mom had died of cancer, he'd been lonely for a long time. Only recently had he begun seeing someone else.

"I understand that, Dad. Now, can I ask you something a bit weird? I've met a woman who claims to be a psychic and this is going to sound absolutely crazy, but she told me to ask you about my older brother, George."

There was a long pause. "Sorry, I'm stunned. Shocked actually," he spoke softly. "When your mother and I first met, she got pregnant. We were both very young and we couldn't afford to have a child. She saw it full-term and we gave the baby up for adoption."

"Let me guess." Carol could feel the hairs on the back of her neck standing up.

"A male and she named him George. As far as I know she never told anyone. Over the years, I regretted the decision, but at the time we didn't know if we would stay together." He stopped, but Carol could hear the sadness in his voice. "Don't get me wrong. I love you very much, but I always wished I'd had a son. Probably why I raised you the way I did, all the sports, always demanding the best out of you. Always thought the next one born would be another male.

Never happened. Even with my involvement in the army I never could find out what happened to him."

"Thanks for sharing that, and Dad, I love you very much and this makes no difference whatsoever. I'm glad you raised me like you did. I've never regretted being in the police department. And of course, you demanded the best out of me. All good parents demand the best from every child."

"Look, I don't know how you met this woman, but she is amazing." "Thanks, Dad. I love you, and we'll chat more soon."

Carol hung up and sat for a moment, still stunned. "Wherever you are Mom, love you too." *How could Agnes have known?* She stepped outside onto her balcony to light up a smoke. The inner harbor unfolded before her, with all the boats and the hustle of the inner marketplace. *Yeah, she picks up things. Man, if I hadn't met Charlie I'd be so totally freaked out right about now.*

She inhaled deeply. *Okay, I'm still totally freaked.*

HIGH TEA AT THE EMPRESS was a very formal affair. Fancy linen table cloth and napkins, matching bone-china crockery, crustless miniature sandwiches, savory pastries, scones served with strawberry jam and rich, thick Devon cream and a selection of petit fours. All served on a tiered silver platter. Sitting across from Agnes, Carol could barely see the old lady over it.

"So, I could ask how you knew about my brother, George, especially since I didn't. But I won't. I've hung out in the past with a man who does a lot of the *Woo-woo* stuff."

Agnes elegantly nibbled at her cucumber sandwich as a traditionally attired maid poured the tea. She reveled in her glory, enjoying the suspense and adoration. She was dressed to the nines in a spring-green dress adorned with daises. Another of her cartwheel hats, this was brilliant white, and elegant sheer white gloves completed her ensemble. "Ah, so you've verified what I told you."

Carol shook her head. "How could you know all of this? How is it possible you knew about George? And Charlie? Well, Charlie I could get, if you can read my history. But George? I didn't know about him so, how could you?"

Agnes slowly stirred a minute quantity of sugar into her tea and blew softly to cool it as she lifted it to her lips, taking her time, relishing her new status in Carol's eyes. "Oh, still a little too hot. You know, the water has to be just off boiling to make a perfect pot and then you have to catch the tea at the perfect drinking temperature to get the fullest experience. Very easy to let it get too cold and I really cannot abide these philistines that will then re-heat it in that new-fangled micro-something machine. This tea is a rare blend, by the way, Tong Mu Phoenix Lapsang Souchong. Bet you can't say that three times in a row."

Carol curbed her impatience. Agnes loved the spotlight, that much was obvious and the only way to move this along was to let her have it. Agnes smiled as she set down her cup, undoubtedly reading Carol's mind again. "How do I know about George and Charlie? Let me tell you a story. It started when I was young, my mother said I nearly died from Scarlet fever. I fact at one point she thought I'd gone to the other side, but she prayed so hard I came back. I don't remember what I was like before, but when I came back, I could begin to read some people's thoughts and pick up other weird sensations. I thought I was nuts inside. We didn't know then what we know now, the power of the mind, spiritual beliefs. I just consider it a gift. I get flashes, sometimes with or without touching someone. But touching or holding hands helps. I've even seen some people's deaths, if they are meant to go shortly. But I've learned not to tell them. Safe to say I don't want to change history. My mom always said when your time is up, it's up, no messing about. And there's the paradox thing."

"What paradox thing?" Carol smiled as she sampled the tea. The temperature and strength were perfect.

"You obviously don't watch a lot of time travel shows. If I knew someone was going to die at a certain time, would I be bending time if I warned them? What if I did, and what if they lived? How much would it affect the time stream? Or is time already written and by telling them I'm only setting the proper time continuum? Love those sci-fi shows. You could go crazy thinking about this kind of stuff." Agnes calmly looked around the busy room.

"I could go crazy listening to this. Sorry to sound impatient but I'm on my break and I hate watching science fiction."

"Okay, sorry. Hey, just humor this old gal."

"So how much do you know about Charlie?" Carol changed the subject. Her head was beginning to hurt from trying to figure out the cause and effect of time travel.

"Charlie? Well, I usually just get a face, a name in this case. Little clues, I call them. If I was a religious person, I'd call them visions. I'm on the ghost tour tomorrow tonight and would love it if you could join me. My old bones aren't what they once were. I could use someone to hold me up. So, is that a possibility? That you'd join me?"

Carol knew the Rizzutos had called limos to take them elsewhere. But the Bellettis were taking the tour tomorrow night, and as she hadn't had much to do with them yet it would be a good chance to get close to that group as well. "Yes, and I'd lie about why but you probably already know." "No, I don't know everything in your head. Yet," she snickered. "But fill me in."

"I can't talk here, but I'm sure you can figure it out. I mean, you've already admitted you know my life's, ah shall we say complicated, haven't you?"

"Yes, dear, that's certainly not new information for my ears. And if other hotel guests are also taking the tour, well, that's just a marvelous chance for you to observe these people you need to know better, now isn't it?" Agnes smiled and nibbled again at the cucumber sandwich.

"It's very frustrating, having conversations with you, you know."

Agnes smiled as she sipped at her tea. "I've learned when to speak and when not to, certainly. And who knows? I might be of assistance in that."

"You'd be willing to do that?" *Not only psychic but brave, especially for...*

"For an old broad. Yes, I am. I've been of similar assistance more than a few times during my career. Agnes calmly spread the jam and cream on one of the scones. "I say, excellent High Tea, better than anything I've had in London."

Carol was impressed. "You're quite the spunky old lady, Agnes. Have you someone in your life?"

"I have had three husbands, one died, didn't actually see that one coming, which was weird for me. He was the one with the crystal skull and maybe that was why, he managed to block my access. Another was delighting his maids on the side. That I did see visions of, though I wish I hadn't, and another I knew wanted to be with men more than me. That one left me in the end. All of them left me with a lot of money. So currently, no, I don't want the complications of anything permanent. Although I do rather miss the companionship, a lady of means has to be very careful. That's where my ability to read people's thoughts comes in handy. I know very quickly whether it's me or my money the men are interested in."

"It will come in very handy as a detective too. Now this ghost tour draws quite a crowd. You told me Victoria is the most haunted city in all of Canada? I could use a little extra education about all that."

"Well, in this hotel alone there's reports of a maid wandering the corridors with her housekeeping trolley, still cleaning rooms apparently. Her uniform is too old-fashioned for this day and age. Two workers just last year, during the god-awful renovations, and please note I still don't like the new chandelier, reported seeing a man hanged in one of the rooms, and other reports of an older, distinguished gentleman who knocks on doors and leads people to the elevators before disappearing."

"I saw him. Just yesterday. Dressed in old-fashioned somewhat distinguished clothing. I wasn't going to tell you."

Agnes smiled "Didn't need to, but I knew already, felt him about the place. Oh, and sightings of a fellow reported to be Francis Rattenbury, the architect of both the Empress Hotel and the Provincial Parliament buildings. His affair with the woman who was to become his second wife, a woman named Alma, caused such a scandal he never worked in Canada again and they fled to England. He was killed there by either Alma or her young lover, George Stoner. Neither confessed and the crime was never solved." She closed her eyes. "So, this might be the man you saw in the hallway, returning in death to his beloved hotel."

"If I were to make a bet, I'd agree. I saw the plaque in the entranceway and could swear that was him. Say, where do you find out about all of this craziness? I never heard about any of this." *Great, I'm in a haunted city, full of pyscho-nutters, with all kinds of ghosts running around. I took this case to get away from mystical Woo-woo crap. I'm beginning to think I should give Charlie a call and have him help me with this case.* Carol shivered. *Why do I just know I'm going to end up with bugs all over me and in my hair, again? God, I hate bugs.*

"Let's just say when you're in the field you keep abreast of all the information and besides, Google is a wonderful thing." Agnes laughed.

"Charlie taught me there's so much more going on in the world that meets the eye and I'm trying to look inside people, but I can't do it like you do."

"Okay give me your hand and let's try a proper reading."

"Here in the tearoom?"

"Yeah, it'll be the first done here. You can put that into your promotional brochure."

Carol held out her hand, thinking of all the old movies with the crazy old gypsy woman in a circus tent. *Damn, gotta quit thinking like this while she's around or she's soon going to hate me.* Out of nowhere, a barely visible woman walked elegantly into the room. The waitress strolled right through her. The woman sat down at table just two over from them. *Let me guess, another freaking ghost.*

Agnes opened one eye. "Yes, Margaret is another freaking ghost. Actually, I quite like your sarcastic sense of being. Reminds me of mine. Now try to think of nothing, wipe your mind clean." She closed her eyes and quickly opened them. "Yes, spirits, I get... Sprity. Someone named Sprity. Earth nymph and ... you are connected."

"Maybe. When I worked with Charlie, we encountered a native spirit, the Haida call her Gyhldeptis. He tried to tell me she was a Buddha/Hindu thing, a future reincarnation of me, or some eastern meditational babble like that."

Agnes stared blankly at Carol, closed her eyes a moment. "He speaks a lot of truth, that shaman. I'll bet he watches a lot of time travel shows. I think his waters run pretty deep." Her eyes rolled back. "There's more. Aw, careful, danger, great danger ahead. A ghost, not nice. And another, rather unusual, feisty female you haven't met yet."

"Great, I keep attracting crazy broads and I'm really not into them. I prefer my bread buttered on one side if you know what I mean."

"Shhh, you're interrupting the flow and yes, I prefer hot dogs to buns myself." Agnes blushed and dropped Carol's hand like she'd been stung. "What? Oh my!"

"What? What's wrong?" Agnes' blush deepened.

"Ah look, if I'm going to die or something awful is going to happen to me you better tell me now."

Agnes turned even redder.

"Okay, to heck with the rules of modifying the time stream bull. What the hell did you just see about me?"

"Excuse me a moment. I need a little, er, medication." Agnes pulled a small, curved metal flask from her inside pocket, unscrewed the cap and took a long sip. "Care for some?" She handed the flask to Carol, who took a sniff first. *Crap, straight whiskey.* Out of politeness Carol took a small swallow. "I'm not saying much but I can tell you this — you're going to get 'a good seeing-to.'"

"Mrs. Van Lunt!"

"It's Agnes. And you asked, I'm only telling you like it comes to me. It wasn't my choice of words. Although come to think of it I wouldn't a bit of a seeing-to myself now and again." She smiled wistfully.

"Oh, my. You're amazing, Agnes. I never expected that from your lips." Carol slumped back in her plush chair, trying not to visualize what Agnes just said.

"Darling, I'm seventy-one, I'm not dead. I'll even supply the Viagra should I find a young, handsome stud about sixty or so."

Carol laughed. "I hope I have half your spunk when I'm your age." Carol felt her cheeks getting hot. "Oh, I think I'm blushing now."

"You just wait, darling." Agnes smiled slyly. She picked up Carol's hand again but dropped it like it had burnt her. Then her head dropped forward, and she fell back in her chair.

"Are you alright, Agnes?"

Agnes' mood had darkened dramatically. Her hands shook as she opened her eyes and struggled to sit upright. "Danger; extreme danger. You will need to be cautious with whomever you... how do I say this? Let into your life. Now excuse me, I need to go to my room, take my pills. My heart is racing. Can you help me?"

"That's the whiskey. May I ask what you saw?" Carol helped the old lady to her feet. "Agnes, your hands are shaking, are you sure you're alright?"

"I've said enough and seen too much, I'm afraid. Help me to the elevator. I've taken too much in, sometimes it gets overpowering, even after all these years. I need to rest and cleanse myself."

Whatever she'd seen, it'd frightened Agnes half to death. Carol knew to tread ahead lightly.

She knew Agnes well enough to know she didn't scare easily. She'd proceed with one eye open and felt better for having her ankle holster on, which she thought would be a wise idea, now that the mob were all here.

CAROL WATCHED FROM the window as members of the Rizzuto and Belletti families piled into their black limos, undoubtedly headed back to Hatley Castle. The wedding venue priced, on the average, at $4,000.00 an afternoon and had been booked by Lorenzo Rizzuto for the entire week. Just like last night. And just like last night, nondescript grey sedans pulled into traffic seconds behind them. Money might not buy happiness, but it sure as hell could buy an exclusive meeting place.

She texted Louie. *Hatley Castle again tonight?*
Confirmed.

She checked her phone, but no new news on Barb.

❦   ❧

"CAN YOU HELP ME, SON?" The older lady smiled at the six-year-old boy playing in the Quadra Elementary school playground; it was October 1990.

Jordon Gibson looked at her quizzically. "I'm not supposed to talk to strangers," he replied, and looked over at his mother. Samantha stood just the other side of the park nattering away on her large, almost foot-long top-of-the-line Motorola cell phone. The glint of the antenna caught the sunlight. She was semi-watching her husband, Bruce, playing soccer in the warm spring weather.

"Well, I'm just a little old lady, and I need help getting this shopping to that van over there. Oh, and I have some very nice candies here, you can have them if you help me." She held out her hand, showing him the wrapped toffees.

Little Jordon got up and walked over to Gladys. As he reached her, she checked to make sure the mother was still talking and no one else was looking. He helped her lift the bag. "Thank you, you're such a sweet lad." As he turned away, she reached into her pocket and withdrew a rag that reeked of chloroform. "But you really should have listened to your mom." She clamped it around his nose and held tight. He slumped, unconscious within seconds. She struggled to lift him into her tan van and quietly drove away.

Mrs. Gibson looked up a minute later to see how her son was doing. No one was in the playground. Suddenly the call to her friend didn't seem that important. The bulky phone fell from her fingers as she ran to the play area. *"Jordon!"*

❦   ❧

THE BLUE EMBRYO THROBBED again and exploded the sewer room with light. Two small bodies lay there, awash in liquids, their bodies attached via an umbilical cord. "What are we?" asked one.

"Unknown," the other responded, before the two grabbed hands and pulled back together.

Doubling again in size, the egg shook with life as memories began to filter in.

Chapter Six

C arol met Agnes again for afternoon tea. Although the hotel's real General Manager still did much of the background work, as Carol could not be expected to manage after only a week of training,

however intense, Big Dan had requested he step in and do more, allowing Carol as much free time as possible. "Every time I turn around I'm seeing a ghost. Is it just me?"

"No," Agnes said as she sipped slowly at her tea. Today Agnes looked like a forties fashion model, dressed in a long flowing red and white checkered dress. Her signature cartwheel hat was red, pinned slightly back. "It's a side effect from that being you told me you met. The forest sprite. She's enhanced a sixth sense in you via the vomeronasal organ. Everyone has the ability although few use it or even know it's there."

"The what? I thought the sixth sense was an intuitive thing."

"It's an organ located in the nose, and detects chemicals and pheromones in minute quantities, something a lot of animals use in detecting their prey or fear in humans. Some species may even communicate via this organ, like dogs, and also to sense when humans are scared of them. Now give me your hand again."

She let Agnes concentrate for a moment before replying after she let her hold her hand, "Glyffy? You're talking about Glyffy? The thing Charlie said was me in a future incarnation? Is this permanent?"

"Yes, these Sprity beings most likely communicate using the vomeronasal organ and your Charlie sounds like just the kind of chap I'd like to date."

"He's a little young for you, though, and besides, he's hopelessly hooked and in love with his childhood sweetheart who died when he was a teenager."

"My kind of guy though if he's into ghosts and the deceased. Feel free to hook us up. I've got nothing against a young stud in my bed."

Carol closed her eyes. "Eww! You've just turned me off sex for the next year." They both laughed.

"Okay, yes, this creature, this Glyffy as you call her, did change something inside of you. So, the answer is yes, you have been gifted with a most unusual ability, you're able to sense, feel and occasionally see, spiritual beings and ghosts. I think maybe she intended you'd be able to detect when she was near you."

"Great, I'll smell her coming a mile away. But it's only around here that

I'm getting more and more visions."

"No, I think it has to do with the ley lines and earth energy that intersects here. They attract corporeal energies and awaken your powers even more."

"Great. How do I put that job skill in my portfolio?"

"I think hush-hush is a better approach."

Carol's nose twitched again, and her senses were suddenly on high alert, just like when she saw the ghost in the hallway. She looked up and watched an elderly lady walk into the dining room, sit down at a table next to them and begin to sip at her tea. Her clothing was similar to Agnes' highend forties fashion. "A spirit just walked in. We saw her yesterday when we were here, didn't we, Margaret?"

"The one who dresses elegantly, feather in her hat?" Carol nodded.

"Yes. She's quite harmless."

"But you do see her too, right?" She watched the woman calmly sit down and like the day before, take her hat off and pull one of her long white gloves off. Carol could see through her to the couple behind.

"Occasionally, just a glimpse, like most people. Only most people will talk themselves out of it. I mainly just pick up her thoughts. She's quite distinct and has very strong energy."

"But the hat. I get something about the hat."

"She thinks about it a lot. Looks at it in the mirror and adjusts it before she comes down at precisely three o'clock for tea. Every day. Very prompt and fastidious. Does everything on a set schedule and has for years, possibly decades."

Carol looked at her, sitting there so primly. She closed her eyes and concentrated. "It's the hat. A man paid her a lot of attention when she wore that hat. He came back and talked to her a lot over the next few days. He was supposed to ask her out for dinner, but never did. She returns here every winter in the hope he'll come back to her, like he promised." A tear threatened to roll down her cheek. "That's so sad. She's come back here year after year, just hoping he'll come back and ask her to dinner. She hopes he'll ask her to marry him."

Agnes watched Carol wipe her eyes. "So, not the cold-hearted, cool-headed realist you lead others to believe. Yes, she loved him dearly and died in her room on the sixth floor a spinster."

Carol glanced at her watch. "I've got to go. I need to make an appearance at Reception. Shall we meet in the lobby around seven for the ghost tour?"

"Yes, please. It sounds like a fun night. You think our friend the hunky American or the equally hunky Italian will be joining us?"

"Hey, I didn't tell you about any hunky... oh. Right."

"*Exactly.*" Agnes picked up her last tiny cucumber sandwich. "You go ahead, my dear. I've got a busy afternoon of massages and shopping. Right after I have another cup or two of this wonderful tea."

I really hate her reading me like a diary.

"I know." Agnes smiled serenely as Carol walked away. *Now, to get back to my room and ask Cider a few questions.*

CAROL SAT BESIDE AGNES on one of the wrought-iron benches strategically placed under the Empress's portico.

"Oh, look, dear! Here comes our tour bus!" Agnes pointed to the red double-decker bus pulling into the reserved spaces in front of the hotel. *Victoria's Ghost Tours* lettered the side of the bus in ornate cursive. The bus door opened, and the tour guide hopped out to collect his evening's charges, a clip-board in his hand. His top-hat and tails warred with the deep-red t-shirt under the coat that sported the same logo emblazoned on the side of the bus. Apparently, the tour company didn't know whether to go formal or informal, but the odd compromise seemed to work for them.

Agnes tugged on Carol's arm. "Oh, good! I do love it when the tour guide's a hottie, don't you, dear?"

Carol laughed. "Agnes, behave yourself."

"Good evening, ladies!" The tour guide bowed theatrically and flipped a page on his clip board. "Adam Johnson here! You must be...let's see..."

"Agnes Van Lunt and my young friend, Carol Moore. I had the concierge call and add her to the tour this afternoon."

"Yes, you certainly did and you're both right here! Now, we're only waiting on...ah...the Belletti party?"

Carol looked back through the lobby's big glass windows and pointed. "And here they come now, I see."

Tony Belletti led the Belletti party through the lobby. Carol ran through her own personal mug-book containing photos of the main players of the Rizzuto and Belletti families. Tony was a Belletti family son. His picture didn't do him justice, though. Tony Belletti's looks made Lorenzo Rizzuto seem ordinary. In fact, Tony was the type of drop-dead gorgeous women couldn't help staring at. He smiled at Carol and she smiled back, then glanced down at her watch, hoping the gesture made her seem shy. Men like Tony Belletti loved to play the big hero to shy women. He kept staring at her as she looked back up. Their eyes locking and the first thing that entered her mind was, *Oh God,* as flashes of memories not yet lived flashed through her, *not him.* He kept staring as if he couldn't tear his eyes away before he had to look in the direction of the tour guide.

"Wonderful!" Tour guide Adam Johnson flipped the pages of his clip board back in place. "We're ready to start tonight's festivities! I don't know about you folks, but I'm just *shivvvvering* with excitement! And since beauty *always* comes before age, let's get Mrs. Van Lunt seated first, shall we? Right this way, now!"

The crowd giggled a bit and Carol held Agnes' arm and guided her toward the London bus. It was an older model, with the jump on-jump off platform at the back. Two four-person bench seats faced each other, their backs to the windows, just inside. The more normal five rows of two by two-seater seats took up the front.

"Ah, Ms. Moore!" Tony Belletti touched Carol's arm lightly. "Please, let me help you two lovely ladies get settled in your seats. Beside me, if I could be so lucky?" He steered them toward the first of seat. His eyes never leaving Carol. His touch sent shivers through her and flashes of knowing.

It is said that you can meet people and know in the space of a heartbeat or a touch that you've been together or are meant to be together. Or know that you will be, but not him. *Lord, why him?*

Agnes elbowed Carol. "He hasn't taken his eyes off you. I think he likes what he sees."

Carol elbowed back, "makes two of us." She couldn't help herself, this man, the enemy, had already dug deep into her. *Instant attraction. I read about it in trashy romance novels, but to feel it firsthand was exhilarating.* The attraction to Jake was more physical due to the fact he looked a lot like her deceased fiancé. *This is deeper.*

"How lovely to find chivalry alive and well in Victoria, Canada!" Agnes flirted back, breaking the silence. "And aren't you handsome and smooth talking. I've been told Italian men are very amorous in bed."

Carol blushed, caught off guard by Agnes' comment. *She didn't just actually say that, did she?*

"If I was ten years older, I would gladly show that you are correct in what you've heard. But in any event, if you and Ms. Moore allow me to join you on the tour, we can see where that leads, no?"

Agnes put out her hand for Tony to assist her up the small step to the long bench seat. "What fun these seats are. I feel very tall and regal. Now, Tony, you sit here," she patted the seat on her right, "and Carol you here." She patted the other side. "I shall be a thorn between two roses."

Carol grinned. Certainly no one was going to argue with that. The two men she'd already pegged as Tony's bodyguards didn't look terribly happy, though. They sat on the opposing bench seat.

Agnes smiled and let her hand fall against Tony's outer thigh. "Oh my, judging by the hardness of your leg muscles, I'd say you must work out."

He laughed lightly and actually blushed. "Well, I play a lot of tennis and golf, I'm not bad, actually. I made professional football in Italy, in fact."

The bus drove along Government Street and the tour guide started his spiel over the PA system.

"Okay folks, how's everyone doing? Where are you all from?"

He responded to several of the crowd before continuing. "Now, there's going to be a lot going on tonight, so let me give you a little overview. Victoria, if you haven't heard, is ghost central. Easily the most haunted city in all of Canada. We have so many ghosts the government is proposing a boo tax." Everyone groaned "Some sites I'll point out to you and tell you their story, but we won't be getting off the bus and touring. And why not, you ask? Well, some of the ones we won't actually go inside 'cause the current owners haven't invited us. That legal issue thing, you know. And some we won't go into because we want to make sure all our guests who start the tour return from it, and if we actually disturb the ghosts at some sites, they might not.

That's why you all signed waivers!"

Ghostly music played over the PA, and the spiel continued. "Now, for those of you feeling particularly adventuresome, there's another tour that takes you to a time vortex. What's that you say? Time travel? Yes, indeedy! Right at the spot where Shelbourne Street crosses Hillside

Avenue, it's possible to time travel! Sometimes. If you're lucky. Some say they've been driving along on a very ordinary suburban street and suddenly found themselves on an old dirt road. But that, as they say, is another story! I can sell you tickets for that tour, if you'd like."

Agnes looked at Carol and Tony and grinned. "Take my hands if you feel scared, my dears. Don't you just love the scare tactics? The only spooky thing about these tours is the exorbitant price."

The other two smiled. "By American prices, this is inexpensive for a tour of this nature,"

Tony replied, his eyes catching Carol's smile.

Carol just shook her head. "I'm just along for the ride, never done anything like this before."

Tony smiled at her. "Then I, for one, am glad Mrs. Van Lunt convinced her niece to join her tonight."

Agnes pinched his leg. "Oh, he's a flirt and a charmer as well."

The bus stopped in front of an old brick building and the guide's voice continued to flow from the PA system.

"This is the former Windsor Hotel. And even though it's been closed for the last eight years, many say shadows play across the windows." The guide's voice deepened and lingered over the words as he told the story. "Oh, yes, many passersby insist figures move inside, casting the shadows, and sometimes the shadows scream and thump. And now and then, folks say they hear little children playing inside."

Suddenly everything blurred. Carol closed her eyes and lowered her head. "What?"

A vision filled her eyes as she stared out the window. Like watching a private video clip of her driving along a street, this street. Late at night when an elderly woman dressed in black fills her view through the car's windshield. She tries to swerve, but it is too late, slamming into her.

The body is flung like a disjointed ragdoll through the air. "Oh God." She slams on the brakes and runs to the woman's aid.

Even in her panic, the odd graffiti scrawled on the door caught her attention. She looked down and felt for a pulse, there wasn't any. The elderly lady lay very still, blood oozing from her mouth and her hand clutched a ... "Carol! Are you okay?" Agnes shook her, and everything vanished.

Only the empty store front stared back at her.

"I, I, thought I just saw something. My imagination, I'm sure." With Tony sitting there she didn't want to go into details about a vision. "I'm alright. Sorry if I gave you a fright, though."

Agnes patted her arm. "That's perfectly fine, dear. You probably just had a hot flash from sitting close to such a gorgeous man. I think I'm getting one too."

"Agnes! Really!"

Tony laughed. "Oh, don't mind me. I haven't been this, how you say, *intrattenuti*, entertained in a long time."

They stopped next in front of Roger's Chocolates and everyone disembarked. Carol and Tony helped Agnes off the bus, one on each side. "This is now a historic site. Back in 1885 Charles Rogers moved here from Massachusetts. He originally just set up a grocery and sold imported chocolates from the US which people were buying up like mad."

"I guess they were just as crazy for chocolate back then as they are now," one of the tour group said as the tour guide unlocked the door and let everyone in. Lights flickered eerily on.

"Yes, some things never change. He ended up meeting and marrying Canadian Leah Morrison. Now good ol' Candy Rogers, as he was nicknamed, decided to try his hand at making his own chocolate. Which became the privately-run Roger's Chocolates brand. It was rumoured that they often slept in the store and the kitchen."

Agnes closed her eyes. "Hang on, I'm getting something."

"Sorry, ladies and gentlemen, she really is a psychic and sometimes gets visions." Carol said trying to calm everyone.

Agnes laughed to herself. Obviously regaling in the attention as everyone turned to stare her. "Now I know why they slept here, used to slather the stuff all over themselves and have a fun time licking it off," Agnes spoke out loud. "Victorian kinkiness, love it." Several chuckled and some of the older crowd gasped at her remark.

"And you're probably going to saying that they never left." Agnes muttered as she turned to the tour guide.

He nodded in affirmation.

She closed her eyes and turned to Carol whispering, "I get why, there's something not right in this store. A creepy feeling, I don't usually get. There's something else in here I don't like." Agnes smiled at the others and said out loud. "Yes, I do get a lot of hot, chocolatey passions in here."

Carol looked about, but nothing came to her. She inhaled deeply, but nothing, not even a single twitch from her nose.

"What was that earlier when we were at the other hotel?" Agnes said as she pulled Carol aside.

Carol quickly explained. "It was me, everything blurred and it was like I'd been thrust into a vision, or maybe a memory, but how can it be a memory when it's not something I've ever done? I'd struck an older lady and killed her in the alley behind the Windsor Hotel. Why I would be driving here at breakneck speed and strike a woman crossing the street I don't know. It was so vivid, so real."

"That is called retro or post-cognition. Encountering something unexplainable by any normal means. Either an event from the past or possibly one that will happen in the future."

"Like *déja-vu* in reverse? I've never been down that alley before we drove by it today."

Agnes nodded, "If this hasn't happened to you yet, it will in the future. Post cognitive."

"Not possible."

Agnes grabbed her, "I think our man Adam wants to get on with his spiel and we're delaying him. We'll talk later."

Adam smiled at the two. "I'd be honored to get more of your visions on this tour. I don't get many mystics joining us. Now, many people have heard and seen shadows moving about the store and the smell of fresh chocolate still wafts about."

Agnes closed her eyes and half whispered to Carol on a light note as she shook her head. "Sorry I get these visions, from people alive mostly. But occasionally in haunted areas I get voices and other strange happenings." "They actually slathered each other with chocolate?" Agnes nodded.

"You're so bad. On the other hand, that would be kinky fun to try some day," Carol replied, realizing how much hell Agnes probably went through and the things she must have experienced. "Small wonder you're still sane after all of this."

Carol caught a shadow flicker over a mirror in the corner of the room as her nose suddenly twitched to the smell of chocolate. "Pardon me." She walked over and stared at her reflection in the mirror.

A bearded man stared back at her, somewhat distinguished looking. He looked quite like Francis Rattenbury, and the man she'd seen before. Although most gentlemen of the day looked very similar it could have been either of them or it could have been one and the same. She glanced behind her to see him better in person, only there was no one there. She turned back to stare in the mirror and only saw her own reflection. *What the...*

She walked back to Agnes, who was perusing some of the items in the store. "Did you feel something just then? Anything weird?"

"Just my cucumber sandwich. I really shouldn't eat the stuff. Love it, but it always seems to repeat on me."

"No, I meant..."

"I know what you meant. I'm getting some really heavy vibes in this place. There's a lot of esoteric shit being stirred, and it has nothing to do with the tour." "What do you mean?" Carol was curious.

"When I'm in a place with a lot of ghostly hauntings I tend to get this creepy feeling down my spine. It's my divining rod." Agnes replied.

"Nothing to do with burping cukes?" Carol tried to make light as she began to get shivers as well. Tony and his gang had already slipped outside for a smoke.

"Ladies, we must be getting on with the tour," Adam said to them.

"No, that was my sarcastic humor. It's not like being able to read people's thoughts, can't with the dead, which I could have made a fortune with. It's this sense that I almost feel like something is watching me."

"Yeah, I swear there was just a guy in the mirror just watching me, only there's no one here. He looked just like the man I saw in the hotel."

The tour guide looked at them. "Pardon me ladies for interrupting, but you may want to see this as we exit the store." He pointed up. "There's no explanation for this."

Some of the group gasped as he shone his light at a mirror high above the door. A small child's handprint could be seen. "It is rumored that one of their children died at an early age and still haunts this store. That handprint has been wiped off many times and always reappears. Now to our next stop."

Agnes smiled. "No, it's not their child doing that. Although I can feel the presence of the Rogers in the room and I think we should leave ASAP."

The smell of chocolate wafted in the air and whisperings echoed. Adam turned white as a chill filled the room. "Yes, agreed, I think our couple wants to slather some chocolate on themselves. The next stop on the tour tonight is Helmcken Alley. The rest we'll see on the second night of the tour."

Everyone hurried from the room and stood outside shivering as they boarded the tour bus. Tony stared quietly at Agnes as they drove on like he wanted to ask a question but didn't know what to say or how to ask it.

Minutes later they got off the bus again. They walked to the entrance of a dark alley. "Along Helmcken Alley, on the left once stood the first jail of Fort Victoria. A ghost is often seen, rattling his chains here. There are rumours that they had the wrong man but that The Hanging Judge, as he was known, Chief Justice Sir Matthew Begbie, didn't care. He ordered him hanged anyways as he was in the mood for a good hanging. It was reported the man was also beaten to near death before he got to the gallows. In another case, it was also noted that once the Chief Justice got so annoyed with the jury, he threatened to have them all strung up. Begbie's ghost is reported to have been filmed near Saanich along his beach-front home where he rather liked to hang out."

Carol watched as Tony performed the signs of the cross on himself, as did the others of the Belletti group. *Okay, that's of interest to note. Need to research the names of the men that were hanged here.* "He must have been a very powerful figure in his time to leave such strong residues behind in his death."

"And sometimes the unjustly accused also leave powerful residue with their passing and don't rest until justice is performed, or in this case possibly a curse," Agnes blurted out, disturbing Carol's thoughts. "Something I've learned in my days as being a psychic."

"Funny, I was just about to say that," Adam said in response. "You must be getting some kind of visions here. Care to share them?"

Agnes closed her eyes as Carol stared at her phone as a text came in.

'The Rizzutos gang, except for Antonio, have left and appear to be heading for Hatley castle again' She turned it off and stared down the short dark alley. *I think I need to pay the castle a visit next time they head out.*

Agnes opened her eyes. "Sorry, I got nothing. But yes, I get the sense of strong injustice here. I think many a scoundrel met his maker at the end of the judge's rope."

A circular concrete area shone in the single street light. "Dare to walk the alley of death to the gallows which used to hang on the other side? Many a scoundrel, as our esteemed psychic has already mentioned, did indeed leave his last breath there." He teased her and the rest in the group.

"Yeah, why not?" Carol and Agnes slowly walked down the cobbled alley behind the rest. As they did at the back of the group, due to Agnes' slower pace, Carol caught something shifting in the darkness. Shadows of fires, flickering. She stopped. "Did you see that?"

"No, my dear. But there is much unrest and I really get that someone or something left a curse here. I saw the reaction of the Italians at the mention of his name."

"I know, I did as well." Carol breathed in deeply again. The weak outline of a man pulled from the shadows. But not the reported figure in chains. It was the same bearded, distinguished man who appeared to be following her. He mouthed some words before pulling back into the darkness. "What the..."

Someone from the front of the pack screamed as the sounds of chains echoed. Agnes stopped. "Go ahead, dear, I want to take a breather."

Carol rushed ahead the fifty feet or so to the group as the haunted figure of a man in chains shuffled along. "Oh my. This has never happened before," was all Adam said.

The same thing Agnes said. Wanting to make sure Agnes was okay Carol looked behind her and watched the old lady talking to vague figure she'd just seen herself in the shadows; "her" ghost, as she was beginning to think of him. Carol strode back to the old gal. The figure tilted his head and removed his top hat, like they did in the movies, and pulled back into the darkness. "You okay? What the heck was that all about? He appeared to be talking to you."

"An old friend I haven't seen in quite a while," was all she said. "Time to head back to the bus."

"But I'm sure he's the same ghost that seem to be following me," Carol said.

"Oh, you know, gentlemen of that era all seemed to look the same," Agnes replied vaguely. "I think I'm beginning to understand the cause of the curse involving the mob. We need to go to the Saanich beach house and pay Judge Begbie a visit. There's a lot more here than we know."

⚬⚬

A MURKY FIGURE TORE open the thin blue embryotic skin and lifted itself free. It stared around the awful rank-smelling chamber. *I am us?*

No, we are us. The other half of it responded.
I do not understand.
Nor do I?

They lifted their arms. *We are now one and yet two. How is this possible?*

Unknown. The cycle calls us, we shall sleep and grow some more.
We are young, still being born.

The blue being spun around itself a silky veil, collapsing into a blue embryonic shape and fell asleep. This time it began to dream.

AS CAROL AND TONY ASSISTED Agnes into the lobby of the Empress Hotel, Samuel came over to her. "Ms. Moore. May I have a word?"

Carol turned to Agnes. "Sorry, duty calls." She signaled for a porter to help Agnes to the elevator.

"It's okay, need a bit of a lie down anyways. We'll talk later."

Samuel waited until Agnes and the porter were far enough away so as not to hear him. "We've got a problem. Mr. Rizzuto Senior's room."

"What's the problem?"

"Housekeeping noticed that at 7:18 the sensors on the mini-bar went off," he told her.

"Sensors?"

"Yes. The mini-bar has sensors that alert them if items are removed so they can re-stock and charge accordingly. In Mr. Rizzuto's room they all went off together. Housekeeping called in to alert us as it seemed strange."

"All of them? That suggests that either a thief was at work or the cabinet could have been knocked over."

"Correct. So, I sent Security to see if there was a problem, but Mr. Rizzuto hasn't responded to any calls either on his room's phone or through the door. Security unlocked the door, but the anchor is still in place. They have just requested our permission to break it down."

"Tell them to wait, I'm on my way. Does anyone else know?"

"Not yet, as far as we can tell."

"Samuel, stay here on Reception. And act as normally as possible. I do not want this to get out."

Carol looked at her watch as she rushed up the stairs. It was 7:56 just under forty minutes had elapsed. Time was of the essence; he could have suffered a heart attack or something.

As Carol ran down the corridor towards the Rizzuto suite she spied Carson and Vidler, two of the Victoria PD's undercover sergeants, who had also responded, and the hotel's own Security stood some few paces away. She ran up to the door, trying to peer through the half inch that the anchor allowed. "Mr. Rizzuto, are you okay in there?"

No response. She looked up and down the corridor, it was empty. Most of the Rizzuto clan members had gone on a tour of Hatley Castle to inspect the facility before the wedding. She knew he had elected to stay behind.

"Shall I break it down?" Carson asked.

"No, don't want the noise to alert others. Watch and learn." Carol grabbed the plastic hotel card and bent it in slightly. She slid the plastic in the gap, with the bent part pointing to the outside of the door. She quickly caught the two metal rods and shoved. The metal moved back effortlessly.

Carol caught something flicker in the light.

"Haven't seen that move before."

"I've had to break into a couple of rooms without anyone knowing." Carol pushed the door open and they entered.

Inside it was a mess. The liquor cabinet was toppled over, and drink cans and bottles decorated the floor. Carol edged around them as she made for the bedroom door and spotted a pair of feet with very expensive leather shoes jutting out from behind the four-poster king-sized bed at the far end of the room. "Crap! Mr. Rizzuto?" She rushed around the bed, he lay there, eyes wide.

Carson and Vidler rushed in behind her. "Carson, check all the rooms and closets in this suite, make sure there's no one else in here. Check also for any escape route."

Carol searched for a pulse, but it was obvious he didn't have any. His body still felt warm, so it would seem he was not dead long.

"Is he?" Vidler enquired.

"Yeah, dead and cooling. I'd say he died around the time of the cabinet going over." Carol stared hard at his neck. "What the..."

She pulled on the latex gloves she kept about her person in case anything like this ever happened and she didn't want to disturb evidence.

Voices were heard in the hallway.

She pulled his collar aside. "Holy. Vidler block the entrance. And have Security keep everyone out of the corridor. I don't believe this."

"Is that a noose?" he blurted out as he ran to block the door and anyone from entering.

"Yes, and somewhat old looking. This is now a crime scene. Don't let anyone in and call the police and forensics."

"But we are the police."

"Yeah, undercover remember. No one else knows that, especially not the mob."

"Sorry, moment of stupidity. Man, this is going to cause an uproar." Carson flicked on his cell phone as he exited the suite. "Immediate backup to the Empress, the Rizzuto suite. Forensics too, apparent suicide."

Carol stared at what looked like the murder weapon. She took a couple of pictures on her cell phone before lifting the noose slightly. There were ligature marks underneath. "Crap, it appears that he's been hanged or strangled." She stared around the room and looked up at the four-poster bed. *Would that be sturdy enough? If it's a cheap copy, probably not. And not high enough. He could have supported himself on the bed. Unless...*

Carol carefully checked his head for signs of blunt-force trauma and found it. *That explains a lot; incapacitated first. Probably what caused the mini-bar to go over and nothing else. Out cold before he hit the ground.*

Murderer could take his time after that, and maybe hang him from the bed. Only why not just leave him there? Why cut him down?

"No sign of anyone, and no obvious escape route, all doors and windows locked," Carson said, as he reported back.

"Thanks Carson."

Carol turned back to the victim and examined his face. No bruising or swelling other than a slight blue tinge to the lips.

A loud commotion at the door as Jake came bursting into the suite, pushing past Vidler, and then past Carson into the bedroom.

"What the hell is going on here?" Both agents were about to grab him.

Carol blurted out before too much noise and possible commotion was raised. "It's okay, he's FBI and also undercover."

Jake's eyes caught the sprawled body. "Shit, not Antonio Rizzuto? Oh, this isn't going to go down well with the clan."

He glanced around the room, quickly sizing up everything. Something Carol didn't miss. "Is that an effing noose?"

"Okay." She stood up, further blocking any view or access to the body. "Not your country, you've no jurisdiction here. I was told there's FBI in this undercover, but officially I haven't been told who or how to deal with them. Back up before I have you arrested." She held her hands out in front of her. "I thought we were working together on this?"

"I have no commands or directives from my seniors. Only your words. Again, I was told there was an American FBI agent here, but nothing about working together." Carol stood there arms folded, holding her ground.

Jake gritted his teeth and gave her a cold, hard stare. Neither was going to back down. He pulled his smart phone out from his jacket and handed her a card. "Calm down, lady. Better call your supervisor on this secure line." He stood back as Carol stared at the number on the card and at him. It was Big Dan's private cell number. *How the hell does he know this number?*

"Okay, back up, you're not getting any closer before I call."

Jake took two steps back into the lounge area of the Bob Hope suite and folded his arms.

Carson stood nearby prepared to grab Jake as Vidler stood by the hallway. "All clear so far."

"Lady, I ain't the enemy here."

"Until I hear otherwise, I believe and trust no one. Except my boss. Now again, back the hell off." Carson escorted Jake back into the corridor and stood next to Vidler, both blocking Jake from re-entering the suite.

Dan answered immediately. "Thought you'd be calling. Yes, you will allow him to be involved in this matter since the New York Mafia are of obvious interest to the American

Intelligence Authorities. This is a joint operation between both our countries security forces."

"You could have told me earlier. Thanks." Carol hung up before he could respond and indicated to Carson and Vidler to let Jake back in; he'd already contaminated the crime scene anyway. Handing the phone back to Jake she said, "Son of a... I guess we're working together on this one."

"As soon as we heard the commotion, we knew there'd be trouble, but not like this."

"Heard? How?"

"We planted microphones." He made it sound so nonchalant.

The yanks had 'phones planted. Even we hadn't set those up yet, couldn't get the warrants in time, and in our country. The nerve.

Jake pointed to the center of the room in front of the liquor cabinet. "Seems maybe Mr. Rizzuto surprised an intruder. We'd a tip that the clans are here for something else. Maybe they aren't in this wedding together and one clan wants to wipe out the other, or it was rumored possibly a third clan might step in from Montreal to bust this joining up. Or maybe, there's a more bizarre reason they're here."

"Wipe each other out? Not what we're getting from the underground. But, yes, I can say we also got reports from our Quebec sources that the powerful Montreal mob is aware and doesn't want this to go through. Bizarre reason? Like what?"

"An old curse, we're told."

"Old curse?" She scratched her head. "Is this the Federal Investigation Bureau and not the Facebook Old Granny Conspiracy Theory Group?"

Jake laughed. "I was told you had balls. Okay, if you believe in Woowoo stuff, this happened well over a hundred and fifty years ago, around the time Victoria was just being settled and there was still the possibility it might join America instead of Canada. It had something to do with someone about to be wrongly hanged by Victoria's Chief Justice, the right honorable M. Begbie. The victim's name escapes me right about now, Marshall or Marchiotti, I think, but the man cursed everyone in the room, one of whom was a Rizzuto, possibly the man that hanged our victim. As you know, the Italians are a superstitious lot, and they believe the curse will be broken by marriage and consummation here. Along with some other weird observances, like cutting off a bat's head, drinking devil's blood, etc, blah, blah, blah. Otherwise the family will be doomed to forever lose their first-born sons, and from the research, that is exactly what has happened to every family affected by this curse since then. One of the reasons they haven't been involved in setting up business on Canada's West Coast."

"What? And you think that person has come back and exacted their revenge by hanging Mr. Rizzuto? You Americans are nuts. Woo-woo stuff; no such thing," she lied. It was the Woo-woo stuff with Charlie Stillwater that got her elected to be on this case. There were hints of occult based reasons why the mob might be here, as well. *Is there anything the Americans didn't know about what was going on here?* "I'm beginning to really hate you. Okay, take a look, but don't touch anything."

"If you're wondering, our dead friend here was the first-born male, so the curse continues." He grinned smugly at her. As he brushed past her into the bedroom, his hand rubbed along her leg. A shiver went through her. *Bastard.* She was truly beginning to hate that assured smile on that handsome face.

Crap this is going to be trouble trying to work on this case with this hunk beside me. Either I break his nose for touching me or take him to bed, or both.

Like her he glared at the noose, the end roughly cut. "Well, it appears, or has been made to appear, that he's been hanged."

"My thought exactly," Carol replied as she stared at the noose.

"He must have been incapacitated first as otherwise we would have heard more commotion."

"Yes, he was. I found the wound. Killer could have done what he wished after that."

"Yeah, but the only possible place he could have been strung up is the four-poster."

"Okay smartass. If he was hanged from the bed and then cut down— and the end of the noose appears to have been cut—where's the other end? Why isn't is still hanging from the bed frame? And why cut him down anyway? Why not just leave him hanging? That doesn't make any sense."

"Never does with ghosts."

"I'm not buying it; something doesn't smell right here." Her nose has twitched several times.

Just then two police officers strolled in and a fully-dressed forensics team followed. Between the white boot covers, white coveralls with hoods and white face masks they looked like ghosts themselves. You could just about make out their eyes behind the goggles.

Carol and Jake exited the suite to leave them to it. The corridor was still empty.

"Not like Grissom's lot," Jake said to Carol.

"You watch CSI as well?"

"Yeah, love seeing how bad they've screwed up the scenes. No protective clothing, not even gloves sometimes, shedding hair and sweat and breathing all over everything. Crime scene's contaminated already. Really need a professional adviser," he replied.

Carol laughed. "That's what I think every time I watch it."

"Hey, at least we got something in common, lady."

Carol bristled at that remark. *Arrogant, handsome prick, I need to keep my cool before I nut him between the legs.*

Carol's phone beeped. "I just got reports that limos are pulling up in front, so beat it. You need to get out of here before anyone shows up and you blow your cover." Carol looked down the hallway, there was little activity at this time with everyone out. That would change very soon. "We gotta go."

Jake glared at her and turned to leave. "Did I mention that bossy women turn me on?" he yelled at her as he retreated.

Ignoring his last remark, Carol turned to the medical examiner. "First impressions?"

"Death by asphyxiation probably, and it appears the noose is the murder weapon. It's old looking but appears strong enough still. I'll have the fibers checked for origin and age. Can't see any defensive wounds, so the blunt force trauma," he indicated the back of the dead man's head, "would have caused instant incapacitation. Ensure the forensics team know to look for a weapon. There would probably be blood and hair on it." Removing his thermometer, he stated, "Time of death approximately sixty minutes ago. Obviously we'll know more after the autopsy. Don't want to say anything else at this stage."

Her phone was ringing, she was needed downstairs. As she exited the room, she spied an open pack of dental floss on the sideboard near the door. *Odd.*

She rearranged her collar and made sure she looked prim and proper. *Lady, its show time and this is more than likely going to get ugly. Now what am I going to tell the mob? Break in?*

Heart attack?

AGNES CLIMBED OUT OF the cab. "Here's for the fare, and here's another fifty for you to wait here while I do something." The dark-skinned taxi driver nodded in agreement, staring at the red bill she'd placed in his palm. It was the biggest tip he'd ever seen.

I'm glad Carol got called away, gives me time to check this place out.

Agnes strolled over to the park bench. *I figure I might as well start earning my pay for this assignment.*

Agnes knew all the details having read over the case many times, trying to get some kind of intuitive feel for what happened and who took Jordon Gibson from the Quadra Street playground in October 1990. She sat on the park bench just beside the playground. On her lap in a cloth bag rested Cider. Nothing came to her. "Odd. I usually get a vision or a sense of something. It's almost like there's been an exclusion zone wrapped around here."

She reached into the cloth and with one hand touched the cool crystal head of the skull, caressing it. "Okay, Cider, ol' gal, show me what happened and don't spare the grisly details."

Everything faded around her as the crystal skull pulled her back threw the veils of time.

Agnes watched as the boy of five ran across the parking lot to the small playground. On the other side his mother, Samantha, watched as she talked on her large cellular phone. Agnes spied an idling tan van, just behind the corner of the elementary school. From it emerged what appeared to be a slender, older woman walking towards the lad playing by himself. *Odd, I expected a man.*

The woman stood wisely behind a large fir tree, years smaller than the one Agnes sat near today, blocked from being seen by anyone. The woman's hand extended as a cheer ran through the men playing flag football nearby, drawing Samantha's attention.

Candies laying in the hidden woman's palm, caught the eye of the lad and he approached her. From her jacket a damp cloth sprang free as she grabbed the child who quickly went limp, inhaling chlorophyll.

She stared hard at the rear of the van, BCD 053 as the woman tossed the young lad inside.

The woman spun around and glared directly at the park bench, staring, it appeared, straight into Agnes' gaze. She pulled a pendant from her blouse and waved one hand in a pentagram, much as the Catholics do making the sign of the cross. In the air the panicked cries of Samantha calling out her son's name resounded.

She shoved her hand towards Agnes. The elder lurched backwards as the vision went black and she felt as if someone had just heaved a mental slap at her.

Agnes shook her head, stunned. Her cheek went red. *Well that's never happened before. She knows someone was watching her through time. Not your average abductor type then, no wonder I couldn't get a lock on anything here.*

Agnes summoned the cab driver that had been sitting there the whole time waiting for her. She quickly got into the backseat, clutching the heavy crystal skull tightly. "Empress Hotel and step on it." She took a long swig from her flask. *And if she knows that, the next question is, does she know who I am and how to track me down?*

Chapter Seven

Carol had barely sipped her morning coffee when Giovanni Belletti, the Belletti capo, stormed in with three thugs in tow. "What the hell is going on? There's paramedics all over our floor and they've cordoned off Mr. Rizzuto's room." His party had returned from their visit to Hatley Castle the night before and had been kept away from the dead man's room. Carol told them she didn't really know what had happened, other than Mr. Rizzuto had been taken very ill. They had been very careful to keep the police and forensic officers out of sight; they, and the Medical Examiner removing the body, had used the service elevators, well away from prying eyes.

"I don't usually have guests in my office."

He slammed the door behind him. "Don't fuck with us, Ms. Moore. You tell me straight up what is going on or there will be hell to pay. I haven't been allowed near his room, nor anyone else, and no one has seen Mr. Rizzuto since we left last night. Lorenzo and his wife have been down to police headquarters, but we've heard nothing, and from what I understand, they've been told nothing." His three men stepped forward. "Trust me. What you may have heard about the Mafia and their enforcers is true. How do I say this, a little unconventional chiropractic adjustment is not out of the ordinary even on holidays and special wedding events."

These guys don't mess around. "Okay, call off the dogs and I'll tell you what happened."

He nodded, and they stepped back. She sat down and began to shake, faking tears. "I, ah, I don't know how to tell you this." *I've got to let go of my cool otherwise they might suspect I'm undercover.*

Mr. Belletti senior nodded and one of his men pulled forth a handkerchief. "When you are ready and able."

She almost suspected he already knew the answer. "Mr. Rizzuto is dead."

"What! Hail Mary, Mother of God." He formed the four points of the cross on his chest, as did the others. *Yeah, they know. Lousy fakers.*

She looked down at the hanky and noticed the emblem on it. An inverted pentagram, and inside of it, a picture of the being with horns and a beard. *Agnes is right.* "All I know is that I was called to the room when he didn't respond. I used my master key and found him hanging from a rope. The room was locked from the inside, so no one else in there with him. Probable suicide, the police tell me." She blew her nose heavily. "It was the most horrible thing I've ever seen." She began to shake, doing a masterful impression of a woman having a fit of hysterics.

Giovanni directed one on the men forward as he caught Carol staring at the emblem on the hanky. "Santa Maria. It is not possible. Some son-of-a-bitch killed him and set us up. There will be hell to pay and I need to talk to the Rizzutos right away before they blame us." He nodded to one of his men. "Check on Rizzuto's wife, Carmella. Make sure she is safe and break her the news."

"Alfredo, give her your hanky. I think she will need a second one. I am rather fond of mine." He did and as Carol took it, he retrieved the first one. *Small wonder no one hears much from any of the mobs' wives, they're probably scared shitless most of the time. Or would rather not know what these clowns get up to.*

Mr. Belletti ordered the others from the room. "I want to be alone with Ms. Moore here."

They closed the door behind the two and stood just outside. "Now that we are alone, I can say this. Ms. Moore, Mr. Rizzuto did not hang himself. You are very aware of who we are. You are talking to members of the New York Rizzuto and Belletti cartels here." He leaned forward, grabbed her by the back of the head and pulled her to him. "Also, now that we are alone, No Mr. Nice Guy. You tell no one else about this. Very still lips."

"Yes." She smiled at him more from suppressed rage than fear. *If I had my way, I'd break every finger in his hand, before cuffing him.* "When any news comes to you of the police investigation, you tell me first. *Kapiche*? It is better I tell the Rizzutos what has happened. I will mention a heart attack. Understand? He had a weak heart. Any news of anything else will lead to an open gang war and I know you don't blood shed on these wonderful new carpets."

"I understand," she said, willing tears to stream down her face. "Please don't hurt me. I only work here."

He let go of her. "You will need to recuperate. I suggest you take the rest of the day off." He stepped to the door and opened it. "Heart attack; and you appraise me of any developments. I trust you like the use of your legs without crutches."

Italian bastard. He closed the door behind him. Carol looked at the second fine linen handkerchief. Other than her smeared makeup, it was blank. *No wonder these guys are so powerful. They don't screw around and I have to be very careful around them or I'll end up in Giovanni's back bending classes. I need to talk to Jake about these guys, he knows more than I do, and Agnes. She seems to know a lot more than she's been telling me as well.*

Just then her hotel desk phoned buzzed. "Carol, we need you at the front desk. ASAP."

"What now?"

THE BLUE BEING ROSE from its cocoon and sat still looking at its thin elegant hands. *I dreamt of being a blue fairy from movies I watched. That could help people, children. Children like I was?* Wings behind her fluttered. She stood up and attempted to twirl on her tip toes slightly before stumbling. *I have wings, I remember. I was Cindy Amberside, I am not now.*

Another voice inside the creature said, *I did not, I lived in these dank pipes full of rot and excrement. I wish to walk the earth.*

> *Who are you?*
> *I am, I was a Lekwungen.*
> *I don't understand. Nor do I?*

I cannot leave, the curse keeps me here. I can feel it, even though I am not Lekwungen any longer.

> *But I am not so.*
> It thought a moment. *Then let us try, I remember a former life.*
> *I too remember, a time before.*
> *We need, we must be free of this place.*
> *You are me, I am you, we are one.*
> *But not.*
> *Yes.*
> *I/we sense that is dissolving. Yes, the next cycle of growth begins.*
> It folded its wings in on itself assuming an egg shape again.
> *Will we remember more of our former lives?*
> *Unknown.*
> *Mine was not nice.*
> *Nor mine.*
> *Then it is hoped we do not.*
> *Agreed, when we begin afresh.*
> *I like the wings.*
> *I like our long pointy ears.*
> *We will keep those and dream some more.*
> *Agreed.*

THE REDHEAD STOOD THERE, impatiently clicking her heels. "Let me see your manager on duty," she demanded of the clerk at the front check-in desk as Carol strode up. *I really don't have time for this, what with the Italians freaking on me, one dead guest, and my missing nephew.*

Carol approached the indignant woman, noting the bearing the Bettie Page or what is now called the Bettie Bang style of haircut with light green eyes and overly thick eyebrows that were the modern style. The woman flicked her 1950's style shoulder length hair over one shoulder. "How may I help you?" Carol's attention wasn't on the full pouty lips, perhaps plumped, but the hard look in her eyes told her that this someone that was quite used to getting her own way and probably didn't take kindly to the word no.

"Are you the manager on duty?"
"Yes."

"Then I'll deal only with you," she said, in a when-I-say-I-want-champagne-I-don't-want-sparkling-fizzy-lime-water-or-the-cheap-stuff-but-only-the-Bollinger-will-do, voice. She flashed a quick, forced smile trying to be somewhat polite, but obviously pleased with herself for getting the person she wanted and nothing less.

The woman pulled a picture free from her purse. "I'm led to believe you have this gentleman, one Luigi Penchanto, staying here. If so, I need to know what room he's in."

Carol glanced at the picture of Jake Holden. Her eyes lifted slightly, caught off guard in moment of rare surprise. "First of all, lady, ah Ms..."

"Becca, short for Rebecca, Casavanio."

"Ms. Casavanio, under this hotel's confidentiality rules we are unable to release a guest's room number without their consent unless you are with the authorities, and then I'll need to see some proper identification. Or you are of some relation to this gentleman?" "I am his fiancée," she blurted out. *What?*

"And your face tells me you've seen him. Then I shall check-in and find him anyways. My plane was delayed, but I am part of the Rizzuto party attending the upcoming wedding."

"Wait a minute, I don't recall a Casavanio booked here." Carol looked through the booked guests listed under the Rizzutos and then the guests listed under the Bellettis. "Nope, not on either guest list. You sure you have the right hotel?"

Becca stared hard at her, melting steel with her bare eyes. "Lady, don't try screwing me over, you won't like the bad side of me. I'm booked here. Look again." She rolled her eyes upward. Carol held her ground and looked through the entire hotel's bookings, confirmed, and expected. "Nope, however there's a Best Western up the street, I can see if they have any availability and shuttle you over."

"Do I look like I stay at Best Westerns?" Her face flushed, the anger flashing across her eyes. The woman breathed deeply, realizing this wasn't getting her anywhere as Carol stood her ground. "Sorry," she said through gritted teeth.

A word Carol knew she rarely spoke and never willingly.

"Bad flight delayed for several hours. I'll take a room anywhere in this establishment for the next two weeks if you have any vacancies at all."

Carol waited for the please, which never came. *But, if she is who she says she is, I want to keep her within my radar. Mr. Holden has a few questions to answer.* Carol tapped at the keyboard, glanced through the open room list and picked one two floors away from the bulk of the guests and Jake's room. She knew better than to say the hotel was booked solid, besides, it made sense to have her here and find out what Jake had to say about her. *What was the old saying 'keep your friends close and your enemies tied up even closer in the closet.'* "I do believe

I have a spare room in the back of the hotel. Street level so may be a bit noisy, but..."

"I'll take it. In addition, leave Mr. Penchanto a message that I am here. Doubt the bastard will come looking, but you never know." She smiled with the sweet grace of a leopard itching to pounce on her prey. "Then I'll find him myself."

He definitely wasn't the person he portrayed. *Just when I thought the crazy stuff was over and done with. Yes, Big Dan did say there'd be days like this. Now to deal with the Italians before they start a gang war in the middle of the hotel.* She texted Louie, asking him to find any details of Begbie and any case involving a Marshall. Jake hadn't responded to her earlier text. *Bastard. Okay before this shit gets real, as they say in the movies, it's going to be show time.* She sent Big Dan a text as well, explaining what was happening and indicating she might need armed backup.

Louie responded quickly. "On it, but this is going to take awhile."

Carol hurried up to Agnes' room and found the old gal having her hair done. "Sorry to barge in, but I need a favor and quickly."

Agnes looked at her like she was on drugs, "Can't you see I'm rather busy trying to make myself gorgeous. When I was younger it took twenty minutes, now I need at least four hours or so." She laughed. "What's up, honey?"

"Is it possible for you to contact Begbie? My guy says he'll look into it, but I'm not confident he'll find much in the case involving him and William Marshall. I've got real trouble with the mob downstairs and need some answers, pronto, before we have a bloodbath."

Agnes closed her eyes, reading what was going through Carol's head. "Okay, girl, I'm on it." She waved the hairdresser out of the room. "I'll see what I can do while still in my curlers.

Man, I must like you. Might have a few contacts that could shed some light."

"Lady, thanks, but man, you keep some strange friends."

"Just remember you're on that list, now beat it. I need some peace and quiet."

"Thanks again. I think."

Carol glanced at her phone and sent a text to headquarters. No, fresh info on Nathan. *Damn, time is beginning to run out on finding him alive.* She knew after three days the likelihood of him alive shrank dramatically. And there had been no contact from the abductors. As she went back down the elevator Big Dan texted, "Full SWAT team on stand-by if needed." *Okay, boys and girls, it's party time.*

❧　　　❧

AN HOUR LATER CAROL had gathered the two families in one of the empty conference rooms, away from prying eyes. "As Manager of this hotel I thought it wise that I get both parties together to discuss what happened the other night before the news gets out."

The Rizzuto clan sat on one vast, plush sofa, the Bellettis on another opposite. The young wife of Antonio Rizzuto, Carmello, scantily clad in a black mini-skirt and black lace veil, sobbed as Carol continued. Carol wondered if it was an act, as unless there was some sort of pre-nup, she was now a very wealthy woman. Margherita Belletti, Giovanni's wife, stared at her in distaste. Carson and Vidler patrolled the hallway outside as back up for Carol should anything kick off and goes totally sideways. She knew in the next room to them the SWAT guys were also waiting if shit hit the fan.

"Preliminary findings are that Antonio Rizzuto died of a heart attack in his room the other night." She had talked to her advisers and Big Dan and everyone had agreed to use Mr. Belletti Senior's line for now in order to avoid any further possible bloodshed. "His room, though, will still be labelled a crime scene just until the autopsy and all tests are completed. My understanding is that you all still wish for the wedding to commence in honor of Mr. Rizzuto."

"Such is life, laughter and dancing one night and ..."

"Death and grief the next," said first by Lorenzo Rizzuto, now the acting capo and senior member. It was seconded by Mr. Belletti senior, the other Bellettis nodded in agreement.

Carol frowned, caught off guard as Giovanni Belletti stood up and walked across the room. She didn't miss the clank of metal. *Damn it, they're packing heat in here.* "You, not being Italian nor Cosa Nostra, would not have heard of this saying of ours. It is one of the codes we Mafiosi live by. Or as you Canadians might say, 'life is life and whatever may be, may be.'"

The Belletti capo put his hand forward after making the sign of the cross on his chest. "We are in deep sorrow and regret Antonio Rizzuto's passing.

He was a well-respected man among the Cosa Nostra and ourselves."

Lorenzo Rizzuto rose and took his hand in his. They shook, much to Carol's relief. This meant that all was forgiven, and the peace still reigned between them. In their world a handshake was better than a hundred signed pages backed up by a dozen lawyer's signatures.

"On behalf of myself and the hotel, I would also like to express my sincere condolences to you all. If there is anything we can do at all, please just ask. As a sign of our respect we shall serve our traditional High Tea to our bereaved guests of the hotel."

The doors opened and several waitresses entered bearing pots of tea and silver trays. Watching some of the men staring at the tiny sandwiches seemed ludicrous, especially when most were swallowed in one bite.

As Carol left the room, she heaved a huge sigh of relief. She spotted Jake chatting with the two armed men, as if he was an old friend.

"I thought I'd join the party, in case you needed back up."

"Thanks. You could have texted me at least. I know how to look after myself, but I was pretty worried this could have gone totally sideways."

"Yeah, I had you covered, just in case, skirt." He lifted his jacket and a mini hand-held UZI gleamed under the chandeliers.

"How the hell did you get that across the border and into this hotel?"

Jake simply smiled. "Well it wasn't under my bath towel when we first met, I must say, although I had other tools that I was packing at the time."

More than anything Carol wanted to grab him by the nuts and squeeze hard enough to make him cry then and there. But a scene like that wouldn't be good with the High Tea-ing Italians just behind the door. "You are such a man-pig. Oh, and *don't* fricking call me skirt. Especially if you hope to get anywhere with me." She turned and walked away, giving her hips a slight side-to side sway, teasing him like Big Dan had instructed. It was better to keep him off guard and interested in her.

⚬⚬⚬

"FAN TAN ALLEY, ONLY six feet at its widest, is the entrance to Chinatown and reportedly haunted by the ghost of a young boy, Chung, who cut off the head of a young girl he loved but couldn't have. Her name was Yo Gum," Adam from the Victoria Ghost Tours said as he stood in front of the group and pointed down the narrow alleyway on the second night of the tour. "Now, before we begin, I did a search for our esteemed guest." He pointed to Agnes and bowed politely. "This lady was in vaudeville and Vegas known as Mystique or properly, Ms. Teak if I am right. I like the play on words there."

Agnes adjusted her large red hat which nearly filled the alleyway. "Yes, my good man, you are absolutely correct." She leaned over and planted a big red lipstick stain on his cheek. "There.

I usually don't do autographs, but that will suffice."

Adam blushed. "Now are you getting anything here?"

As he spoke Carol watched Agnes go suddenly pale.

"Yes, I'm getting a young Chinese boy and an older very petite and beautiful Chinese woman."

Adam and the half dozen others all opened their eyes as Carol held her up and shook her head. *She is a true showman.*

Agnes leaned into her and whispered, "That's show person, dear. Show person. Get with the times."

Carol just smirked to herself. *Damn mind-readers.*

They walked along slowly, the group allowing Agnes a moment to catch her breath as she took off her large brimmed hat and waved it in her face. The old gal had this usual measured slowness and pace. It was like walking with the Queen of England on tour, besides Carol wanted to soak in the feel of the place. *Either her usual demeanor or more of the show.* Carol had already learned it would be best to humor her and walked slowly with Agnes. Besides, Italian hunk, Tony Belletti, was eyeing the both of them, and Carol in particular. *Why do I keep getting flashes of something every time I'm near him?* He was a bit of a distraction she didn't mind right about now, especially if she wanted to get in close with the mob to find out answers, because with the Rizzuto Senior's death all concerned lips had tightened up considerably. *To be expected if either side thinks the other did the killing even though the official cause of death was a heart attack.* As far as she knew no one knew about the noose. "You okay?"

"Do you see the young lad coming towards us?" She lurched backwards pushed into the wall as Adam continued to speak.

"People claim they see a young boy running to them and feel themselves pressed to the wall before everything returns to normal," he said, virtually as Agnes flattened herself to the wall.

Everyone turned as Agnes gasped and Carol gripped her to stay standing. "It was him, just then." Agnes went blank as she slumped into Carol's arms.

"You pay the old broad to pull that stunt off?" One of the Italians spoke up as everyone turned to watch Agnes struggle to return to consciousness as Carol clung onto her.

Adam blinked in disbelief. "No, apparently Chung has returned to his haunts again. The rumor is true folks, he's still running through the alley trying to escape his pursuers." Nonplussed, he went along with the unexpected turn of events.

Agnes clutched at Carol's arm. Tony waved his men back and also rushed to steady Agnes. As he did he stared into Carol's eyes. *Man, he's even more handsome up close.* She inhaled deeply. *And smells damn good too. If that's what hunky Italian male smells like normally, I want some of that.* His eyes burned into her.

"Normally no. I've met a few in my time." Agnes winked at Carol and pretended to swoon again.

Tony squatted on his heels and helped Carol lift Agnes to her feet. "Are you truly psychic?" "Yes." she held his arm and slid her hand down into his.

Cagey old broad, she set this up to touch him. Gotta give her some credit for that.

Carol reached over to grab his arm. Firm hardness didn't flinch under her touch. *Oh, and Agnes is right, he's solid romance cover testosterone fueled hardness.*

Tony smiled deeply into Carol's eyes and looked at Agnes. "We, as you know are in Victoria for a wedding. But could also use the aid of a trained psychic, that's why we took the tour. With the death, we need some help. I thought the guide could be of help, but he's just a mouthpiece for the company. You, on the other hand are the *cosa vera*, how you say, 'real thing'. None of us, including the guide, saw the boy."

Agnes stared hard into his eyes. Carol could see the mists run through them, like what happened when she did a reading with her in the tearoom. "I can't help you."

His face dropped. "But there is a curse here. It has already cost us one of our kind."

"I know. I said I can't help you." She pulled her hand away. "Carol here might, you need to ask her, but I need to cut this short." She stood up. "This has exhausted me. I need to get out of here, now. Carol, take me to the Gate of Harmonious Interest just around the corner and then back to my room." Agnes stood and began to walk through Fan Tan Alley away from the group, bee-lining it for the gate, which was next on their stop and just around the corner in the opposite direction of the hotel. Carol would have to double time it to keep up with the old gal. Tony after her, bemused as he was being stood up, not one used to being turned down.

"I apologize for my friend's rudeness," Carol said to Tony. "Let me talk to her and see if I can get her to change her mind."

"Yes." He smiled at her. "Perhaps dinner would be nice. You and me?"

"Okay," Carol stuttered caught off guard. "Let me deal with Agnes, leave me a message at the front desk as to when." She looked up at the others. "Continue without us. Sorry, Agnes and I are calling it quits for tonight. She's frail and that was quite the shock."

Adam stared at them and pointed down the street. "Well okay then, not everyone has a pleasant time on these tours, I did warn all of you that you may encounter the unexpected. The next stop on the tour, Bard and Banker

Pub, we can stop in for a drink and I'll tell everyone the bizarre events that unfolded there that ended up making one of Canada's famous poets."

Carol nearly ran to catch the old broad who was moving a lot faster than she'd ever seen her move. "Hey, slow down. You okay?"

"No, around the corner and away from the mob before I speak." She began to nearly run as they exited the alley, turned right and quickly stood under the huge oriental structure, which was just at the end of the block. "The gate was cleansed of all evil spirits when it was raised and is like a haven or refuge if one is in need and I am in need."

The great Chinese Lion at the far end of the red and gilded twenty-foot high gate glared down at them. Agnes reached into its mouth and caressed the stone ball there, obviously knowing to do so granted good luck.

"What are you yammering about?"

"Sorry, but one never gets used to looking in the face of Bathomet." She pulled a metal flask from her jacket chugged a quick swig before handing it to Carol. Carol snapped her head back and gagged on the straight bourbon whiskey. "A dram of whiskey is good for ya. Settles the nerves." She took another swig and put the flask back into her pocket. "I just stared into the face of the devil. They are definitely calling him up. The Mafia are reported devil worshippers. I heard the stories and met some people that had been involved with them. The stink of hell is a smell most foul and he oozes it. They are here for much more than a wedding. They do bring a curse and it has stirred the gathered spirits, which I've already sensed beginning to happen. I think we need to bring forward that visit to Judge Begbie."

Carol stopped as Agnes spoke. "Lady, what kind of crap are you spouting?" *Maybe she is nuts.* "But I agree I think the key to the curse lies with him."

"Not nuts." She tried a weak smile. "This is why I've lived most of my life alone. No one wants to live with this cursed affliction I have."

"Sorry, a subconscious thought."
"It's okay I'm not offended, I got used to it a long time ago."

"Okay, you've thrown me here. Devil worshippers? The Devil? Isn't that worse than some displaced ghosts?"

"Carol, you've spent time with a shaman and a native sprite. You already know there's way more out there than most of us realize. I can only say there are also evil spirits, some more foul than you can even imagine. He goes by several names, Bathomet, Isthar, Lilith, Azazel, Bast or, as we usually call him, The Devil, is one of those. He is not the devil of the Bible nor the king of hell. But the damage he inflicts and the corruption he can raise is tremendous. Watch your back with this lot and be very, very careful. I've said enough, back to my room, I need to cleanse myself and you should as well." Agnes abruptly strode off towards the hotel.

Cleanse? I just had a bath this morning. She's doesn't mean the cedar branch whipping thing Charlie does to himself, does she?

"Nothing that drastic," Agnes blurted as they walked along. "Sorry, your mind is an open book to me. Some incense and smudging yourself in white birch fungus and sage should do it. And as you were about to think it, no people don't get used to me reading their minds. No matter what they might tell you."

"White birch fungus and sage. Thanks lady, but I had dessert earlier. Now if they're not here just for a wedding, can you tell me what the hell is going on?"

"Whiskey first, we talk later. Not sure myself right now. Need to talk to Cider." Carol's thoughts strayed to a vision of the crystal skull.

"At least she converses with me, unlike your secret friend; Bob, is it?

Carol blushed, she knew Agnes was talking about her Battery Operated Boyfriend. "You drive me crazy."

"No, that's Bob's job."
Carol smirked, "Man, nothing gets by you."

"Yeah, not much. Now get me to my room. I need a stiff one of a different kind."

Carol shook her head. *I could get used to hanging out with this crazy old broad, she has a sense of humor similar to Charlie's, only she was a whole lot more civil. But the reading of the mind thing is still unnerving.*

Could do with a shot of whiskey or three myself.

"I've got more in my room if you want to join me," Agnes said, obviously reading her thoughts again.

"And quit doing that. Whatever happened to personal space?" She glanced at her watch as they rounded the corner nearly at the hotel. Carol called on her phone, all was quiet there. Then she called Jake, he answered and agreed to meet with her for dinner. "Otherwise engaged for dinner but I'll talk to you after if you're still up."

She checked her police phone still no news on Nathan. *Damn, I'm this close and I can't get much time to help with the investigation. I feel so handcuffed.*

"Ah, the bath towel hunk. But tell me who Nathan is to you?"

Carol jumped. "Quit doing that! Sorry, I apologize. Didn't mean to bite your head off"

Agnes pursed her lips. "As do I. It is hard not to pick up some people's thoughts, yours come to me very easily. Again, I'm sorry."

They walked a little further before Carol let go of her anger. "Nathan is my nephew, but you probably already know that. He is the second abduction this week. My sister Barb's only son. I can't pull myself away from this case to help much and that is driving me crazy."

"Well, if you don't mind, I'll see what I can find out through Cider. I get a sense there will be more before this wedding is over."

Shit, Carol thought. *Maybe I should quit this case in order to devote more time to helping Barb.*

Agnes shook her head, "The needs of the many outweigh the needs of the few, or the one. Sorry, I'll not intrude into your sub consciousness any more tonight."

They walked down the promenade just outside the Empress Hotel. "I know, breaking this case could lead to stopping the mob from setting up a whole new operation in the West Coast. Still he's my nephew." Tears threatened to stream down her face. "And I love him, the closest thing I have to a son."

"I know, I will see what I can do trying to find out about your nephew and Begbie."

CAROL AND AGNES SAT on the Saanich beach in front of the house Judge Begbie. This was the spot where Adam from the ghost tour reported the judge had been filmed haunting. Cider had indeed confirmed that his ghost was felt hanging out here. "Thanks for this, I owe you big time." Carol smiled.

"That you do lady, that you do." Agnes rubbed in.

"Hey, I gotta say the hair looks perfect." What she could see under the large green hat.

Agnes smiled at Carol as she unwrapped Cider, it was beginning to get dark. "You need to take a course on sucking up to people."

"You really got to stop reading people's minds."
"Occupational hazard, I'm afraid."

"So, here's some history, if you didn't already know. Back in the 1800's Jacob Sehl came to Victoria from Germany. He bought the land at the end of the inner bay and began to build his furniture factory there. Clearing the land, the workers complained of boxes falling out of the trees, along with bones and bodies. Not being very respectful of native traditions, at that time, they either burnt or tossed everything into the ocean. The Lekwungen chief was outraged, claiming they've disturbed the dead and the spirits were now trapped here, as they believed the dead spirits still live and had set up an entire village for them to dwell in. The Lekwungens moved away from the area, fearing for what might happen. A few years later, Jacob's house caught on fire and oddly enough at that same time a mile away, his factory did as well. Mrs. Sehl claimed she saw beings, hair aflame stoking the fires.

She died a few months later of insanity.

Beings with hair aflame. I saw that somewhere.
William Pendray then bought the land, several years later.
"Did you say, Pendray?"
"Yes, the same family that just had a son abducted."
"Does nothing get by you?"
"Very little."
"Occupational hazard," they said at the same time.

"And Google is a great tool. Now you're messing with my story. The land was now known as Deadman's Point when he decided to build his own factory on it. He installed a very advanced sprinkler system, at least for its time, in the factory, obviously being somewhat cautious regarding what happened to the previous owner. He went to inspect the factory one day shortly after opening and a large chunk of the sprinkler pipe overhead broke away falling thirty feet, crushing his head.

His only son, Ernest, came racing up to the factory the next day on his horse drawn carriage when the horse jolted to a stop and Ernest was flung off the carriage onto the ground in front of the horse. The horse bolted right over the prone man crushing his head. Their ghosts are the ones believed to still inhabit Pendray house at the sight of Huntington Manor Hotel next to Laurel

Point, as it is now called. His foreman, one William Marshall, was convicted of assaulting a Lekwungen shaman for trying to protect his people. In an unprecedented judgement, Judge Begbie charged him and had him hanged. One of the first times a native man won the case."

"Wow, you know a lot of this area."

"I do my research and these matters are my hobby. Only I don't know what caused the Judge to try the man. Seemed very unusual for his time. That is why we are here."

"What has this got to do with the mob?"

"My visits with Cider have told me Marshall was not his true last name, but Marchiotti."

Carol sat on the sand rather stunned as Agnes ran her hands over the leather packaging she had Cider wrapped in.

Behind them a moaning began as a shadowy figure parted from the trees. "Someone calls me."

"We come seeking answers to an ancient curse."

Begbie glared at the leather package Agnes held. "Ask the one inside she will tell you the truth. I have nothing to say."

Agnes stared at him and at Carol. "The man is of obvious intelligence to know what I'm holding."

Agnes carefully exhumed Cider from the many layers of wrapping she was placed in.

Agnes spoke up, her voice a little shaky. "We come seeking information. It is reported that you hanged a man for beating a native man nearly to death and for that he cursed you."

Begbie turned to Carol and slowly approached her. "I am trapped here because of him. I did what was right by law. You know nothing." He seethed, his eyes glaring red. "Again, I will not talk of this matter, see inside her. She will show you what happened."

"Now, Cider will and you sir, had better not be telling me a lie, or you will stay trapped here a long time." Carol spoke trying to gain some control over this strange turn of events.

Begbie crossed his arms, "I am a judge of the United Colonies of Vancouver Island and the Province of British Columbia. I do not lie, nor do I find humor in your accusations." With that he faded back into the trees.

Carol sat beside Agnes as she began to concentrate on Cider's crystal head. "You gotta say the man garnered a lot of respect in his day."

"Yeah, so did Richard Nixon, before he got caught cheating. Now, shh."

Agnes closed her eyes. The beach began to swirl away and take on the confines of the provincial courtroom.

A gavel hammered on an oak block.

The weak Songhees First Nations man, his face swollen and bleeding under the bandages, was placed under oath, swearing on his medicine bag. William Marshall, the accused, had earlier held onto the pendant around his neck. The young Judge allowed this in his courtroom for those that chose to do use something more sacred to them than the Bible.

A younger Begbie rose, his face red. "This Songhees man claims that he was savagely beaten by you, William Marshall. How do you plead?"

"I plead not guilty, Your Honor. This savage was interfering with my job to clear Laurel Point of the trees, and as we soon learned, of the vile bodies they left hanging to rot away in them. He would not leave nor would he get out of our way. Every time

we cut one down, he'd rush in and dance around like some drunken madman, yelling and screaming at us. I had enough."

Begbie looked at the battered man, his face shattered, one eye swollen shut, lip still oozing blood. In Songhees Begbie asked a few questions.

Marshall's eyes opened in in shock at the white man yammering in a native tongue. "He tells me he is a shaman and was trying to quieten the souls of the ones you disturbed in their village.

Souls that will be very angry for what you have done."

"His village? Your Honor, Jacob Sehl bought the land for his new factory, my job as foreman was to clear it. We did not expect to find revolting corpses hanging in the branches, maggots rained down, the smell was beyond revolting. These people are the worst savages I have ever met. I never know heathens could be so filthy and vile. They need to be sat down and taught the ways of our Lord, if that is even possible."

"*A'si'em nu schala'cha*," replied the shaman, barely able to sit, let alone stand.

Begbie closed his eyes a moment taking in what the injured man barely clinging to consciousness had said. "You destroyed their village, it was where they let the dead of their tribe reside. You burnt the bodies, tossed the ashes into the ocean. He was very upset at the total disregard for their traditions and ways."

"Their traditions? Your Honor, these are savages, they do not bury the dead, but let them rot in trees. They are beyond disgusting. In the end when he got in our way, I had to stop him before he hurt one of my men. I had to stop him. There was no reasoning with him."

"You could have confined him and brought him to the police station. Instead you beat him to a pulp." Begbie seethed.

"Your honor, he deserved everything he got, he's lucky. I should have slit his neck and I wouldn't be here today, wasting my time. Now clear me of the charges and let me get back to my work. I have no use for this filthy savage."

"No," Begbie slammed his gavel down. "No, you sir, will be charged with attempted murder, as you have just admitted in front of this courthouse. I have no choice but to convict you and sentence you to be hanged by the neck until dead. This man was merely trying to protect his people."

"People? They were maggot filled rotting corpses." Marshall screamed and fought to break free from his manacles.

"Into the courtyard. I have to leave in the morning. Hang this man, here and now."

Marshall screamed his rage as two men dragged him kicking and screaming from the courtroom into the dusty yard in front. A small crowd had gathered, half expecting to watch the Songhees man be hanged. They were shocked when Marshall was dragged to the gallows.

"Any last words?"

"I curse you and the vile likes of them." Marshall spat in Begbie's direction. As his hands were unchained in order to put them behind his back. he kneed the hangman, who collapsed in pain. Another grabbed the man before he could escape. Marshall pulled a necklace from around his neck. "These are my last words."

Begbie held his hand up, allowing the guard to wait a moment. "Speak as you are entitled and let the assembled crowd hear what it is you want to say."

The man began to whisper to himself a moment. "My true name is not Marshall, but Marchiotti. I am of Mafioso blood, we are warriors. I place the curse of Satan on this Shaman and his village of the deceased. They shall live below the ground, like the Bible states. And you," he pointed at Begbie. "You shall not ever rest, above or below, the earth. Nor shall you marry, nor bear any children but endure a lonely and diseased life and die alone. I send Satan to end the life of this disgusting savage worm." He pointed to the shaman who'd been brought out to the proceedings by two others.

"Hang him now, he has said enough." Begbie decreed.

A black shadow lifted from the man as he chanted and wrapped itself around the weak shaman. Growls rent the air, and everyone gasped as bite marks appeared on his body as if he was being attacked by some savage unseen creature.

The shaman threw his medicine bag to the ground and waved at the contents spilling forth. Blood spurted from his body. Two other dark shapes leapt forth to attack the unknown being attacking him. Screams and growls of a bestial nature tore into the panicked crowd, which began to race from the madness of the court yard.

Marshall laughed. "He will join me in death."

The hangman dropped the noose over his head. Marshall muttered his incantations over and over. The shaman clutching at his chest, where blood poured forth raised his hand to the man about to be dancing in thin air. *"Hay'sxw'qa gwns âne 'techul Lekwungen Tung'ex. Hay'sxw'qa si'em nakwilia,"* he gasped with his dying breath.

Begbie stood back, speechless as the floor beneath Marshall gave way and he convulsed several times before the pendant slipped to the earth from cold fingers.

The shaman fell to the ground in silence. The dark figures faded into the background.

Begbie strode up to the dangling man and bent to pick up the five-sided pendant. He dropped it in horror as it burnt at his fingers. He pulled his own cross from around his neck and began to perform the sign of the cross before him, over and over.

"Have any of the proceedings in this courtyard stricken from the records." Begbie tore the last pages from the book the court recorder was feverishly writing in. "No one can know what just happened here. The records will simply show that the man was hanged, nothing more, and woe betide any here who ever say otherwise."

He stared up at the horrified crowd. "Go to your churches and pray for the souls of those affected today and wipe from your memory this event. To repeat it to anyone would be aiding the devil's evil work."

The cleric looked up at Begbie. "What did that shaman say to Marshall before he died?"

"He cursed him in return. His kind, the first-born male shall always die early and horribly until the instrument of the Lekwungen people's imprisonment breaks the curse or is imprisoned like them."

Begbie calmly walked from the court yard into the court room. His head already filled with visions he wanted to put into drawings as he so often did.

Agnes opened her eyes. "Now, this makes a whole lot more sense. Explains why Begbie doesn't want to talk to us, and why Marshall cursed him. Although obviously guilty Marshall did not see anything wrong in what he had done and so considered himself innocent."

They both repacked Cider. Begbie was nowhere to be seen. "Yes, I get he's more than a little angry over this." She stared into the dark trees. "Like you I work for the Justice system of this province. If there is some way, we will get you free from this."

From the darkness a voice echoed, "Thank you." "We will?" Agnes glared at Carol.

"Yes, we will. The man was only doing his job and..."

"And you're a Justifier, I get it. Although in my mind I think Robin just looked at Batman and said 'how in jumping Jehoshaphat are we going to pull this one off."

"To which the Bat dude would reply, to the Batcave and step on it." Carol shook her head and laughed as they trundled back to her car.

"HEY LOUIE, THAT CASE of William Marshall I asked you to look into, I know a bit more about it. He was hanged by Matthew Begbie back in the late 1800's in Victoria. I need whatever details you can find but specifically if Marshall was his real name. I believe it could have been Antonio Marchiotti. Need to know if this is there any relation to the Rizzutos or the Bellettis and history of first-born males."

"Man, Big Dan told me you'd be asking some strange shit and that's why he put me on the backup team. But how in hell did you come with this information? You a psychic or something?" "No, I just hang out with one for the occasional tea," she joked.

There was a moment of silence. "You're for real, aren't you?"

"Yes. She's a hoot, even though she can read most of what I'm thinking. Hey, by the way, look up Agnes Van Lunt, she's around seventy or eighty, went by the stage name of Ms. Teak, and let me know what you get." "Any news on the toys?"

"So, the weird thing about the two pics you sent me of the toys is that they weren't made after 1990. They are of a limited giveaway set. The first one is Donatello and the second one is Raphael, both Teenage Mutant Ninja Turtles, from Kellogg's Corn Flakes boxes. They were the hottest rage back then.

"How do you know this?"
"I'm a toy aficionado."

"A what? Okay stop, I don't mean to be rude, but man, you need to get a life."
"I know. Spent most of my life in front of the TV and playing video games or looking on Ebay for old toys and researching their backgrounds and origins. Didn't think it would ever come in handy on the job though. What I'm looking for currently is a 1953 Lone Ranger doll, I'll send you a pic, in case you ever come across one."

"How about we focus on the job but send the pic anyways. I apologize if I sounded rude, but right now I ain't got the time."

"Sorry."

How do people spend their lives on such mundane triviality? Trivial lives, I guess. But the question remains now, are these clues? Especially the masked turtles. Is something being covered up? Or hidden? What happened around 1990?

Carol dried herself off from the shower and lay on the bed, finishing her second whiskey despite the late hour. She had felt as if she needed it. *Is it possible that ghost I saw earlier in the hotel has up and strangled one of the mob? What about "my" ghost, who was at Antonio Rizzuto's door.* Carol closed her eyes. *I'll have to get Agnes up there. She'd know or sense some kind of Woo-woo vibrational kinda stuff.*

Carol decided on a power-nap and set her alarm for thirty minutes. As sleep claimed her, in her dreams Carol found herself in a hotel room. Jake locked the door behind her, wearing only what he wore when she first met him. He lifted her effortlessly and flung her onto the bed. Only when she landed, she was in the back seat of a car. A shadowy figure was in the front driving her car along Victoria's streets. *What the eff is going on here? Someone's hijacked my bloody dream.* "Who are you?" *Damn can't even get lucky in my dreams.*

"We've arrived," was all it said and vanished. *That voice; Agnes?*

She looked up at the street sign. She was on the corner of Shelbourne and Hillside. *Wasn't this mentioned in the tour? Something about a vortex?*

Only what am I doing here? And what the hell happened to Jake?

As if answering her thoughts, the sidewalks dissolved around the car. Carol opened the back door and instead of stepping onto asphalt her foot crunched on a gravel road. From in front of her mists formed and a man stepped through them. He was distinguished, dressed in Victorian style business clothes. Carol blinked in disbelief. It was him; "her" ghost. "Sir Francis Rattenbury, I presume."

He walked towards her and stuck out his hand. "My fame precedes me even here. It wasn't dear Agnes who hijacked your illicit dream, but me."

"You know Agnes?"

"Ah, Ms. Teak and I have chatted over tea on occasion via her friend Cider."

This has to be a figment of my imagination and sarcastic humor run wild. Okay got to play this by my guts. "To what, sir, do I owe the pleasure?"

"It is the approach of the full moon and the gates between realms are thin. In addition, much unrest has been stirred by the arrival of personages that you are in acquaintance with."

Carol thought for a moment. "You mean the Mafia that have come for the wedding?"

"It is they. Some have deep curses on them brought about by an ancestor involved with that heretic Chief Justice Sir Matthew Begbie." Carol remembered the signs of the cross the Belletti group made while her and Agnes were at Helmcken Alley. "Curses that bring much unrest and threaten to awaken he-who-cannot-be-named, among others."

Ah, man here we go with the Harry Potter crap. Wish I never saw those damn movies. "Okay, so the he-who-cannot-be-named dude is coming by for a visit. So, what can I do to help?" *I'm not liking where this is going.*

"You are a justifier."

"Are you kidding me? This is because I helped Sprity in the past, isn't it?"

"The earth knows and remembers."

"Ah crap! That's what I get for not caving in and getting lezzie with her isn't it."

He stared at her blankly. "The earth doesn't remember everything, and the term "lezzie" is unfamiliar to me."

Carol quickly filled him in with the details how Sprity admired her and at one point grabbed her and kissed her deeply, supposedly as part of her ritual to change her into an earth spirit. "She was a little disappointed, I could tell, that I didn't reciprocate the passion of that kiss."

"Ah! Kissing someone of the same gender is not anything widely practiced in my time. In any case these Mafia persons do have amongst them one that is very bad and has a curse placed on him. The curse needs to be satisfied, or the deceased will begin to exact their revenge."

"How can this be?"

"Very powerful energies do the Mafioso manifest. Part of the curse involves the unrest of the dead. The living cannot live as the need for justice grows."

This isn't sounding great. "But the head of the Rizzuto clan is already dead."

"He was not the cursed one. My time is closing, I can't talk anymore. This will be the first of many meetings."

"Not the cursed one? Then who? Many times? But do you know who you are, you've been dead over a hundred years."

"Last time I checked, my passport said Sir Francis Rattenbury."

"How is this possible? Legends say that you are a great architect that was killed brutally by your estranged lover or her young boyfriend. You're not telling me that you want me to find out who killed you?"

"No, I know who killed me and that doesn't matter. I am not here for myself."

"Oh, wrong guess, then. But you were buried in an unmarked grave."

"Does the world have to know who I was? If my birth was marked by a civic holiday and marching bands went up and down main street celebrating my passing in front of the legislature I built would that make me a greater person? Or this a better world?"

"Unlikely."

"No, but your ghost is reported in the Empress Hotel and the Parliament buildings you designed and built." Carol had no idea, for once, where this conversation was going.

"Well, one cannot fault a gentleman for wanting to admire that which he is proud of, even after he has passed away."

He looked up. "The vortex is collapsing. I must be quick."

Carol looked around, only grass fields seen everywhere. "I don't see anything."

He pulled her close and whispered in her ear as he vanished. Concrete erupted under her and a car honked its annoyance at her standing in the middle of the busy road.

Carol woke up before the alarm. *Okay that cuts it. I'm staying off the whiskey and switching to red wine. At least I hear that is healthy for you.*

⚓   ⚓

THE BLUE BEING SAT in the corner of the sewer room, tears streaming down its face, the dreams still fresh in its mind.

The dreams, I remember so much now. My mom was obsessed with running. I hated her.

She'd make me run to the school bus stop every morning, loaded with my back pack. When my sister was born, she'd push her in the stroller and make me run in front.

I lived off scum, I used to live in a native village on one of the hillsides where you have buildings in the harbour. I went there once through the sewers to see. The sun hurt my eyes, someone walking their dog saw me. I smiled, and they ran off, screaming. The dog howled and wanted to tear my flesh. I was horrid to them, ashamed I returned here to live off the filth. The stink of excrement is what I awake to, urines cloying acrid sting. Acridness cast from the sting of memories. It cried a while before continuing, *I remember the offending smell of trees and flowers that day. That smell, distasteful from what I live with now. Yet, I remember that smell. Why is it?*

They both begin to speak together. *We hated our existences. Never a hug nor a smile. Just run to the bus stop. I asked once in grade one to leave early so we could walk. She slapped my face several times a day sometimes and washed my mouth out with soap. I never asked, nor disobeyed her again. I learned not to speak. Yelling, always her yelling at me. I don't remember my mom ever saying much kind to me. She often blamed me for everything wrong with her life. Her pregnancy left her trapped with my dad. A man that threatened to beat her silly and sometimes did at night after they'd had a few drinks or did some drugs.*

I ran away from home as soon as I could, lived a life as a hooker, eventually getting hooked on the drugs I swore I'd never do. But they took away the pain, made my life bearable.

The half that was Lekwungen was silent for a long moment, absorbing the other's misery.

I live shivering in the cold dankness of the sewers. No breakfast, no warmth, no love. Always shivering. Run away from the ones awaiting our caress. I have only vague memories of my former life before being down here. We don't seem to age, just fade away, one day here, suffering in the dankness, then when we give up, gone into the blackness.

We found the effect of living off the drugged ones; by absorbing their residue we get sustenance and numbness, it makes the being down here bearable. We could even enjoy touching one another.

Always shivering for a hug, they both thought.
We shall no longer.

Agreed, we must begin by forgiving and find the reasons for our entrapment.

For now, we must rest and be reborn again.
We are weak, but we will find strength from our misery.

And we must not be found. The others, the Lekwungen will not understand. They will destroy us.

Agreed, we are truly alone.

The blue being folded in, forming a blue haze around itself in a safe cocoon.

Chapter Eight

Louie called Carol on her cell. "If there are any records on the Marshall/Begbie case they'll be stored in the BC Archives and God only knows how long it might take to get them. I've put in a re-quest anyways, but in the meantime, I've done a little digging via our old friend Wikipedia. Your information is correct inasmuch as William Marshall was hanged by our famous hanging judge, Mr. Begbie, back in 1860. There's scant info about the case, its only oddity seeming to be that it was expected the native would be executed, not the white guy. Everything else is mundane, nothing out of the ordinary. I have found also that Marshall's body was taken back to California and buried in the San Francisco Mission Delores Cemetery under the family plot of Moretti. The Morettis moved back to New York shortly after the great fire. They merged families with the Rizzos and became one of the five New

York mob families."

"Let me guess, the Rizzutos."

"You got it. This psychic you're hanging out with knows her stuff. I'm impressed. Not only that, but every Moretti, Rizzuto first-born male from each generation has died prematurely and usually in horrible circumstances, and strangely each first-born male has fathered a male child. Everything from several gunned down, to heart attacks, to being found hanged, like Mr. Rizzuto, no signs of someone having been in the room. Also, two of, get this weird fact, spontaneous combustion. Now, what's the odds of that happening you might ask?"

"I know you get off on this stuff, I don't want to know stats. How about Ms. Teak?"

"Let's just say it's twice as likely that hell would freeze over, and that family really should buy lotto tickets. Your sidekick is legit. A long record of being this psychic stage person and several cases of her aiding police in solving weird cases, some rather famous."

"Thanks, gotta run."

CAROL ALREADY HAD THE boys at CSIS verify what Rebecca had said when she arrived at the hotel by the time she sat down for dinner with Jake at the Bard and Banker Pub, which Carol wanted to visit since it was reported to be haunted by the famous poet, Robert Service. The restaurant was a convenient place to reconvene as it was close enough to the hotel to rush off if something came up, but far enough away not to get any prying eyes or ears. "So, this place was once owned by Robert Service, a famous Canadian Poet, who wrote The Cremation Of Sam MaGee and The Shooting Of Dan McGrew."

"Those sound vaguely familiar those poems. So, I vaguely remember his story, didn't he trip over a corpse or something like that?"

"Yes, and it haunted him for the rest of his life."

"So, you're telling me that this guy became a famous poet because he tripped over a corpse? I guess good stuff comes out of weird happenings if you want to believe in this mumbo jumbo voodoo like of crap. This is a load of shite as far as I'm concerned, do you believe this BS?" Carol watched the figure of Robert Service quietly walking up the stairs, journal in hand, and he appeared to be in deep thought writing as he walked. *Ah, the precursor to texting while you walk, only he's lucky he only had horses to run him over in his day and not an automobile.* She knew better than to tell Jake based on his last remark. "Well, there are supposed to be a lot of ghosts in Victoria, so it is quite possible. However, there is a rather important thing I want to talk to you about that came up yesterday."

"Not a ghost, I presume?" He smirked in that cocky sneer of face.

We'll see just how long Mr. Smart-ass holds that grimace in about ten seconds. "I ran into someone quite interesting at the hotel today, she showed me this photograph and said the person in it is her fiancé, a Luigi Penchanto. Got any explanations?" Carol put forth the photograph that Rebecca gave her. "There is no mention of him in any database. If files ever existed, they have been wiped."

"Fuck." Jake closed his eyes and put his head down. "No! It can't be."

"Be what?" This was going to be anything but a quiet dinner. *But that wiped that smug smirk totally wiped off his smug face.*

"Rebecca is on the loose and probably looking for me."

"Oh, she's looking for you alright. Are you telling me you are scared of a woman? Big badass copper, Cole Brady, er sorry, need to keep names in context, Jake Holden. You afraid of a little skirt, er woman?"

"Put that skirt on the Tasmanian Devil, throw in a reject from WWF fan club, complete with wooden chair to belt you with, add a pinch of the cast of

Inglorious Bastards and stir with a healthy seasoning of a female Fifty shades of Grey and yes, you just got Rebecca."

"Sounds pretty kinky. Now tell me how you two got together?"

"At the time, part of my job. I had to go undercover and that meant I had to seduce her in order to get inside the mob. Which is why I was put on this assignment. Kinky doesn't even begin to describe her. I knew she liked me and when we got close, I discovered she's a part-time dominatrix." "Okay that explains the "don't mess with this bitch" tattooed all over her forehead. How close?"

"We got engaged."

"That's pretty close; and while I shouldn't ask this, and probably don't want to know, for I belong to the-whatever-flavor of fun you have in your bedroom is your business, how kinky is kinky?"

Jake looked coolly at Carol. "You know, spanking, hot wax, bondage. The usual stuff. There wasn't much she wouldn't do."

"Wow, you really go for the wild ones. Does that explain the scar just above your left ear, looks fairly recent?"

He touched the scar, almost fondly. "Yup, she got too excited with the whip one night." Jake closed his eyes, lost in thought for a minute. "Now, where was I? I think the last time I saw her was in court. She had to have an ankle monitor. She swore she'd never ever let me go. I got a call two weeks ago, a week after it was placed on her. How she found out I was here I have no idea.

That woman has contacts in pretty darn high places."

"Apparently, as she is an invited guest to this wedding. How'd she get it off?" Carol asked.

"Probably gnawed it off, if I know her." Jake didn't miss that look of distain on her face. "Just to spite us. We found it on a dog in her house. White poodle, with a red collar, cherries adorning it. Answers to the name 'Twinkles.'"

"And you know this how?"

"I wanted to keep some contact with her after the case. The bureau did warn me about her, but I didn't think she could ever find out where I was. Like I said, she has her ways, probably blackmailed some judge."

"You liked her then?" Carol bristled."

"We were engaged, I had to get as close to her in order to infiltrate the mob. Didn't know she had any connections to the gangs out east, and yes, it's hard sometimes to not get emotionally involved." He stopped, lost in thought for a moment. "Yeah, I liked her a lot. She had passion and a zest for life, reminded me of something I'd lost over time. As you know dealing with criminals can leave you a bit jaded and wondering sometimes is everyone out there just trying to bust your ass or wanting to con someone out of something. I guess I never thought I'd run into someone that I could fall in love with. As crazy as that might sound. But enough of that. I've got reports from a source that there's talk of the mob meeting an arriving ship from Asia on some sort of business. Not sure when, my contact will let me know as soon as he does."

"Let me guess, they're trying to set up some kind of coalition with the Asian gangs out here."

"Oh, you got the tip as well. Care for a hot date?"

"You've got the nerve to ask." *Where did this come from?* "Okay, sorry. I'll need to get aboard that ship to plant listening bugs. Care to join me? Could be exciting."

"Maybe. I'll see if the boss approves it."

She got up to use the washroom as Jake paid the bill. *Least the Yank can do after this nightmare. I don't think I'm letting him within a foot of me.* Carol entered the stall, several scribbles were scratched into the paint, including one of a being, his hair askew. *Strange, probably done by some broad strung out on mushrooms.* A shadow crossed just in front of the closed stalls door, as her nosed twitched and the room went cool. Didn't know Mr. Service was a peeping-tom. Carol closed her eyes a moment trying to concentrate.

So, I've got to ask CSIS why the hell hadn't we heard about this vessel in our own waters? In this very bay.

By the time she got out, the room felt warm again. *And the bigger question. What do the Americans know that we don't?*

❦   ❦

"EVER WONDER HOW THE Mafia got so powerful?" Agnes asked as they sat having tea the next afternoon. She had on an elegant red and green flowered dress and her usual wide brimmed hat.

"Ruthlessness and a very structured hierarchy I'm told."

Agnes smiled and spoke slowly, like she was reading the Sunday paper. "They have been known to employ the services of the incarnate one and in return give him souls to devour."

"What? That's not possible. And why here on the West Coast?"

"Simple, no guns, laxer laws, smaller police presence. Victoria is not that far from Seattle via boat and offshore is Vancouver. Two of the biggest ports bringing in the Asian markets. They want to strike up a deal with Bathomet, Set, Shiva, Satan, whichever is your preferred name for the infernal lord of downstairs, to give them protection and guaranteed success when they start tapping into the burgeoning Asian markets."

"How do you know so much? You're some cagey old broad."

Like I said before, I do my research, like you. Besides did I not mention I was psychic?" She laughed and bit into the dainty triangular cucumber sandwich with no crusts.

"This is nuts. You know more about what's going on here than the RCMP or CSIS. We only got alerted to the upcoming wedding three weeks ago via an American contact. But we've never heard anything at all about them being devil worshippers."

"Let me tell you a story." Agnes took another long sip of her tea. "It started when I ran into a rock group. Told me they were going to be the next big thing, like the Tumbling Rocks. You know, the band with the lovely lead singer with a pair of lips that could French kiss a moose"

"I think you mean the Rolling Stones?"

"That's them. Their lead singer was Nick Juggler, anyways this other group was scheduled to go on with the Rolling Rocks and they were very concerned as all the Horoscopes were saying bad karma." Carol smiled to herself but let Agnes continue. "I forget the name of this other group, so couldn't tell you what became of them. Anyway, it was the sixties, 1969 to be exact, long haired hippies running about, peace, free love and all that jazz had just kicked in. I was doing a show of psychic readings in San Francisco in a club next to the Fillmore West. This was a major venue then and we had a lot of huge stars roll in after shows. These five arrogant punks rolled in and wanted to do a reading. They were trying to get a feel for their upcoming free show to be performed at the Altamont race track in a couple of days."

"The Fillmore West? Didn't a lot of great acts perform there and wasn't the Altamont gig where some people died?"

"Carol, darling, you're interrupting the karma again. Besides at my age I tend to forget what I'm talking about if I get interrupted. People had been warning them about this event and they wanted some information wondering if it would be wise to proceed. I consulted Cider and told them Venus, Mercury and the Sun are all in the Sagittarius quadrant, while the moon is on the cusp of Libra-Scorpio. This is very bad karma. I thought it odd, but I remember their lead singer smiling and saying something like, 'that's perfect.'"

She paused. "That threw me a little and I said again 'there's a good chance of something going very tragically awry.' He just smiled back as I took his hand. And I saw the same vision as I did with Tony. I knew there would be trouble at that show and there was. A few people died and oddly enough the Hell's Angel's biker group were used as security."

"I get it, very bad karma."

Death calls silently on some but leaves a foul stench on others."

"You think a killing is in the cards?"

"Or several. You must use extreme caution with the Cosa Nostra. I know they are not here merely to watch a wedding and in the upcoming days, the quadrants are aligning in very similar patterns. I warned the authorities back then, but no one took me seriously. The other band didn't come on to play, they backed down in the end. I never worked in San Fran after that and was very ill for days after that trying to get rid of the devil's taint on me. I'm warning you now."

Carol sat stunned. "So, if that is the case how do we stop this pact from being formed out here?"

"Not we, you. I'm too old for this. On the night before the wedding, downstairs in Hatley Castle, they will be performing the last of the nineteen keys of the Satanic ritual of the inverted pentagram. That has to be stopped before it is completed."

"Can't I just walk in and arrest them?"

"No, timing is critical. If you stop the ritual before completion, he is trapped inside and doesn't have a way out. Starved of spirits he will wither away. But he needs to be called from his usual place of residence."

"Hell, I Presume."

"Carol, stop." She waited a moment like a petulant teacher. "He is weakest when he is in the pentagram, called there he is trapped until the ceremony is complete. That is why there are sacrifices, to awaken his need, his thirst to be called to that place where he is vulnerable."

"You are not shitting me on this are you?"

Agnes slowly blew on her tea some more. "Wish I was. Now it's time for my beauty makeover and massage, and trust me at my age, this will take most of the day. But you must wait for them to begin chanting in the archaic language of Enokian."

"E-what?" Carol watched her get up and walk slowly away without responding. *I guess I'm supposed to look this up.*

"Yes, that would be wise," Agnes said as she stopped and rearranged her large, elegant hat.

It's not every day you sit down for tea and have your entire, orderly, existence puked into your lap. How am I supposed to deal with this? Like her I doubt anyone else is going to believe me. Devil worshippers? The old gal is crazy, but I sense she's talking some truth here.

She glanced at her watch, most afternoons were quiet, unless there are special guests checking in or it's the weekend, then it's generally just nuts. Carol texted Samuel to man the fort while she went to her room. *Research and some tea. Although a stiff drink might settle the nerves better.*

⚬⚬   ⚬⚬

CAROL SAT BEFORE HER laptop. *So, I've Agnes, mad Italians and Satanic rituals. Only she knows something I don't and won't tell me. Why?*

Carol first looked up Enokian. *Okay, she's got me there, apparently one of the oldest languages known to man and used at the rituals to attract the Devil and is repeated in translation at all the ceremonies in the current language.*

There were a lot of reports and arrests over the years of Satanic cult members and Satanists in the Victoria area, Carol found out as she went through the webpages and police reports.

She Googled haunted sites of Victoria. Dozens of webpages came up. "Wow, she's right, there's a lot of locations here as well." She spent the next couple of hours scrolling through page after page.

Carol grabbed a tourist map of Victoria, tacked it on the wall of her room and began to mark with a pen all the known hauntings and sightings. *So, if Agnes is right about this Ley Line stuff and that in England all the old sacred sights and churches travel along straight lines, except where they converge in certain major earth energy centers, like Stonehenge.* What she also learned is that the energy centers were male and female charged, positive and negative and that they also wound back and forth across each other. *And I can detect them via a dowsing rod, good to know. So, if this is correct then there should be something strange. Or maybe there's something to see that sticks out.* She stared at Hatley Castle which seemed to stand all by itself across the bay to the east. She drew a line towards it then drew another from several of the known ghostings; St. Ann's Academy, the Victoria golf course. Then she drew a line on an angle down through Fan Tan Alley, Bard and Banker Pub. The lines intersected, like at Stonehenge. Carol ran a Google search and indeed they were ley lines and where they intersected were centers of earth energy. *No surprise that this is where our Eastern guests are holding their ceremony. The castle if this is correct is an area of sacred earth energy. They must use Google too.* Carol ran across several articles, including some on the use of dowsing rods, some from two pieces of copper and another cut from the branches of trees. *On my next day off I gotta try this.*

She found a few blog sites about ghosts, hauntings and underground tunnels in Victoria and responded to a couple, hoping to get some response that might help her. Carol shook her head, most of the bloggers had unusual monikers, like Danglepuss. *Probably some pimply twelve-year old kid in glasses. The internet is a funny place where you can be any kind of alter ego you like.*

She put in a request on most of the sites, if anyone had any unusual things to report, ghosts, or beings with hair aflame, she added at the last moment and signed them all with Justifier.

THE BLUE HAZE POPPED and crackled, a young girl with large eyes awoke and emerged from the matrix, long elfish ears and hair sparked with blue flames. She shook herself and her wings fluttered behind her. *We dreamed of being a blue fairy.* It fluttered off the floor of the dank sewers a moment. *Now, we are one.*

Only we are alone now. The others trapped down here, the Lekwungen will not understand.

They are angry, very angry.

And will kill us for being different.
We are different, we are not them.
We are not either of us.
We are new and alone.

I dreamt of my former life as a human. My mother never once told me she loved me. She said because of me she was stuck with my dad, who was never home. He worked on the oil rigs of Alberta, drank, made my mom do drugs with him. She eventually became addicted to them like him.

We are alone, And trapped, Unwanted.
Why then are we here.
Unsure?

It curled in on itself.
Tears streamed down both sides of its face, of its being.

Chapter Nine

Carol sent Jake a text asking if he wanted to join her for dinner that evening but he never responded. Odd. She went to see if he was in his room. Muffled voices echoed as she was about to knock. Carol listened, one was Jake and the other was definitely a woman. "You will learn to satisfy me or else." *What the... it sounded like he was being ordered to do something and the females voice sounded vaguely familiar.*

A moan echoed. *Bastard, he's got a woman in his room. And obviously he's not giving her a tourist view of Victoria from his window or he's got one of my maids in there and he's showing her more than just his bed sheets. She knew Marilyn, a younger buxom blonde, usually called on customers for room service on this floor. That's it, I should storm in and fire her ass.*

Would be a legit excuse to barge in. Then the smart snap of a whip sang out.

His voice gasped on the other side of the door. *That's not bloody Marilyn. Didn't he say Rebecca was some kind of crazy dominatrix? How could she have found him already?* Carol wavered between entering and leaving when another crack of the whip echoed, and his voice gasped, "Stop." Rather loudly.

Or was he in actually in trouble? Only one way to find out. She quietly bent the master card, slid it into the slot and softly entered the room. What she expected to see, Carol wasn't too sure. But she didn't expect to see a big hunk of a man like Jake Holden naked on the bed, his hands cuffed to the bed rails and Rebecca sporting only a black leather corset. She had her back to Carol and was about to straddle his face. The faint smell of chloroform filled the room. There on the bedside was a rag, which Carol surmised was drenched in the stuff. Jake, judging by his lack of hardness, wasn't a willing participant. Carol stared a second or two longer than she should at the size of his thickness laying between legs.

Jake looked up at Carol. "Help me," he groaned, more, it was obvious now, from the aftereffects of being drugged than finding a voice to speak.

"Honey, no one's going to help you. Now you better get down to business and finish what we started last time. Cause you know a slave's job is to pleasure the mistress. Otherwise, I'm just going to have to whip you some more." She snapped the whip again. He jumped; redness adorned his body in several spots. She'd been whipping him more than a few times, it was obvious. "Carol, help."

"What?" Rebecca looked behind her and realized they were no longer alone. "Get the hell out of here, right now."

I have half a mind to let the bugger suffer and leave. But I don't think he did this willingly. Carol took a step forward.

"She drugged me and tied me against my will," Jake blurted, trying to get the energy to push the dominatrix off him.

"I said leave, before I take the whip to you as well." Rebecca rose off her knees and tried to stand on the bed in her six-inch stilettos as Carol ran at her. The whip began to snap back as she tackled Becca like a linebacker sacking a quarterback.

The two crashed onto the other side of the bed and vanished from Jake's view. They rolled around on each other twice. Rebecca tried to slam her long, manicured nails into Carol's eyes before the detective grabbed her head in both hands and slammed the back of Rebecca's head into the floor, twice. The woman went limp. Carol got up and grabbed a handy pillow, tore the case off it and flipping the redhead over, tied her hands behind her back with it.

"Where's the cuffs key?"

"In the top dresser drawer."

As Carol searched for the key, she asked, "Now, what the hell is going on here?"

"She knocked on the door. How she found out this was my room, I don't know. She had a wig on and said something about hotel cleaning staff. I let her in didn't really pay attention to her as I was on the phone. The minute I turned my back she chloroformed me."

"Well, neither I nor my staff would have told her. Our confidentiality is very strict." Carol couldn't help noticing there was a goodly number more welts than she first realized. The woman had been having her way with him for quite awhile before she showed up. Beside the bed was a wig and what looked like a hotel maid's outfit. "Let me guess, one of our staff is also probably bound and gagged somewhere?"

"I hope its Marilyn, I'll help untie her."

"No surprise you know her name, I'm sure your eyes never left the view of those two mountains she keeps under wraps. And how do you know her?"

"She was flirting with me yesterday. Told her I could take her out for a drink later."

"You are the worst piece of male disgustingness I have ever met. I had half a mind to leave you here cuffed up and let our redhead have her way with you." She twirled the key ring to the cuffs as his manhood stirred. "I see the blood is coming back to you then."

"Sorry, it's just you're so sexy holding that key, and having two women fight over me is quite a turn on."

"Men? Even tied up they can only think with the wrong head." Carol clicked open the cuffs. "I, for the life of me don't understand how being tied up and whipped is a turn on. Must hurt like hell."

Rebecca began to stir so Carol placed the cuffs on her. She struggled to a half-sitting position and smiled evilly. "Don't knock it until you try it. And lady, I'd put you over my knees and have my way with you any day."

"That ain't going to happen, this bread is buttered on one side only. The only comfort you're going to enjoy tonight is a cold cell."

Carol picked up the hotel's phone. "Samuel, get the police on the double. I have someone that just broke into a guest's room and assaulted them."

Minutes later a police officer arrived and hauled Rebecca away still cuffed.

"Lady, I ain't done with him, nor you, yet. Until next time." Rebecca glared at her evilly.

Carol glanced over at the bag of bondage goodies left open beside the bed and spied a ball gag. "Wait a moment officer." Carol grabbed the ball gag.

"You wouldn't dare, bitch."

Carol stretched it over Becca's head, let it go and pinched her nose until the redhead had to inhale. "I would, bag. There is a little of your own medicine." She grabbed a pillowcase and stuffed it over her head.

"Hey what the..."

"I'd rather not have the Italians or anyone else see you being hauled out of here. Make any noise and I'll authorize the arresting officer to use his baton to quiet you. Got it?" She grabbed a bathrobe hanging on the door and threw it over the trussed woman. "And I can't have our esteemed guests staring in shock at a nearly naked woman dressed in hooker-Saturday-night special clothing being detained either. Take her out the back service elevators." The policeman dragged her from the room. *Man, that felt good. Okay I got rid of crazy bitch, now I can concentrate on this murder and try to not have more dead Italians on my hands.*

"Okay, we're done with the Ms. Crazy dressed in cow hide and corsets. Explain to me how you two got mixed up?"

Jake adjusted his shirt. "You're not into leather? Too bad, you'd look hot in a black leather corset. How about we do dinner again, I've worked up a bit of an appetite."

"Are you kidding me?"

"Darn, I was just beginning to get aroused. Oh, I wouldn't have done that, you better be very careful with Rebecca, she's extremely jealous and clever. I doubt we've seen the last of her."

"I'll have her behind bars for a couple of weeks until this is all over."

Jake grinned, "Oh, I doubt that. She has money and her ways. Keep your back covered. If she thinks we're involved emotionally with each other, there's no end to what she's capable of. I know from experience." He winced as he bent over to pick up his shoes.

"And that looks so enjoyable? I think I'd rather go bungee jumping in the nude." She patted his back firmly.

Jake winced and hissed loudly in pain. "Naked Bungee-jumping. Now that's kinky, can't say I've ever done that before. Thought I read somewhere they do that further up the island." Carol shook her head. "You are worse than disgusting." *Man, are all men pigs? To think I found him attractive.*

⚓   ⚓

AGNES SAT BY HERSELF in her room. Several incense sticks lent the room a smoky quality.

"Okay, my old friend, let me know about Nathan Evans. I've gone through the deck of Tarot cards three times and nothing." She focused on the face of the lad in the picture Carol gave her earlier as she shoved the large cards aside and put her hands on Cider. Agnes closed her eyes, after long moments only blankness returned. *You ain't telling me he's dead, are you?*

"*Okay, find me the plate number BCD 053.* After long moments of haze, the words, 'my boys,' floated in front of her vision and the scene of five boys playing a card game in a room and an older lady laughing in joy at the sight. *What the hell has that got to do with the abduction? There are times when even a crystal skull has a twisted sense of ha-ha.*

As Agnes pulled her hands away from the cool surface of the crystal skull the woman looked up and stared directly at Agnes.

It's her.

The elder placed her hands back on the skull and was immediately hurled backwards off her chair. The words slammed into her skull. "You shall pay for this. The master doesn't like interference."

Agnes coughed twice as she slowly got up. "No broken bones. Man, that chick packs quite the wallop."

Two eyes looked up at her as she went to cover the head. "I will find you and make you pay for this. No one must know."

"Great I've got a stalker, never had a stalker before."

⊰⊱   ⊰⊱

I THOUGHT I'D HAD MY plate full of whack-jobs with this assignment. Having gone back to her room to tidy herself up, Carol rode the elevator down toward the restaurant. *Dealing with dead Italians is one thing, now a whip cracking dominatrix as well. At least she'll be behind bars for a while.*

Whatever happened to staid, stiff upper lip English Victoria, where you sit around and talk about the weather, who finds the one cucumber sandwich where they missed cutting the crusts off and just how bloody marvelous was that cricket game. Shit, what next a raving mad clown that spouts Shakespeare as he stabs his victim and eats their kidneys with his popcorn at the local cinema? Or just a raving...

Her rambling thoughts ceased immediately after the elevator doors slide open outside the hotel gift shop. Staring straight at her a man, beady eyes, jet-black hair, and a large, hooked nose...He turned away, incongruously engrossed in the assortment of Empress Hotel chocolates and perfumes.

"Are you FUCKING kidding me?" Not believing who she was staring at.

Two people strolling near her gasped.

"Look, I do apologize. Didn't mean to be offensive." They smiled timidly and sped up.

Great out of left field a wicked curve ball.

She was about to simply stroll past and let it go, only the whole Jake and Becca situation had infuriated Carol more than she thought. *Bugger this, I've reached my limit.*

Instead of walking past, Carol stormed straight into the store, careful to keep her eye focused on him, which wasn't hard as there wasn't too many others about at this time of day. She took in the dark overcoat and blackbrimmed hat on and knew it *was* him. His eyes opened as she strolled up. "Mr. Martin Crow? May I help you at all?"

"Perhaps," he clacked almost sing-songlike. "I've come to these waters looking for some aquatics of a more stagnant nature." His nose wrinkled as he sniffed at one of the perfume samples and just behind him hung a rack of long 'Raven Lunatic' tee shirts, showing several night-capped Ravens. *Somehow quite appropriate, given the circumstances.* "Not these of the more putrid, foul kind."

Again, he plays in riddles, always riddles. "Okay, I'm in, Mr. Rumple-tell-me-who-I-am eat-me-stiltskin."

Carol breathed deeply and thought a moment. "These are ocean waters in this part of the town. They are never still, and since laden with salt, are usually of a more malodorous nature.

That one which you seek you'll not find in this store, or this city. Perhaps inland, but not here."

"It seems I have come here for nothing." He clacked his teeth together.

"It appears so. Port waters are usually flowing, and I suggest you would be wise to do so as well." She pointed to the exit.

He tipped his hat to her. "Then I shall get my leather bag and get cracking." He smiled slyly as exited from the gift shop. *Damn innuendoes. I'll let Charlie deal with him, I've got my plate full of Jack-in-the-boxes to deal.*

"Excuse me." The middle-aged store clerk interrupted her. "I don't think he paid for those chocolate nut bars in his hands."

Carol already knew this outcome. "Go ahead and apprehend him and I'll call security." She lifted the handset on her belt and waited before paging code blue as the clerk turned the corner and came back moments later clutching only the black brimmed hat. *Well that is a surprise.* Carol nearly mouthed the virtual words she knew the clerk would utter.

"He's gone. It's like he vanished into thin air." Her eyes were wide open, threatening to crack the layers of makeup she had obviously taken hours to put on.

"Good riddance. One less nut bar in town. Put it on my tab so that you don't get in trouble. Oh, and pull those 'Raven Lunatic' nightshirts from the rack and dispose of them immediately." Carol grabbed the hat and walked out of the store leaving the woman standing there totally bemused.

And one less nutso to not add to my collection of whack jobs in this assignment. I may have said this before, but time again for a smoke and one hell of a stiff drink. Think I'll need to visit the local chapter of the AA before this is all over.

She glanced at her police phone. *Nothing on Nathan. Crap, this isn't good. I'm running out of time.*

⚓ ⚓

EARL LOOKED UP FROM his gardening duties at St. Ann's Academy located a few blocks behind the Fairmont Empress Hotel, as thunder cracked the skies. Clouded over, rain threatened any minute to unload. He'd just started his rounds on the ride-on lawn mower and was hoping to get them finished before nature decided to unload its drawers, as he called it. It took nearly an hour to do the grounds on either side of the elegant walkway up to the Victorian building. "Gimme a break, motha nature. I's got a lot to do today."

He caught a glimpse of mist rising from the ground on the other side of the walk, behind a copse of well-spaced trees. The guardians he called them over the years, for every time he stood in the middle of the grove he felt safe and protected. He glanced around, there wasn't mist anywhere else and it hadn't begun to rain. "Where in hebe and gamorra is that coming from?"

The mists rose from various points in the ground, but instead of spreading it began to swirl on itself turning into thick white blocks. "I's neva seen the likes in me twenty years here." He spoke in his thick Irish accent. "Or as me relatives in Newfoundland might spout, 'Lord Tundering Jesu.'"

Shutting the mower off he stared as the mists continued to swirl away in several places as the dark clouds rumbled again. Light sprinkles plinked on the hood of the mower. "I's can't cut the grass now anyways."

He got off the mower and walked towards the copse of trees. Quickly the splatters turned into a light drizzle, he flicked the hood to his jacket over his head. Earl stared bewildered, the rain didn't do anything to dampen the swirling mists. It was as if they weren't being touched.

He counted the columns that seemed to be coalescing into humanlike forms. "Nine, begorra. Only once had he ever seen the ghosts of the nine nuns known to haunt the grounds and that was on a full moon night near All Hallows eve, when he'd staggered onto the grounds in a semi drunken stupor. He'd been doing cleanup on a wedding party, as the hall rented itself out on many an occasion. Under no circumstances are staff allowed to consume alcohol while on the premises, for any reason. He quit after that night taking the nuns as a sign.

Only that night they were mere shadowy figures, barely visible as they walked the grounds clutching their prayer beads. These were far more solid, he could make out the faces in the dimming light caused by the clouds. "Hey, I ain't had a drop since," he sputtered at them. The nuns, all dressed in white habits, ignored him as they began to move in a circle in the center of the copse. An area he often stood at, sensing the energy there. Like being in a rain like this, others laughed when he told them, he felt tingles coming up from the earth. He stopped telling people and when alone out here would often enjoy the sensations. "Good Karma," he whispered. But today was different. The nuns began to circle faster in a clockwise manner, clutching bibles, crosses and prayer beads. He could hear them chanting the Lord's Prayer.

Our Father, who art in heaven, hallowed be thy Name. Thy Kingdom come, thy will be done, on earth, as it is in heaven. Give us this day our daily bread. and forgive us our trespasses, as we forgive them that trespass against us. And lead us not into temptation, but deliver us from evil. . Amen.

They repeated the verses several times, each time getting louder, the words thrumming into his head. Words he knew from his Catholic upbringing back in Ireland. The rain began to fall harder, still not touching the spirits walking. He was to retire this year if he wanted.

His hands shook as the figures began to swirl into one and lifted heavenward like a giant winged angel.

We have been released.
Amen.

"Feck, this is absolute cack and shite. I's never seen the likes. I's handing in me resignation today and taking up the bottle again." His hands shook as he jumped on the mower and with the blades still engaged cut a single swath through the wet grass in a waving line back to the storage sheds.

Chapter Ten

"Are you kidding me? How is this possible?" Carol sputtered.

"You found the car running, the attending officer cuffed to the steering wheel and Ms. Casavanio gone?" The police officer nodded. "Yes, the officer has quite the lump on his head. Oh, and a ball gag in his mouth. And his gun is gone."

After Carol's encounter with Mr. Crow, she had been summoned to Reception only for a uniformed officer to inform her of the impossible.

Rebecca had escaped.

"Samuel, get security footage up and running from earlier yesterday. The redhead, Rebecca what's-her-name-pain-in-the-ass. I want pictures given to everyone on duty and headquarters. She just escaped police custody and is considered dangerous. Get hotel security into her room, round everything up and place it under police custody, immediately. And make sure there's a least two guards."

DUCKING UNDER THE POLICE tape, Carol held it aside for Agnes to enter the crime scene.

Outlined on the floor was where they found Antonio Rizzuto's body. The room was still technically off-limits, but Carol wanted to know what, if anything, Agnes could sense, and as Jake had blown her off for dinner, again, it was the perfect opportunity.

"Agnes, you're awfully quiet."

"Sorry, there's a lot in here and I'm trying to get a feel for it. I can hear the man dying. But there's ... old spirits. And more."

Old spirits? Could there really be a ghost involved in this?
Agnes frowned heavily. "Something's not quite right."

Carol kept quiet as Agnes slowly walked around the room and bent over the chalked outline. *Maybe I shouldn't have brought her here, but she said she did this before with other police departments and we haven't found any evidence leading towards a suspect.*

"Honey, I have. I was involved in the Boston Strangler case back in the sixties. Now stop thinking. It's mucking up the air."

"Sorry, don't think I'll ever get used to you reading my mind."

"Yeah, it's like ordering Diet Coke, just ain't right. Now shh." Carol tried to think of nothing. It was more difficult than she thought.

Agnes stood quietly for a few minutes then slowly headed for the door.
"Leaving already?"
"I'm done."
"So?"

"Lady, there's a shit load of disturbances going on and I need to chat with Cider over this."

"That's it? That's all you're going to say."

"Yes. Except for you to cover your back and sleep with one eye open." Agnes frowned.

"What the hell does that supposed to mean?"

"Just what I said." Agnes quickly opened the door and left as fast as her old legs could move.

Well, that went well. I've never seen the old girl move that fast. Which means she saw or felt something in here. Carol stared around the room. *I agree with Agnes, I need to come back later.*

Something doesn't feel right, and my intuition doesn't usually let me down.

⚜   ⚜

"SO, TONIGHT'S THE NIGHT. The ship is coming in." Jake had texted her earlier.

Carol sat in her car as she called him.

"I thought being an undercover cop you would thrill on excitement like me. Anyways I only have tonight before this ship leaves, bound for San Francisco, and I've been ordered to plant a couple of ears on it. Are you in? We could do dinner and wine after."

She did like living on the edge, wouldn't have been a cop otherwise. That and upholding the law. "Dinner and wine, man, you never give up? After that outrageous scene with Rebecca in your room, I shouldn't even talk to you. But I'll consider this part of the assignment and not pleasure. And if you think of trying any funny business, I'll slap my cuffs on you so fast you'll think you just got booted out of an airplane. Got it?"

"Got it."

Yeah, he got nothing in that last sentence. I'll have to watch him like a hawk. "So, we run out to this boat, without being spotted, board it and plant bugs? How are we going to do this?"

"I've got it already planned, some of my men will run another ship very close to them as they 'quote' leave the harbor and we'll be suited in black gear, a black ops dingy, muffled engine and slide right up to them. I'm told tonight most of the crew is on shore leave and only a skeleton crew are on board. We've had satellite surveillance and drones watching the ship all day."

"You Americans have all the coolest gear."

"You haven't seen the half of it. Are we on?"

"Let me check with my office, but I think we've a deal, not sure I can get the proper warrants in time to allow the Canadian authorities to do this. Given we've let you Yanks into this whole operation, or should I say you've barged in, without being asked, I don't think that would stop you from doing this anyways."

"Lady, we're the ones that told your boys about it in the first place."

Carol called him back after Big Dan called her back. "So Big Dan says I'm on my own. Deny everything if I get caught as I can't get documentation in time to allow me to legally use the information if required, but I don't think you care about that, unless you've got what you need from your people."

"By the time we're back, I'll have what we need drawn up. So, it's a go?" Jake replied.

"It's a date. As long as I can plant our own ears aboard. My guys want to know what's going down on this vessel as well. Could be crucial to finding out what is really going on with the mob out here."

"Great. Meet me at pier forty-six by the boat named Seahorsey and don't worry about what to wear, we've got all the gear we need to do this with."

"Seahorsey? Your great undercover super-secret balls-to-the-wall loaded with all the newest wangle-dangle circuitry boat is called Seahorsey?"

"That's her."

HOURS LATER, AFTER dark had fallen, Carol hung onto to the sides of a small black dingy as her and Jake were being towed along. Both wore black fatigues and had blacked their faces as well. She'd never done anything this risky before which in itself was exciting. He was right it was a turn-on, the living on the edge of danger, part of her life as a police officer. Jake's earpiece beeped. "Okay head down, we're going in." He released the rope and started the small engine. Even from inside the boat she couldn't hear it run. "Electric, produces less heat for an infrared signal and far fewer decibels. Not to mention the paint and the material of this dingy is nonreflective."

They lowered their heads until she could barely see over the side. Quietly they whispered closer to the calm vessel wallowing in the waters of Victoria's inner harbor. *He's so calm under tension he's done this kind of operation before. I can only guess at the madness he's gone through undercover with the FBI.* Meanwhile her insides were turning to the consistency of quicksand. These moments of danger and thrill were what she lived for. *The edge. Crap, just realized that. I'm one of those crazy thrill seekers that like to jump out of airplanes and dance over beds of hot coals.*

As they pulled up alongside, he glanced at the small screen in front of him. "No heat scores on top, they are all either in the bridge or below deck." He pulled a small gun like affair from a covered case and aimed it above them.

A silent whoosh and a projectile shot up. It popped itself to the side of the ship and then dispersed a load of plastic looking pouches. Instant footholds, she knew. He counted to ten and pulled on the rope before nodding it was safe. "Wait until I'm over the side, in case I have to deal with anyone.

The rope should hold two of us, but I'd rather not chance it."

For all his size, Jake was extremely agile. All too quickly he was up, over and signaling her to join him. They ran along the starboard side, ducking under windows. From the dark waters of the inlet the hum of a large vessel approaching alerted them of its approach. It was a darkened large luxury cruiser, over thirty metres in length and headed in their direction. A large part of the bow lowered, and the roar of several black painted jet-skis erupted as they ejected from the vessel. Jake pulled a small pair of binoculars from his pocket. "Crap! We've company. They all in black commando outfits and bearing weapons." He spotted the Uzi's strapped to their backs, faces were blackened as well as partly covered with ski masks.

"They'll spot us if we go back over the side." He looked around as the vessels quickly approached. "Shit, under the lifeboat."

The two dove under the covers as excited voices from inside the ship erupted, alerted to the approaching jet-skis. "This wasn't part of the plan?"

"No. Don't know what's going on." He pulled a gun from under his jacket, as did Carol, and both waited under the cover of the lifeboat. Her heart thumped hard.

A small explosion rocked the boat, followed by semi-automatic fire. The boat was obviously under attack. "Do we make a run for it?" she whispered.

"No, we wait it out. Lay out as straight as possible and I'll get on top of you. This will make the boat as centered weight wise as possible."

More shots rang out and somewhere a body thumped to the ground. Tracers ripped by them. Carol hissed and Cole clamped a hand over her mouth as he climbed on top of her. Her eyes opened in panic catching his cold hard stare. He replaced his hand with his mouth and kissed her deeply. *What the...*

His hungry tongue dove into her mouth. *What?* The man was psycho, or ... *It's that fricking edge thing.* She felt herself wanting to respond to his kiss.

"Jake, what are you doing?" she whispered in the dark when he moved his mouth and ran his hands over her breasts. She could feel the throb from between legs.

"You excite me. I can't help myself but be aroused when I'm next to you."

"Are you kidding me?" she whispered. "We're in a life boat hiding from killers."

"Hey if we're meant to go today wouldn't you rather go this way?"

"I'd rather try to get out of here alive."

"And if we don't?" His hand trailed down her midsection. Carol fought the urge to deck him, anyone nearby would surely hear and the gig would be up.

"We might as while enjoy our last moments in style."

Son of a bitch, bastard. This wasn't the time or place for this. She wasn't exactly a willing participant, either.

God damn him, it felt good, too good as his fingers caressed her between the legs. NO! I can't. He's FBI and I'm police.

"I can't, we can't."

Carol reached down and grabbed him hard by the crotch.

"Oh, that's it, baby," he moaned into her mouth.

She crushed his balls in her hands.

"What?" he muffled his cry of agony.

"Now, get your bloody hands off my pants," she whispered into his ear. *It is said in the depths of emotion and despair you discover your darkest side. Bastard. I just discovered mine.*

"But you're turned on, you can't deny that?"

"I know, not here, not now. This is work and there's guys with guns out there. *I'm on duty, what if he ever said anything, to anyone and being undercover police, I couldn't even think of raising this through any kind of Me Too Movement?*

Carol continued to squeeze his sensitive parts harder as more shots rang out.

"Okay, I give, I give. Let go of my scrotum."
"Let go of me. Deal?"

He pulled his hand free. "Fuck lady, you're a teasing bitch. Oh, my balls, I don't think I'll be able to walk."

"If wanted you I'd have told you."
"But."

"No buts. I may want you. Not here, not now. Get it. We need to get our shit together and figure out how to get out alive."

"Just wait 'til I get you alone someplace private."
"Keep it quiet," she spoke softly. "They'll hear us."

More shots were exchanged, some from silenced weapons, others thundering away. Footsteps thumped closer.

"Over here," a voice yelled. Someone screamed while bullets ricocheted off the side of the lifeboat's hull. "We need to leave, now." A walkie talkie sent a line of garbled voices into the darkness.

"And I thought you liked feisty women? What do we do now?" she whispered.

"We wait. Not when they're crushing my balls, you malicious bag." Jake held his crotch.

Thump, Thump. Someone grunted as they ran by.
What The fuc...
Tracers zipped by, tinging off the metal of the life boat.

A barrage of gunfire erupted from a semi-automatic gun nearby. Voices cried out in what she thought was Asian. Something splattered near them and then silence.

Finally, someone moaned, before something splashed into the water. *Shit, those are bodies being heaved overboard.* After a few moments the sound of a boat's motor restarting echoed in the sudden quiet. It quickly faded into the distance and silence reigned.

Jake listened for a few more moments before lifting the top of the lifeboat's cover. "All clear."

They scrambled out in the dark and spotted what looked like the Skidoos fading into the darkness. "What the hell just happened?"

"Don't know, another gang? Someone else found out about this ship? Or the Italians want to already start getting rid of the Asian gangs. Could mean the start of a lot of trouble." Jake moaned as he readjusted himself and walked tenderly. "Man you've got quite the grip. Damn."

All around the deck blood splattered bodies lay. Bits of flesh clung to the walls; gore splattered like in some bad horror movie. Holes in the walls where bullets had gone through or ripped along. Four bodies at first count, a few more floating on the dark waters. Jake grabbed a semi-automatic and checked how much ammo was in it. He headed into the ship. Ahead of him one body moved. He put a bullet through the man's head, before Carol could react.

"Sorry, can't have any witnesses. Plant what you want out here, I'm going to look inside, stay here. I'll see if there's no one else aboard. But I'm pretty sure they took everyone out. Might not be any point in planting bugs, probably just get your guys to haul it to the docks."

"Only why show up, kill everyone and leave? Didn't make much sense." Carol walked slowly about, checking the pulse of everyone she found that looked like they had a remote chance of being alive. A couple were so shot up it didn't matter; chunks of flesh were splattered everywhere. She took a couple of pictures with her phone of the ones that had enough left to maybe identify and began to climb the stairs to the command center thinking she might find some answers when Jake came bounding outside from below deck, high tailing it as fast as he could.

"Carol! Run like hell."
"What in the...?"

"Bomb," he yelled and lifted his gun and ripped several rounds at the nearest lifeboat's restraining cables. The small craft fell to the still waters. Carol ran towards him. They didn't have time to get to their dingy, if indeed it was still there.

Jake tossed the gun aside and effortlessly picked her up by the waist as he ran past. He flung them overboard. Carol inhaled deeply as a horrendous explosion lit up the otherwise dark sky just before they hit the water. Something slammed into her as she breathed in salt water and lost consciousness.

⋖⋍⋗   ⋖⋍⋗

MY MOTHER! I MUST FIND her. I remember now where she lives. They flew off in the sewers until they got to View Towers off Quadra Street in Victoria. *We cannot stay long, the curse pulls against us, it is night. We can stand the night much more than the day.*

It fluttered into a small apartment and there in her bed lay the former Cindy Amberside's mom, Donna. Beside her a full glass of rum and bottles of prescription and illegal drugs.

She has strung herself out on drugs. We have got here just in time to save her life.

What do you care? She was horrible to you.

The elfish being leaned over and stroked her hair. *I know, but she is still my mother and I love her. We must save her.*

The half that was Lekwungen thought a moment. *Okay, then we will feed off her and take this poison from her.*

The blue fairy leaned over her, stroked her hair and breathed deeply taking the intoxication into itself, like a purple undulating mist, sucking it out of the woman.

This feeds us.
It felt itself filling inside. *But she will do this again.*

No, we will transform that energy into this part of us. It reached into itself and pulled out a small wriggling blue essence. *Our love.*

It opened her mouth and placed it inside where it glowed a moment, before dissolving. *It is done, she will hate us, at first, thanks will come later.*

We must go, the curse is calling.

The blue winged creature bent over in agonizing pain. *We need to return.* It cried in agony as jolting tremors shook its body. *Yes, we must go.*

Quickly it visualized itself back in the cool security of the sewers.
I hate this place, the stink.
I hate this also.
We must be free of this confinement.
Agreed, we will find a way.

Chapter Eleven

Carol moaned into his mouth as he began to stroke her. "You bastard. Take

me here and now before I change my mind, and yell rape and we both get

shot full of holes. This is crazy and dangerous."

"Admit it. You're loving it."

"You're such an asshole. Now take me before I regret this." She pulled his mouth to hers and reached down to unzip his pants. His hardness sprung free. *Son of a ... he doesn't even wear underwear. Damn it, this was hot and absolutely crazy. And I want him. What is wrong with me?*

He slid his finger between her legs. "Oh yeah, you're wet."
"Quit stating the obvious."

She moaned as his thick hardness entered her. He entered slowly, filling her. All she could do was moan into his mouth. He pulled back out and again slowly pushed himself into her. *I need my head examined. I shouldn't be doing this.*

The feel of his throbbing hardness tore her away from all else. Filling her. Carol gasped and clutched him to her. Yells filled the air, thumps of bullets, bodies falling. *They can blast away, this feels too damn good.* Thrusting up, pulling the entire length of his desire fully into her, she bit at his neck, *Shit.* Every internal nerve danced like hands juggling a pot aflame trying not to scream. He kissed her, and she gasped. *So fucking hot. I shouldn't be thinking like this. What am I, some sick kind of kinky perv, like Rebecca? I can see why he liked him woman on the edge.*

This is so bloody American and PC incorrect.

But Christ he feels good, deep inside me and gone again. Like ocean waves battering at the fragile coastline of my sanity. Sanity? No, this was insanity. She cried into his mouth lost in the erotic sensation of being flung over the edge of reason and caution. *This is so frigging hot and most definitely not the right thing to do.*

All too soon Carol felt the convulsions building inside. *So kinky, so sexy, to be making love like this.*

Thump, thump. Gunfire continued to explode all around them.
Oh, god I'm coming. She opened her eyes and stared into Tony's.
Tony, what the...?"

Carol woke inside the ambulance as it caromed around a corner. *Just a dream? It wasn't Jake I desired, but Tony. Even my subconscious knows who I really want.*

"You're awake, that's good. I think you're going to be okay, Agent Moore. You were moaning a lot while you were unconscious," the attendant told her.

She blinked twice, focusing, and realized it was Vidler.
"We're on the way to the Victoria General."
"Was there a guy with me?"

"Jake Holden, FBI. You mentioned his name before coming to. He contacted us and then left when we got to the shore where you'd washed up. He resuscitated you. You've taken on a lot of sea water, but otherwise I think you're going to be okay." Vidler kept his face expressionless.

God, he probably knows what I was dreaming about. Still he's a consummate professional. She tried to sit up and realized she was strapped down, vaguely remembering something slamming into her as she struck the water, *Jake? Resuscitated? He probably enjoyed sticking his tongue down my throat. Oh well, at least he was gentleman enough to make sure I was okay.*

"Is he here?"

"No, said he had other matters to attend to and took off with a couple of other agents in a blacked-out SUV."

Other matters, like taking an ice pack to his balls. She giggled to herself.

When the attendant wasn't looking, she reached down and checked herself. *Man, why do I have a serious consciousness and why couldn't I live like my dream? Why, because I take my job and my oath too flipping serious, that's why. Only I didn't dream it was Jake, but Tony.*

Damnit! My subconscious is telling me something.

When this is over, I need to talk to a psychiatrist, about a dark side that until this assignment I never realized I had. Damn, that Jake.

⚓   ⚓

HER PHONE BUZZED THE next morning. Samuel texted her that Tony Belletti wanted to meet her in his room. Oh hell, I hope this isn't more Italian Mafia crap going down. Carol sneezed twice. Think I might be coming down with a cold. I know one thing, he wouldn't pull the kind of crap Jake does.

Tony Belletti stood as one of his minions opened to door to his suite to let her in. Another minion hovered nearby. She had no idea what this was about and as per Big Dan's orders she was miked-up with him on the other end of the wire, just in case it got rough. She calmly sat where indicated on the sofa and he sat down beside her. He reached up with one hand as if to shake hers and as she lifted hers to meet his grasp, he turned it palm down and kissed the back of her hand. "Ah, Ms. Moore, glad you could make it."

Carol blushed. "Hello, Mr. Belletti. How may I be of service?" She pulled a hanky from her pocket and sneezed deeply. The dipping in the cold harbour water last night, had plugged her sinuses. "Sorry, think I'm catching a cold."

"Ah, I did not ask you here on work related matters and your explanation to both parties earlier seems to have settled the peace. While this is a sad event, the wedding still goes on and for that I am, *grato*, how you say, grateful. I wish to get to know you better and find you very attractive. There is a certain wild Canadian charm, I find very sexy, what we would call, *provocare*, about you. I have asked you here to take you out to dinner as I mentioned earlier on the ghost tour." As he spoke, he ran his hand over hers. "Care to follow me downstairs? And I presume I can have your company alone, without the elegant, but how you say, *posseduto*, possessed elder."

She laughed slightly. He's already booked a private table for two downstairs, knowing I wouldn't turn him down. "I think the word for Agnes is more eccentric. You are a handsome man, Mr. Belletti, as I'm sure you know. There's something about an Italian accent I find attractive. Now give me a moment to let the staff know, unless it is urgent, to belay my calls and if you don't mind, I'd like to change out of this uniform. Give me fifteen minutes to meet you there."

"I shall be waiting *senza fiato*. Breathless!"

She turned and quickly left the room. Before speaking to the mike, she made sure she was well down the hallway and no one was around. "Well this is a pleasant turn of events. I've been asked out for dinner. I'll de-mike for the dinner."

Big Dan responded, "Why, think he'll ask to have sex with you or something?"

Carol smiled. "You didn't see the lust-filled look in his eyes. Possibly, but after last night, I couldn't possibly." She had debriefed Big Dan on what happened once Jake got her back to shore and the medical authorities had cleared her. Only she hadn't told him about what happened in the lifeboat. She still couldn't believe it. "I think he seems to have the hots for me and I ain't about have an audience. Would take the edge of the moment off."

"I thought you were a dedicated employee." He half laughed, something Carol rarely heard him do. "And if it gets too intense, remember I've got Vidler and Carson ready to intervene in a moment or if all goes well. Remember the golden rule, always raincoat protection."

Carol gasped. "Dedication only goes so far in the line of duty. The rest you'll just have to imagine for yourself. Gotta go."

She rushed upstairs and quickly changed into a well cut red and yellow dress that didn't show her breasts off, just accented them, but did show off most of her legs, which she thought was her best asset. She drew on a pair of black sheer patterned nylons. A glance in the mirror, oh yeah lipstick. She looked over the several shades and grabbed the deepest red. She stepped into a pair of sparkling red stilettos, which again helped accent her calves. *This should grab his attention and if it doesn't, he's interested in the wrong kind of equipment.*

Tony was already sitting at the table by himself. A glance around the room showed there was none of his henchmen gathered. It would be just them.

"*Bellissimo,*" he breathed quietly as she slowly sauntered into the room.

He stood up and moved to pull her chair out.

Wow, don't get many true gentlemen these days.

"I have seen many beautiful things in my lifetime, but few bring such *bellezza pura*, sheer beauty, to my eyes as the sight of you," he whispered into her ear and let his breath wash over her neck. Carol melted into her chair.

Son of a... never had a man do that to me. Who the hell wants to eat?

"You are utterly gorgeous, are all Canadian women of this ah, *meravigliarsi*, wonder?"

His eyes, she knew spoke the truth. Whatever spell she had cast on him was working. He placed his hand over hers and gently stroked her fingers.

Oh god, this man was too much. But this is sheer utter bliss.

He turned his hand under hers and ran his fingers gently down her palm. His eyes seemed to burn deep into her soul. "I tend to like stronger assertive women, there is something about you that is beyond what I have for words and that which I've never found in someone."

Damn it. She felt a deep shudder thrill through her whole body. *No one has touched me that intimately in months, if ever.* It was like the first time Alan had touched her. She wanted to say something intelligent, but couldn't as he stroked her hand and fingers. *Man, what he does to my soul.* Tony handed her the wine list. "As a complete change to tradition I shall let you choose the wine"

"If I know Italian men, I think you like would like a full-bodied red." *I might as well get something out of this undercover operation, always wanted to try some.*

"The only full body I want is yours. But you are correct in this."

She nodded over to the waiter on duty and ordered a bottle of Painted Rock Skaha Blend, one of the more expensive red wines on the list. They waited patiently as the waiter uncorked the wine and pour a small quantity for Tony to scrutinize it. He sniffed at the glass, swirled it and tasted, slowly and seductively. "Is this Italian or perhaps Argentinian?"

"No, Canadian."

"Magnifico, this matches the best of the wines I have sampled from the wine capitals of the world." He tasted again and swished it in his mouth. "I get, Welcome to Canada. The wilderness and open spaces that brings out the strength of character. The living on the edge of nature. A cliff I am finding myself tumbling from."

"I like living on the edge." She smiled slightly as he sipped his wine and sampled some herself as they clinked glasses. *And not like the edge of a boat she was shoved from last night.*

Nor the hell that bastard American placed me in. She fought to keep another sniffle down.

"Very good. Great choice."

"This winery this is from is in the next set of valleys inland from us, the Okanagan, and keep playing your cards right and you might end up on the edge of something else." "Would that be my bed?" he asked from out of the blue.

"Is that all Italian men think of? Sex?"

"No, but the *bella bellezza* of you betrays the desires inside. From our two nights on the ghost tour, I have found myself drawn to you and have had a hard time sleeping without the vision of yourself before me. I am not usually lost in infatuation for a woman. So, this is my way of wanting to get to know you better."

Carol smiled. *Yup one horny Italian dude. Could be a fun night. An unexpected bonus from this job. Well I was told to get close to the mob.*

"I didn't invite you over for dinner to just get you into bed."
"Really, I'm let down. I was told Italian men are how do I say this ...?"
"*Suscitato*, aroused?"
"No, passionate and romantic lovers."

He lifted her hand to his lips and lightly breathed on her skin. Shivers ranged up her arm. "Oh, I see you've found me out. But I do wish to see more of this enchanting island, would you care to show me about. I am not one to jump into the covers with anyone. I prefer to get to know you better first. It's my Catholic upbringing."

Relief welled in her. They talked about various things after that getting to know each other better. Carol had agreed to show him around the island.

God, this guy is too, too much.

⚜   ⚜

"HATLEY CASTLE IS CLOSED to the public for the week. I have already gathered your possessions and you can stay there until the wedding. But you need to keep a very low profile until then. It was bad enough that I had to rescue you from the police car, now Ms. Moore has had the police issue an all-points bulletin for your arrest."

"Bitch. I don't take lightly to anyone interfering in my fun." Rebecca sneered as she got off her cell phone.

IN THE MORNING, DONNA Amberside woke, her heading throbbing. "Fuck what a weird dream that was. I dreamt my baby, Cindy, returned to me aglow, like an angelic blue fairy." She reached for her half glass of rum, smelled the contents and as she was about to take a drink, she felt her guts begin to heave.

Running over to the reeking toilet she puked long and hard. Staggering back to her bed she sat a moment.

I remember now. The bitch did something to me in the dream. She reached for the drugs and went to get a glass of water from the constantly dripping tap. "These will make me feel better." She put two into her hand and tried to put them into her mouth. Her hand began to shake as she fought to ingest the drugs. For long moments the body fought with itself until Donna gave up and tossed them down the sink and turned the tap on. "Fuck, I can't do this. She did something to me.

I hate her." She threw the glass against the wall as tears she hadn't felt in a long time fought their way to the surface.

She pulled up her phone and looked at the one number she swore she'd call one day and never did til now. "Hello, mental health services, I need to talk to someone. I need help. I think I'm going crazy." Donna Amberside sat down and began to sob uncontrollably.

CAROL STRODE INTO THE Q (as in Queen) at The Empress dining room where she knew she'd find Agnes at breakfast. As usual the room was tastefully done in white linen covered tables, royal blue and purple cushions decorated the sofas and the row of benches. Victorian wooden chairs and balustrades lent an air of class. Agnes had chosen to sit against one of the windows and there was no one near her to overhear their conversation,

Carol noted as she sat. "Good thing we're somewhat private here. I was just wondering, is it possible ghosts, maybe even Sir Francis Rattenbury, were involved in the murder of Senior Rizzuto?"

"Unlikely, but I can't seem to see much inside that room. Just feelings."

"Well, he came to me in a dream. He came out of the Shelbourne vortex they talked about on the tour. He whispered something to me just before vanishing as the vortex collapsed."

"And what did he say?" Agnes' eyes opened, suddenly more interested in Mr. Rattenbury than her breakfast kedgeree. Agnes, even in breakfast mode was done up in a pale-pink frock with turquoise trim, reminiscent of a bridesmaid's dress. All frills and flowing.

Man, she looks amazing, like a 1940's catalog. The broad must have a few bucks stashed away. Carol opened her eyes and stared saying nothing with that, *okay come on read my mind, lady,* on her face.

"Okay I'm not God, I don't read everything in there. What?" Agnes slowly nibbled again on her breakfast, losing interest in the conversation.

"Man, I like keeping you on tender-hooks. This is quite a change."
"So?"
"He said to me before he disappeared; 'the earth remembers'."
"I think I discussed that over tea with him once with Cider."

"She told you? You talk to long deceased spirits over bloody tea? I thought I had one on you, finally. This sucks."

"Sorry, bad habit of mine, comes with seeing and reading people's minds. And yes, the earth does remember, hence why the Mafia are stirring up the ghosts in this town. They don't forget curses, nor do they like others interfering in their territory. As you know they have already performed some perfunctory initiations at the castle, as we learned from Begbie, the native band from this area was cursed to languish underground. Which goes against their beliefs. These are arousing even more unrest. I won't say much more than to guard your back at all times." "Back at the crime scene you ran out of there pretty fast. Why?" Carol asked.

"I am still trying to sift through some of those murky details. I was very disturbed, like I said earlier, the whole room has been placed into a kind of morphic field to keep people like myself from finding anything out. Even Cider can't penetrate through."

"So, are you saying it is possible that a ghost is involved in this hanging after all?"

Agnes sipped at her morning coffee. "There is that distinct possibility;

like I said the earth remembers. Care to join me for some breakfast?"

Carol took in the dish of flaked fish, rice and hard-boiled eggs and thought the better of it. *Give me good old pancakes and maple syrup any* day. "Think I'll pass."

Carol sneezed again. The old gal smiled insidiously as she delicately forked her kedgeree to her mouth. Carol shook at the water still stuck in her ears.

"Still got salt water in your ears. Enjoy your late-night dip?"

"I was going to mention it but then thought why bother? I knew you'd already know. But did you know about the gun men? I definitely wouldn't have gone if you did."

"No, didn't know about them. All I knew was that you were on a boat and then you were in the water. I don't get everything all the time. Hope you don't catch cold."

"Now one thing I do want to know about. Why is Sir Francis Rattenbury trying to get in contact with me and from what you tell me you as well and don't give me that 'the earth remembers' crap?"

Agnes thought a moment before responding. "It's a bit more complicated than you realize."

"How complicated?"

Agnes slowly poured herself another tea and added sugar with the dainty spoon. "Now I've dug into some of the background stories that as a mystic are rather troubling. I can't say much more than that. There are things going on you need to discover for yourself."

"Agnes, how do you know this stuff?"

"Again, I can't tell you. I've said too much now, you need to do the digging and perhaps one day you'll find out. Just use caution."

"Man, you use one riddle after another. I get the feeling there's a lot you're keeping from me."

Agnes sipped slowly at her tea before simply saying, "You, my dear are most astute. I will say this much only. Visit the Pendray house, check the history of Deadman's Point first."

"Sure, will do. Now Agnes. Tell me really why you are here? And don't tell me for the Mafia or the ghosts tours or like I said earlier 'the earth remembers' BS. There's something going on here bigger than that. Isn't there? You may forget first and foremost I'm a police officer and know when someone is lying to me." Carol stared hard at her, telling herself to try and keep her mind blank.

"You, my dear can be hard to read sometimes. And you're right, I came here because I was hired by someone to find their missing child. The Gibsons. Have you heard of the case of missing Jordon Gibson?"

Carol blinked for a moment. "Yeah, vaguely, but isn't that a really old case. I don't know much of the details."

"In October of 1990 Samantha Gibson, was watching her husband play soccer when four year-old Jordon asked to play in the playground off

Quadra Street. Even though the playground was only a few meters away."

"At four, man, today she'd be charged and have social services take him away."

"Yes, today, but the world in the quiet suburbs of upper end Victoria was a little different back then. Safe, peaceful and very civil, or so she thought. They never found him when they went looking for him. It began one of the largest police searches ever undertaken, with a huge reward. The police got thousands of tips, including the sighting of a man and a tan van in the area, but the boy was never found."

"How horrible she must have felt. You wouldn't expect your child to vanish so close to you. So why are you re-investigating this? The reward?"

"I was offered the $100,000 for the reward. But I took the challenge not because of that, I don't want the money and don't need it. I took it because you asked me to."

"So why the challenge to solve the case, surely he must be dead by now? Hang on, me? How? I haven't asked you to help me."

"Yet. Apparently. That is why I was contacted. Samantha began to get visions in her sleep, and now she's claiming he's trying to contact her, from a tunnel somewhere under the city. The tunnel where he was held and made part of the Satanic ritual."

"Oh, I've heard of the claims that Victoria is full of devil worshippers. And tunnels. Tunnels that many have said exist under the older parts of town. Some claim under the purple lights set in the sidewalks."

"Only no one has ever found the entrance to these, until now. Samantha claims he's trying to lead her there in a dream. She saw me on a TV show and tracked me down via my web page."

"You've got a web page?" Carol didn't even think the old woman knew how to turn on a computer.

"Yeah, just because I'm old doesn't mean I don't know how to keep up with the times. I pay a lovely young man to update my page and keep me on the first page of Google."

"Really? That works? I thought it was just hype by salespeople."

"No, something to do with music, rhyming logs or something like that."

Carol smiled, "Algorithms. It's the way we can use the information in the internet to compile information. The police use it a lot in searching for data regarding a crime or suspect. If we know the suspect is a white male, drives a red Honda and lives in this area, we can log it in and find all the known people."

"Stop. If this more complex than programming my blender I'm hearing blah, blah, blah."

Carol thought about the two new stories that just hit the papers in the last couple of days. "Is this somehow hooked to the two new abductions, one of which is my nephew?"

"Yes, it is related to those I believe, including your nephew."

"Now, being an unclosed case is there any way you have access to the files? Might help me wrap my head around this case and maybe lead us to the other two."

"I'd need to get clearance from my boss, Big Dan. You think they're related after all of this time?" she already knew the answer before Agnes spoke it.

"Yes. I've also heard someone mention the book about a girl who was abducted in Victoria, she also reported tunnel systems under Victoria and Satanic rituals. I just found a copy of the novel in the local bookstore downtown. Michelle Remembers. I'll get you to read it and see if there's any truth to the book."

"And in return for helping you?"
"We might be lead to the two boys and a third about to happen."
"Another?"

"Yes. Ratty is saying there's reports of usually three to five needed for these rituals."

"Crap. I'll notify the chief and get what I can for information. And this is related to the mob being here." *Ratty? She must talk to Rattenbury a lot if she's got a pet name for him. Who else would talk to a dead guy?*

"I'm afraid so." Agnes rearranged today's hat, which was a turquoise that precisely matched the dress's trim, in an indication that she was done and about to get up.

"I have some free time today which I'm going to spend with Barb. I haven't been able to give her anywhere near the attention I'd have liked. Then later I'll get permission to show you my nephew's file and take a look at that book of yours, see what I can dig up on that, then the Pendray House thing. Man, so much to do."

WINGS FLUTTERED BEHIND the fairy being as she walked around the rank confines of the sewer room, talking to herself.

I was young, maybe six. My last memories are of picking berries on a cool fall morning. I heard the snarl of a cougar. The crunch of teeth, my cries as I was dragged from the bushes. My mother screaming as she launched herself at the feline. It ran off not willing to fight another human bigger than it. Her stroking my hair as my blood drained onto her lap. Her singing my name as I died. My name I remember it, in English it means, floats with butterflies. I've never seen a butterfly, would like to.

The blue elfish being sat against the wall of the sewer, talking to itself. *Close your eyes, I remember a place. I will take you somewhere.*

They both closed their eyes and Cindy took them through the earth via its spiritual pathways to a cool mountain slope. The field was littered with spring flowers. *Our school took us here on a field trip. My mom would never do anything like this with me. I remember walking into the field and having all of these things flutter all around me.*

They pulled to the surface of the same field and dozens of butterflies lifted free. All colors and shapes, some small others large danced around, little wings gliding on subtle winds. Several, finding her either none threatening, or of similar likeness, landed all over them.

My eyes hurt, but this is so beautiful. The sun, the warmth. I have never known this wonder before. What are these delicate beings that surf the breezes?

These are your name sakes.

The Lekwungen said nothing for a long time. Cindy, as she remembered herself, knew it was crying and let it have its moment until the pain began again.

We must go now.
Pain seared through its being.
I know.
They both closed their eyes in agony.

Chapter Twelve

Alone in the solitude of her office; a quiet fifteen minutes with a few hours later, after her too-short visit with Barb, Carol lunched ham-and-Swiss suited her just fine for a change. She'd read the headlines earlier. Two more boys had disappeared or been abducted.

Crap and still no leads on Nathan.

A knock at her door signaled the end of her quiet time. Not sure what to expect she opened the door only to come face-to-face with two vases of red roses; two dozen it looked like. Their fragrance filled the small office as he placed them on the table and passed her the card, which read simply, *To my wild Canadian Bellissimo.*

Christ, I could really get to like this guy. Why does he have to be the enemy? The card read,

'this gentleman would be honored if you could show him the wilds of Victoria and Vancouver Island. Leave me a message on my door.'

She knew Jake wanted to take her out tonight and responded with a message on the back of her business card. 'I have a business meeting I can't cancel tonight, will see about tomorrow or the next day. I can get Wednesday off and take you on a trip up Vancouver Island.' Unfortunately keeping tabs on the Italians was more important at the moment that being there just to hold Barb's hand. Would be a different matter if there was anything that could actually be done, and she knew Barb understood.

He responded with another card before lunch, 'That would be great. I shall make my day free.'

CAROL STROLLED OVER to the Royal Columbian Museum, which was across the street from the Empress. She sat in the back area surrounded by the totems set up. "Man, I'm not anywhere near Charlie and wish he knew how to text. Who am I kidding, he doesn't even have a cell phone."

She lit her cigarette, wishing he'd do one of his magical appearing acts.

Man, could use someone to talk to right about now. Carol closed her eyes as she exhaled.

A blue light travelled up one of the totems.
She calls us.
It stared through the blue eyes of the totem.
We haven't much time here.
She is like us. A joining of two inside.
Yes, the familiarity speaks to me as well.

This concrete is unsettlingly. And so close to our former village. We cannot stay long.

It breathed deeply.
She is a justifier. She can set matters straight.
Agreed.
We shall seek her out, another time. Not here the pain is great.
Agreed.
The being retreated as pain wracked its body.

Carol turned and stared at the totem behind her with its large ovoid eyes as several blue tinged butterflies lifted free and flew away.

How bizarre is that and why do I get the feeling I'm being watched?

⚓   ⚓

"I HAVE NEVER BEEN AMONGST such wild splendor. It is amazing to think most of this coastline is nearly untouched and the trees; *massiccio*. Massive," Tony said in complete amazement as they got out of the SUV that Carol had rented.

The road was mostly paved, but the few gravel sections had made her glad she'd rented a more suitable vehicle. They'd spent nearly two hours driving out along Vancouver's West Coast to Port Renfrew in order to reach Avatar Grove, only stopping at what she called some local chew 'n' choke diner for lunch, where Carol insisted on ordering Poutine for the two of them to share. Tony loved it and there was something very romantic in looking into his dark eyes as she fed him fries dripping in gravy and he did the same to her. It was even funnier to watch this chic, high bred Mafia man, so haute couture and PC correct, eating with gravy dripping off his fingers. She was pretty sure he'd never done before. While there were other large trees in the area, including the world's largest Red Douglas Fir and Sitka Spruce, Carol simply wanted to show him this new trail, as she'd not seen it either. Although being in the ancient forest brought back some haunting memories due to her recent dealings with Charlie Stillwaters and the pesky forest spirit, Gyhldeptis.

"This is Avatar Grove, a newly built boardwalk trail allows us safe access to some of the largest uncut trees on the island."

Carol put on her small backpack and waited while he slipped off his expensive leather shoes and put on the runners she had brought for him. She asked for his shoe size yesterday when she confirmed where she wanted to take him. Lunch had been the most fun she had on a date in years. Carol watched the flex of his legs and rear as he bent over to put the runners on.

Stop it, you can't fall for this guy, he's the suspect. The man I may have to throw in jail.

"It has been a long time since I've worn runners. I think the last time I trained with Athletico Madrid."

Carol was taken aback. "Yes, you said you were a professional soccer player?"

"Ah, you North Americans and your soccer. It is football, not like you play football over here. Although your game is very macho, we actually play the ball with our feet. But yes, I did play on the team for two years as a fullback before an injury ended my career."

Well, that explained the size of those massive thighs of his, as Agnes so aptly pointed out. "I haven't been on this one yet, up the island there are more with massive trees as well. But this is fairly close, so I thought we'd enjoy it fresh together."

"Ah, like *vergine*; virgins. I like it."

Carol smiled, his innocent humor was infectious, and he'd also been trying to teach her words in Italian. Yet, being part of the mob, as sweet as he seemed, she knew he'd been involved in many underhanded dealings and most likely a few murders as well. *Was there such a thing as a sincere, gorgeous killer?* "Okay two *vergines* exploring the woods on our own."

She breathed in the clean fresh West Coast air, chilled with mists and salt water. Tony had already thumped his feet down on the wooden boardwalk. A trail of wet slime from large six-inch slugs littered the surface. Dew dripped off the trees, several draped in moss hanging from boughs and branches like an old man's beard.

"Well, am I going alone?" He held out his hand and Carol folded hers into the strong warmth of his. They trundled off along the newly formed upper section of the board trail. Minutes later they both stood below the twisted boles of the tree labeled Canada's Gnarliest Tree, and that it was. For about twenty or so feet up the limbs twisted about each other, like tied pretzels and at the top were several large boles that reminded Carol of the trapped witch in Stanley Park. The one that Charlie helped trap, that nearly killed her.

"It is amazing. I see faces twisted into the wood." He tilted his head one way and then the other. "You have given me something I never imagined I'd ever see. It is *magnifico*. How old is this tree?"

"It is estimated to be several hundred, maybe a thousand years old. The lower limbs have formed as the tree tries to survive and find sustenance due to the fungal bole that is living off its bark." She pointed to the large knobby protuberance sticking out of the tree and reached forward to touch the ancient living being. As she did voices rang out from the forest. Carol closed her eyes. Visions of ghostly natives flooded her mind and animals, all long dead and gone. *Crap.* She opened her eyes. *Agnes was right I can see ghosts on occasion, only how do I stop this?*

"You okay? You look a bit how I say *pallido*. Pale."

"Yeah, just beat from the drive, and hungry. I may have picked up a chill or cold in this clammy climate over the last couple of days." She lied as she sniffled lightly. *Actually, it was from the long drawn out night floundering in the cold ocean with one rude FBI man*, Carol really wanted to say, *and discovering something about myself I didn't ever want to know.*

"Ah, then don't worry, I let you take me here to this splendor, that reminds me of my old grandmother, she looked nearly as twisted and gnarled as this tree."

Carol stopped as she walked along with Tony trying to measure the incredible girth of this tree. A little shadowy creature with elfish features and blue flaming hair popped its head up from a rock and stuck its tongue rudely out at her.

"Did you see that?" She tapped Tony on the shoulder and pointed back to the rock.

Tony stared at the rock she was pointing at. "I see beauty and a rock. But the beauty is beside me as well." He hugged her to him. *Man, I could get really used to this guy.*

"Man, you are something. There was this small foresty fern covered critter. Just there."

He squinted. "No, nothing, you no smoke some of that green stuff or nibble on the famous *fongo*, mushrooms out here." He squeezed her hand as the creature gave her a look of distain, stuck its tongue out and vanished.

"No, I stick to cigarettes and alcohol as my poisons. Yeah, must be my mind playing tricks on me." His hand was warm in hers, tugging at her senses. *I gotta ask Agnes about this, seeing ghosts or sensing them is one thing, but mythical forest creatures is another.*

"Too much late nights and coffee," he whispered into her ear.

Or not enough late nights," she whispered back. *Don't do this Carol, you can't fall in love with this guy.* Somewhere inside her head a little creature like the one she just saw waved its hand and set a little clock before itself and pressed a button to make it count down. *Yeah, I know a matter of time. What is it all those romance books say, 'you just know when the right one comes along.' Fuck!*

"Now, you need to do this, it's a tradition out here that you hug a tree. Especially great trees like this one." Carol walked up to the tree and opened her arms wide. She put her palms to the gnarled surface. He looked at her like she was insane.

"This is *pazzo*, how you say crazy. But I follow your lead." He too put his hands around a small portion of the base next to her. It would take at least ten more people to complete the perimeter in people hugging it.

"Now, shush, no words. You just hug this ancient living being and give it thanks." Carol closed her eyes, the coolness of the bark pulled at her palms.

We are called, we come. Rang out from the interior of the tree.
Carol opened her eyes wide. *What the...*

Tony's hand grazing hers pulled her away with his warmth. He smiled at her, "I thanked this world and this forest for sending me this Canadian Bella Donna."

"You are the most romantic man that I have ever met."

"I am not always like this. It is being with you, that brings these feelings out of me." He grabbed her and at the base of the tree, kissed her deeply. *Shit, that creature's clock just clicked several tocks closer to the hour hand.* Carol didn't resist, letting his lips crush against hers. His tongue penetrated her mouth. She fought hard to restrain herself but couldn't.

When they broke apart his smile, his sheer loving presence was intoxicating. She wanted to have him kiss her again and again. *God, someone just pushed me from the cliff of reason and understanding. This isn't good.*

He pulled back. "You say nothing, but the look in your eyes gives you away."

"Thanks, I guess I just didn't want to say anything that might spoil this moment." Her heart thumped wildly and her legs shook as she pulled away and began to walk down the boarded trail.

He wrapped his arm around her as they walked. The sheer touch of his body, exhilarating. "I think the blood has left your extremities. I shall hold you up. Ah, my *Bella Donna*, nothing can spoil these moments." *Yes, I am in major trouble.*

She has called the others.
We must go.
They can't find us either.
And the pain begins. It screamed in agony.
The others are coming, we must go. They can not detect us.
We must find the release from this curse. As the others want to, as well.
They know.
She is the one to release us.
We know.
The blue fairy pulled itself into the bowels of the earth.

They walked both sections of the trail, for the most part quiet as he took in the wonder of a West Coast rain forest. The lichens hanging like a woman's hair, different colored fungus' that grew out of living and dead trees. Ferns that sprouted everywhere as if planted by a drunken mad gardener.

When they got back to the trail head, Tony excused himself to go to the outdoor washroom. Carol walked several feet away. Something in the darkness of the brush next to her. A glimmer of yellow, burning a second then gone. Flutters of winds on trees and shapes crawling in the dark, flooded into her head. She moved closer, chillness swung over her and a native being decked in ferns and animal skins edged from the mists. *You called earlier.*

Carol had forgotten. *I called who? What?*

I am a shaman of the Songhees. We come, because of him and who he brings and what he has done. Disturbs the past. He spoke directly into her mind as he began to waver as if unable to focus on keeping himself present.

Carol closed her eyes a moment, *the Songhees shaman that Begbie defended.* "You are not so strong here. Why? Is it from his kind?"

Run to the wall and wonder. Seek why it is so? There I can talk with power.

Carol heard the outdoor toilet door open and the being vanished. *Well that made less than sense.*

With that the coolness evaporated as Tony came out of the wooden outdoor toilet.

"I guess it is time to head back to the hotel." He glanced at his watch.

"Agreed, I have to be back on duty in three hours, shame" she replied.

"I could ask you out for dinner and perhaps up to my room tomorrow." She knew what the trip to his room meant. *Trouble, big fricking trouble.*

"I'll check my schedule and if I'm booked, see if I could get free."

He smiled back at her. "Yes, *perfecto.*"

That was the problem, she would love it. I need to talk to the only girl friend I got here,

Agnes. The minute hand clicked one closer. *I know I can't resist him, he is too much.*

❧   ❧

THE NEXT DAY BACK AT work she had to dodge around the dozens of roses that littered her office and a card that simply said, '**To my Canadian love, thanks for the wonderful day.**' She stared at the word, love. *Shit, this has gone too deep. I can't let this continue. Damn, why him? Somehow, I've got to tell him.* Carol fought back the tears. *Shit, because I know it's too late for me.* She checked her watch, the High Tea was to begin within the hour, Agnes said she'd talk to her.

❧   ❧

CAROL STROLLED UP TO Agnes in the tearoom. Oddly enough, she caught Jake sitting beside her. Jake was dressed in casual suit and tie, very distinguished looking. Agnes in a long flowing dress done in frills and lace.

Bastard, with that smug face, I'd love to put a bullet through it. "Ah glad you could join." Agnes smiled, "I had just sat down and was admiring the beauty of this room and its tasteful appointments when this handsome man walked by and, quite out of my nature, I asked him if he was Ms. Moore's bathrobe man?'" She giggled. "And I told her, you must be Ms. Teak. I was told you were staying here. I caught your show in Vegas quite a few years ago," Jake supplied his reply.

"So, I invited him to join me for tea. Gets a bit lonely sometimes not having any adoring fans to chat with."

Jake turned back to Agnes. "Of course, there are ways and means of making these things appears real. I thought it might be props and people planted in the crowd. I dare you, read my mind and I'll buy this tea. Go ahead, prove me wrong," he growled, with that male confident stare Carol remembered from their first meeting.

Agnes' eyes flashed. Carol had seen her get upset before, but to be called a charlatan definitely stirred the old girl's dander.

Agnes clanked her cup down hard. "Close your eyes and just try to blank your mind."

Jake did, putting his hands on his lap. Carol was surprised that Agnes didn't want to hold one of his in order to read him better.

"You are very good at clearing your mind." She frowned as if pretending to have a hard time. Then she opened one eye and winked at Carol.

"I'm well trained in doing that, makes for greater focus in my job."

"Ah, important, for an agent."

His eyes shot open. "You tell her anything?"

"Don't need to, she reads mine like an open book."

"And this." Agnes made the sound of a sharp crack noise of a whip flicking as she imitated someone wielding one with her hand. Jake turned beet red. "An admirer and practitioner of the fifty shades book series then."

Jake rose and waved the waitress over growling, "Put this on my room tab. I'm outta here before they get my bank account numbers and drain them."

He left the room as the two ladies giggled. "Remind me never to tee you off." Carol smirked.

"He looks rather good with his tail between his legs. I do so hate been called a charlatan. Rather raises my blood pressure that does. Now back to a relaxing tea, scone and those terrific lemon cheesecakes which are to die for. Although," she watched the hard confines of his rear as he walked away, "He is very delicious, shame his inside doesn't match his outside. Anyway, let's forget about him. I get you have a much bigger problem with an even more handsome fellow."

Carol closed her eyes, tears welled up and she unloaded everything that happened with her and Tony.

"Oh dear, how distressing for you. I warned you to stay away from though him, didn't I? I saw this coming. You've fallen in love with the enemy and I think he has as well. You've bewitched him, Canadian Bella Donna."

Carol screwed up her face. "Man, I hate that you can read me like a book."

"Then in order to avoid possible bloodshed and respect both your integrities you must tell him and break it off. As soon as possible! As you know they have this code of honor." Agnes raised her voice at the end.

"*Omerta*, yes I know about it."

"Then as you know with the Cosa Nostra; they are sworn to have no involvement with any police or justice system what so ever, no confiding or cooperation. He will be very upset, but potentially in danger if they find out. If others find out about you, there may be a hit put out on you and him possibly as well."

"That's kinda what I thought. Damn, I easily could have married that man. He is incredible." "So, I've heard."

"Don't you mean read?" They both laughed as Carol told her about her hike which she knew Agnes had already picked out of her head, but it lightened the mood and somehow it was good to share details with another woman. After all her mom had passed away a few years ago and other than her sister, didn't really keep any close female friends.

Agnes rearranged her hat, the signal she was done, she reached over and touched Carol's hand, "Thanks for sharing. But you must tell him quickly or I sense there could be big trouble. Oh, and come see me for a séance tonight. I may be able to help you find Nathan."

"A séance? Really? You know something about my nephew?"

"Have I steered you wrong before? I need to get inside your head to find out something I'm missing and again can't say much more than that, here." Agnes strode slowly from the room with the grace of the Queen. She nodded with a tip of her hat to the shimmering image Carol got of poor Margaret, waiting at her table. Waiting for her man.

Now the hard part. But first I need to talk to Big Dan and let him know what's going on.

CAROL SAT TONY DOWN in her office. "Tony, I have to tell you something before I continue this," she touched her chest and pointed to his, "with us."

He quietly settled into his chair, not the confident full-of-Italian-bravado man she fell in love with. "My *bella donna*, you are going to tell me you have another? Or that you will lie to me and tell me you are not, *innamorato*, in love with me, because I see it in your eyes, as I am. If you need time I understand, this is a place to be scared of, we are from different lands and cultures."

Carol held her hand up. "Stop, you are making this hard. First, I have to say that I have never met a man like you. I never believed I could fall this deep, this fast." He began to rise, and she waved him down. "No, sit I have to finish this. More than anything I want to continue, but I can't." She fought back the tears and emotion welling inside. Her hands shook. *Christ this is the hardest thing I've ever had to do. Mom, grant me the strength to continue.*

Carol shook and took a deep breath. She was also prepared if this went bad and he reacted negatively. Yet somehow Carol knew he wouldn't. "I did not intend this to become what it is, and for that I am sorry."

It was awful to watch such a vibrant grown macho man crumble "I-I my love, am crushed."

"This is the hardest thing I have ever had to do, but I have to honor myself and you."

He stared. "I don't understand."

"There are times when two worlds must not, and cannot, nor will ever be allowed to cross. I have read and understand the Cosa Nostra code of ethics. So, I cannot betray the man I am falling in love with. Because..." she choked back her emotions. "I'm involved with the Canadian police. I'm here to watch over the wedding." The explanation was all she was allowed to say, direct orders from Big Dan.

His mouth fell. He stared, anger flashed across his eyes as she knew it might. Then he dropped his head. "As you know, my code of honour as Cosa Nostra forbade this, forbade you." He crossed his hands in front of him in the sign of the cross and slammed his fist into the wood arm of the chair. He closed his eyes, for a moment the man she knew was gone and only a boy remained. A small, frightened lad.

"Yes, I know. Mine as well. I will not go to the wedding with you. Nor can I allow this to proceed. I know your code and I cannot deceive you any longer. I trust that you will tell no one of my background. I need to end this now, while my own heart remains."

"You have broken my heart and that has never been done before." He took a deep breath.

"As have you."

She half expected him to go into some kind of rage, was ready to defend herself if need-be. To her surprise he remained calm. "My lips will be sealed about anything to do with you, with us. On that you have my word."

He took another deep breath. "As are mine with you." He stepped forward. "One final kiss." Tony Belletti waved her arms away and pulled Carol to him. They kissed for several long moments.

The hunger inside threatened to possess them Carol felt her will washing away, in that moment she knew that what she thought she felt was real.

He pulled away, his eyes had gone a deep dark black. "Goodbye my Canadian *Bella Donna*. I shall always remember you." Tony Belletti walked from her life and the room, closing the door behind him without looking back.

Carol crumpled to her desk and held back the sobs.
As shall I my Italian passionate man.
My Uomo Apassionato. As shall I.
Then a flood of uncontrollable tears exploded from within.

⚜ ⚜

AGNES WALKED JUST AHEAD of Carol in the fairly narrow passageway, she'd asked Carol along to recheck something in Fan Tan Alley. "My senses tell me a clue to our cases dwells here."

As she said that a hand from the shadows just past the corner of a building, holding a large pipe, slammed the back of her head as the elder walked past. Agnes fell in a heap. A knife snicked from its sheath, shiny silver glinted in the moonlight. Carol ran forward and kicked the knife free but the assailant slammed the pipe into the back of her leg and she too crumpled in a daze. Agnes moaned as what looked like an older woman raised her hand to administer a crushing blow to her head. Around her neck dangled a five-sided pendant.

Carol pulled her gun free from its hidden ankle holster. Agnes saw her in a haze and threw her arm up, knocking Carol's arm. The explosion deafened them as a bullet ricocheted down the alley, missing her target. Carol fired again. Sparks and blood flew as the hand holding the pipe swung towards her instead of Agnes' head. It hit Carol's hand in a bloody smear. Her gun spun away, and the pipe clanked to the ground bouncing into Carol's foot. Both Carol and the assailant cried out in agony.

The figure began to pull back into the darkness. Carol dove for her and only got one foot as she receded into the dark. The woman shoved hard against the detective with a surprizing amount of strength, her foot catching Carol just under the throat as she vanished into the darkness.

Coughing, Carol rolled, miraculously finding her gun. She stared at the dark area. Nothing moved. Keeping her eyesight trained, she grabbed the small flashlight she always kept on herself. Expecting a corridor or an alcove only brick wall stared back. "What?"

There was no possible place to hide a mouse let along a human. She shined the light upwards, half expecting the person to pull some kind of Spiderman stunt. Only more brick work shone back.

Agnes rose to her feet and grabbed her hat, stumbling slightly.

"What the hell just happened?" Carol shone the light all around them, with her gun following.

"Didn't expect that. Mugger, I guess," the old gal said as she hauled herself up and began to walk slowly away from the scene.

"Mugger? Wait a frigging minute. There's not only no one here besides us. She's vanished into the brick work. You can't hide in two inches thick of shadow."

Agnes kept walking until she got into the streetlights gleam. Carol rushed up behind her.

"Stop. Mrs. Van Lunt what are you not telling me?"

Agnes breathed a deep breath. "Didn't expect that. Let's just say I've got enemies." She shook her head and took a long drink from her flask. "Enemies that are not only after me, which alone is cause for alarm, but can pull off shit without my sensing she was there and deceived me into coming here."

A psychic that couldn't read her attackers mind nor sense her presence. This makes even less sense. "You ain't moving until you tell me what the hell just happened."

"I can't tell you."
"I need to know more than that."

"I can't. If I tell you several people including yourself and Nathan will die. That is all." Agnes moved to go around her.

Carol blocked her way. "Nathan? Damn it, woman. Why aren't you telling me what in fuck just happened? Because I know what I just saw, a woman armed with a pipe and knife emerged from shadows only a couple of inches thick and whacked you upside the head. Then you stopped me from putting a bullet through her."

"I can't. Didn't know she could do that. She fooled me into coming here. If not for you, I'd be dead. People will die, myself included."

"Bull crap. You read minds, a psychic. You probably already knew this was going to happen. You can't get BS past this detective."

"I know." Agnes thought a moment, glancing at her watch and closed her eyes. "The vortex has just collapsed, she's gone and can't return for now. We have maybe a minute in what I call the null zone before another can start. All I can tell you is that she's taken your nephew as insurance against me and you.

If you would have killed her just then, we'd never find him." "He's missing because of you? How..." Carol was stunned.

"I think so. She can't take me out, I thought, but apparently not so. She's marked me and I'm not safe, only I can't take her out. Neither can you now, she has Nathan."

"You're not telling me who she is?"

"I can't."

"His abduction was days ago. He was abducted before I met you."

"Yup, vortex manipulation. You saved my life. She insures you don't go after her. So, I can't tell you and that's it."

"Her pendant. The story you told me about the devil worshippers and the band."

"Just that. I was afraid something like this could happen. She is probably watching us, much in the same way as I do through Cider. Maybe she can read your thoughts as well, not sure."

Carol's head was spinning, trying to put everything together in some coherent order. Mere seconds remained. "You can't tell me anything? I caught the pendant around her neck. She has someone on her side you can't beat."

"Yes, she has access to the vortex in this area, can shift through time and uses it at will."

"That's completely fucked up. So what do we do about it?"

"See me tomorrow for the séance." Agnes glanced at her watch. "Time's up." She began to walk up the street.

Carol stared at her retreating figure as Agnes took a good long pull at her flask and continued walking. Glancing back and forth at each shadow she crossed.

Agnes had managed to get herself in some kind of deep dark trouble.

PURE BEESWAX CANDLES shed a dim light as three incense sticks filled the air of Agnes' room with a serene grounding aroma. The lights in the room were turned off as Carol walked in. "If you're wondering, the electrics interfere with the process."

Carol inhaled deeply, the incense having the desired effect, she sipped at the tea made from lemongrass that Agnes already had waiting for her. Helps clear the mind, Agnes had said. She felt everything with Tony slip away. "I told him, he took it better than I thought. It was harder for me, I think. I knew he was the enemy, but there was something about him that tore at my heart."

"Maybe because he was the enemy and you knew you couldn't have him. I just saw him down in the lobby, on the phone. Sounded like he was booking a flight home. Put me in mind of a love-struck puppy." Agnes said as she watched Carol's shoulders sink. "Once the grief has left you, you'll feel better and so will he." Her flowing cotton gown was woven with glistening colors of green, blue and bright yellows. Tassels adorned the sleeves and hem. A purple silk belt was wrapped around her waist in offset the pale pink and green mottled tie-dyed figures running through the gown, like an old Dagoli print. "I don't get to do this much anymore. Although there are still a few very rich people that I see as clients, they pay extremely well for what you get today for free, so no judgement and let's get on with the show. Besides old habits die hard and," she covered over where the ears should have been on the skull, "Cider here is after all a crystalized rock. A rock yes, but much more. The properties of the crystal conduct vibrational energies, as they are not only connected to the earth, but they are of the earth. Now before we begin, there's something you need to say to Cider first." She removed her hands and gave Carol that condescending parental look.

"Say what?" Carol stared at the hollow crystal sunken eyes and at Agnes. "You are kidding me?"

"From a place of honesty as well. You know I can smell BS a mile away. Or she won't help you, bad time of the month and all. A bit sensitive the old gal, so not my call."

Carol gritted her teeth, fighting off the desire to scream out several profanities. Finding out if Nathan was still alive and saving him was what really mattered. *God, she tries my patience.* "Okay. I'm sorry about that crack earlier. I think it was some of my broken heart lashing out. Sorry. I didn't really mean it and you probably know that, I've already done some wild bizarre things in my time, including travelling through the earth on some odd vibrational plane with a freaky little forest nymph and I know you're more connected to stuff of the psychic world than I am. I trust Agnes and she believes in you. That is enough for me. Again, I am truly sorry."

A low sigh filled the air. Carol's eyes opened, "Did she...?"

"Yeah, just me." She laughed. "I learned ventriloquism a long time ago."

"You are such a bag."
"Had you fooled, didn't I?"
"Yup, and isn't easy to fool a cop."
"Been doing this for a few decades. But man, you have seen your face!

Priceless. Okay give me your hands and close your eyes."
"Can I ask about what happened last night in the alley? You got enemies?"
"I can't say much, she might be watching or listening. It has something to do with Nathan, not sure what. But we need to continue and quickly." Agnes held her hands a moment, whispered some words, breathed over Carol's hands and rubbed hers slowly over them. Shivers ran down her arms. She placed Carol's hands over top of the skull and her hands over Carol's. "Now breathe deeply and relax, let your mind clear. If at any time it becomes too much, and you can't take it, pull away. This is going to be quite a journey."

"What do you mean quite a journey? This is crazy."
"You want to find the kid or not?" Carol nodded.

Agnes grabbed a wooden match and lit it. She started burning something in a bowl. Soon smoldering scents filled the air. She placed this before Carol and told her to inhale deeply.

"Then shut up and don't ask. Let go of all your disbeliefs, inhale deeply, this will relax your mind and allow you to open your subconscious where

Cider can connect with you. Oh, and as another young girl once said, we're off to see the wizard, the wonderful wizard in the Woo-woo lands that live beyond this realm. Now this will probably take awhile. So, enjoy the ride."

Carol felt herself quickly enter an altered state of consciousness as something washed over her. *What is happening, is she drugging me, was there something in that tea?* The smell of incense and peyote faded to be replaced with the slow measured tick of a large wall clock. Ticks that began to speed up until the hands just blurred and Carol fell deeper in the trance.

It really isn't acceptable to go drugging a friend is it? Agnes walked over to the bathroom sink, flushed the tea down the drain and washed her hands. *But in this case, I need answers before that Satan possessed woman finds me. Answers I ain't got and can't get, no matter how many times I try. If Carol has to pay for it, so be it.*

Chapter Thirteen

"This is Inspector Davis of the Victoria RCMP. I've been in-formed that I was to call you, Chief Inspector Carol Ainsworth, if there was anything found in the Nathan Evans disappearance case from 2017."

"What?" Chief Senior Police Inspector Carol Ainsworth gasped. She was about to meet with the Vancouver Council on recommendations on what to do about the homeless camp set up in front of city hall. *Nathan's disappearance*, she stared at the floating three-dimensional picture nearly twenty-six years old.

"The facial reconstruction program and DNA scans seem to indicate one of the five bodies, all of young preadolescent males, found at a demolition site, is Nathan Evans."

Carol hung her head low; the one case that had eluded her after all these years, her own nephew. *I still remember it. He vanished so close to his mother, just like the earlier one involving Jordon Gibson and the two others earlier, all about 26 years apart. That crazy, wonderful psychic, Agnes, warned me before she disappeared.* Her mind raced as visions of those days long past surged through her. *And oddly, that was about twenty-six years ago* "Sorry, Details, give me the details and spare the sentimental crap."

She heard the man swallow. "The Windsor Hotel was being torn down and the workers found something quite grisly in a walled off room in the basement. Five bodies of young boys, all badly shriveled and preserved like they'd been embalmed. They appeared to be positioned to be playing around a couple of balls, like they were throwing it to each other."

"Okay order a 'cease and desist' and I'm on the way over." Carol looked at her wrinkled hands as she got off the phone. More wrinkles adorned her face as she caught the reflection in the mirror. Her white hair — arctic blonde, she described it — was short with a layered cut. Everything about her spoke of being neat, precise and exact.

She stared at the picture of her old boss, big Dan McKinney behind her, or Big Dan as he was often called, although never to his face, due to the fact he liked to snack on the double arches burgers. For many years before she moved to Victoria and went undercover, he was her guiding influence. How many times did he drag her into his office and tear strips off her? Or thank her for a job well done. Or in rare cases poured his heart and soul out to her, often leaving them both in tears.

It was his recommendations that got her current rank, just before he passed away eight years ago. *Speaking of old friends, I wonder whatever happened to that crazy old Shaman. Should give him a call. Oh yeah, last time I checked he still hadn't listed in the Yellow E Pages of digital calling. Besides if I know him, he's probably sitting in the forest on a large old growth stump with a Sasquatch and a Yeti debating if roller skating with Buddhists is more sacred than listening to Roy Orbison while drinking green mint tea and snacking on sage crusted crackers or some such nonsense.*

She could accept the loss of many things and people in her life. Everything except the loss of the one thing she could never get back, her nephew Nathan. Carol stared at the image of Nathan on her desk, supported by the Imaging feature, it updated every year to show what Nathan would look like now if he was still alive. *Nearly thirty years ago, how handsome he'd look today.*

She was sure her sister still secretly hated her for it. *I shouldn't have listened to that old broad Agnes and instead quit the Empress gig in order to throw myself into his abduction. I'd have found him, I know I would have and at least I'd have my sister back in my life.* She visualized the ball games and the school concerts she would have sat through for agonizing hours in support of him and Barb. *In hindsight, I could do it, at the time, if I brought one of Agnes dainty flasks, full of whisky. Now, all I've got are memories and thoughts of what might have been.*

"I'll be right there, put up a police line around this. No one, not even the forensic team, touches anything until I get there. Inspector Davis, get a DNA sample of the four right away and the CDI#12, carbon dating infrared tool to determine the aging dates since death. I want to know who these boys are before I get there and contact Victoria's Chief Constable to let her know I'm on the way down." Carol contacted her husband, "Hate to say this Brad, but I won't be home for dinner, something very urgent just came up. Will let you know when I'm done, I'll send a Vid call later to tuck the kids in." He was such an understanding man, but being married to a police inspector, he had to be. Especially when your wife is the top man.

***

CAROL HOPPED ON THE nearest jet-copter and jetted over. Within an hour she was standing in front of the semi collapsed bricked-in area. Carol stooped low to get into the partly opened room, bricks and mortar had fallen into the area where a wrecking ball had opened it up.

Some of the rubble had disturbed the idyllic scene, dust rained over much of it and a few bricks had crashed into the frozen tableau, but it was as the Victoria inspector had stated. Five boys arranged in playful poses, all focused on a ball set in the floor before them. Some more desiccated than others. Someone had taken the time to not only bring them here, drug them and set them up.

"The environment of this small, enclosed room, like a mausoleum, has kept them very well preserved." She held a cloth to her nose, the stench of decay wasn't strong, but locked up in this room for all of those years, a subtle musty rankness pervaded.

"Did you get the DNA and carbon dating results?"

"Yes." He scratched his head. "The results are rather disturbing and unusual. In that this one is indeed Nathan Evans. We have the names of the others too as DNA samples were collected for each one and kept on computer."

God, how do I tell my sister after all these years that he was right under our noses the whole time? "The others are all from unsolved cases, each around the twenty-six-year range."

"So, who can abduct four boys over a space of a hundred and thirty years? It just wasn't possible even with today's standards of longevity. Unless more than one person was involved."

"Is there any other DNA on the clothing?"

"Yes, all of them, from a Gladys Townsend."

The name was familiar. "The old spinster who owned the hotel up until about four years ago."

"And that's why the hotel was finally being torn down. She refused to sell, was very well off and didn't need the money. She kept it going, even though it lost money most years and became a rundown establishment that Victoria council wanted torn down. She died well into her hundreds and even had it written into her will that the hotel must be left intact. Although it is reported that once every year, even while she was in the nursing home, or at least while she could walk, she'd come to the hotel. To spend a couple of hours there. No one was allowed to follow her."

Carol glanced around the room, it had been set up with old posters to look like a boys' room.

"Let me guess; she had no kids of her own?"

"None."

It has been a long time, but she had been here trying to help Victoria RCMP work on this case when she was here doing the undercover Mafia case from the then Fairmont Empress.

"The other boys?"

"The DNA results indicate that this is the Gibson boy, taken from the Quadra playground in 1990. The only one not in the same time gaps is the last one missing in 2017."

"What? Not possible, Okay, get the scene-of-crime team in here quick. I want all of this taken to Vancouver where I can have it studied." Carol walked out into the alley and stared around. *I stood in this alley all those years ago. I stared at this building, at that door.* Carol walked up to the rusting metal door as it stood there quietly like it had done for over a hundred years and ran her hands over the rough surface. *I was on the ghost tours with Agnes. I saw something. I saw something here.*

Carol hammered her fist on the door. *What, I don't know. Okay. Now the hard part.*

She touched the little emblem on her chest. "Barbara, it's me Carol. I've got something I need to talk to you about, meet me at the sight of the old Windsor Hotel right away at the corner of Government and Courtney."

Carol senior hung her head. *After all of these fucking years, he was here the whole time, and no one knew. I never knew. Only how did this happen? Without anyone being aware? And how is this possible in such a long time frame. It didn't add up. It was like someone went back and forth in time. But that is still crazy, like science fiction. Although recent scanners the police have just purchased are able to pick objects before and behind in time. That was inanimate objects. These were young boys stolen, some from right under the parents' noses, including my sister's. Time to dig into my notes and files I kept at home on my computer. I'm missing something here. Who could have done this and how? Surely not this old gal?*

She glanced up and looked closer at one of the posters, it was from early parts of the century. From a movie about a character called Indiana Jones, the movie was entitled the "Indiana Jones and the Kingdom of The Crystal Skull". Carol looked closer at the poster and swiped at the dust covering it. *Hang on. What was the old girls name, Agnes, Ms. Teak.* The paper had yellowed over the decades. *But...*

She pressed her emblem and snapped away a half dozen photos, including some close ups. There in the bottom left was an image she didn't recall being there in the poster before. Below the Russian lady with the sword in her hand. An older lady holding a skull before her in both hands. The image fit the poster. Carol Senior scratched her head. *Only it didn't. The skull was not one of the deformed ones from the movie. I know that skull.*

She waited for Barb to arrive. *This wasn't going to be easy.*

⇐⇒   ⇐⇒

WELL THAT DIDN'T GO well, as expected. Barbara, who hadn't talked to her in years, while thankful for closure regarding her son's death, called her several choice words, including useless slag and stormed back to her car. *Didn't have much of a sister before, none now.* Carol Senior sat in her living room. Tears streaming down her face. Photographic images were projected all over her walls, the newest in police equipment, she could ask for the time or date of each photo, allow them to age forward in time, shrink or expand any section. These were the photos and notes from her case involving Nathan. It was brilliant what new technology can do these days. She pressed her emblem and new pictures from the hotel's hidden room captured on her vid cam popped up.

So somehow unless there is two people involved this isn't possible to have all these lads abducted. How? Why every twenty-six years, except the last one?

The ones she took of the crystal skull poster caught her eye. "Computer pull up all the known images of one Agnes Van Lunt aka Ms. Teak."

The last time she'd seen the old gal was when she'd taken her to the Shelbourne vortex in Victoria. "Sure, suckered me in that night. Trusted her, she drugged me and set me up. Hadn't heard from her since."

It wouldn't be Agnes doing this would it? No. I trust my intuition, she couldn't do this. Could she and what was his name? Francis Rattenbury! He travelled forward in time, could she to now or the future? Or back to the past?

One appeared of Agnes in her stage act holding up a crystal skull. *Cider, her name was Cider.* Hang on, computer. Super impose that image over the image of the similar image from the poster.

It did and as the two slid together, they appeared to be very similar.

Now, shrink the two to the same size.

As they did the two merged into one.

More images began to pop up.

"Computer what is going on? I only wanted..."

Carol Senior stared at the photos popping up, the advanced system could recognize and pick up any known images requested and threw its entire library of historical photos regarding said Ms. Teak.

One was from a Charlie Chaplin movie, a picture of a woman walking

in the background who looked to be talking on a cell phone, the script read 1912. Another of an odd man taking pictures with a modern looking camera and dressed in clothes that didn't match the period, the script at the bottom read 1947. Another of a woman who no one recognized walking slowly as the carnage of JFK's assassination unfolded. And others.

Then one of Shelbourne vortex that was taken by the original Google camera team back in 2005. The elderly lady appeared highlighted in the left corner holding a sign.

Carol zoomed in.

Not possible, this wasn't here in the original, as far as I remember. I remember staring at that image all those years ago. She scanned her notes and went into the archives she kept in the basement. Carol pulled the ancient photograph from her files that she kept all these years and squinted at the Google photo she hadn't seen in decades. There was no image of anyone holding a card up.

What is going on here? She'd read recently about breakthroughs in possible time travel, bending time into the past.

Carol Senior marched back upstairs as fast as her elderly legs could take her and compared the two photos. She blew up the image until she could read what was on the card. It simply said, 'sorry'.

Agnes what have you done?

Or more importantly, how?

THE CLOCKS ARM SLOWED down until a dull bong echoed over and over. Carol snapped her head back to the smell of incense and candle wax. "What the hell was that?"

"That I believe is a parallel time loop of your life in the future."

"But... I haven't lived it yet... I don't get it, it isn't possible. You saying I don't find my nephew, I have to live with this for the rest of my life." Tears started to stream down her face, "How the hell do I tell my sister I failed?"

Agnes stared at her, "Sorry. I tried several times to find answers, clues to Nathan's disappearance, but failed like I mentioned earlier it was like something or someone had put a filter around him. I can't break thorough in this time frame."

"What the hell do I do with this? This doesn't help me at all."

"Not much, I'm afraid." Agnes walked around behind where Carol sat, staring dumbstruck and shell-shocked staring into Cider's deep recessed eye sockets.

"Wait, several times? What do you mean?"

The old gal pulled a crystal from her pocket and slammed it against the back of Carol's head. The police officer slumped forward, unconscious.

"No, this was meant to help me only.

You can't remember any of this."

With that she dragged Carol to her bed and placed her on it. She stuffed two pills into the back of her throat. "Midazolam. Dissolves fast, wipes out short term memory and you'll sleep like a baby. Sorry about the lump, that won't go right away." She sat down before Cider.

Now the hard part begins.

Chapter Fourteen

"But Agnes, the events to the Jordon Gibson abduction are virtually identical to what happened twenty-six years ago." Carol rubbed her head as they sat having tea in the main room of the hotel. "Christ that's sore. I got it from passing out and hitting myself on Cider?" Agnes adjusted her straw wrapped purple version of a smaller cartwheeled hat. Her dress and top watched in paler shades of stripped fuchsia and a rosy pink. "Yup, and again when you hit the ground. I've had many people either fall asleep or pass out during a séance, didn't expect you to be one," Agnes lied with a smile as she sipped at her tea. "That they are, it happens to involve the Shelbourne vortex, there are times when it is reported that people drive along Shelbourne and Hillside and they say they are suddenly on a dirt road. A minute later they are back in the present. But occasionally the reverse can happen, and time jumps

ahead."

"Not possible."

"Then tell me how you know of Francis Rattenbury?"

"He says he came through the vortex into my dreams."

"Exactly. So, if a ghost from the past can do this, why not one from the future?"

Carol thought a moment. *Wouldn't I have a greater lump in the front of my head?* "So, are you saying this will happen again in another twenty-six years and again after that?"

Agnes nodded her head in affirmation. "Nice tea, have I said that before, as well?"

Carol didn't take the bait. "Are you telling me that someone from the future returns to take a boy every twenty-six years or so?"

"Check the records on unsolved cases and let me know."

"So how do I stop this? I have no clues to his disappearance and obviously won't if he goes back into the vortex?"

"It is you that will solve this."

"Me when? Not twenty-six years from now?" *I thought the old gal was of sound mind and body. I was sadly mistaken.*

"Ah, you are very astute."

She rubbed at her head. "Man, that hurts, swear someone whacked me in the skull. Wait, if I do that, how can I know about this now? I'm getting more and more confused."

"We go to the vortex tonight. I get the feeling that person that was after me is getting closer to discovering my presence. Time is of the essence. You will need to take pictures with your cell phone. The rest I can't tell you about. The photos will capture what I think I need to know in order to save his life."

Carol looked at her strangely. "Agnes, why we?"

"We as in you, me and Cider." Agnes hesitated for a moment. "Again, you need to enter the vortex as well as myself. As for me, I've lived a full life, but have never experienced something like this. Around this time of the year before the All Hallows Eve it is very powerful. I also want to see what Cider experiences. She can see and experience things beyond our realm and possibly communicate with those we need to talk to. Tonight, will be on the eve of similar galactic alignments like during the rock concert in California with Venus, Mercury and the Sun all in the Sagittarius quadrant, while the moon is on the cusp of Libra-Scorpio. Very powerful alignments, I also found out, for non-relevant time experiences or déjà vu encounters. Or so I'm told and maybe, just maybe, help find Nathan."

Carol shook her head. The old gal talked to that crystal skull like she was a living creature.

"You forget I can pick up thoughts and she, Cider, is living to me."

"And you forget I'm a cop and I know when you are lying to me." Agnes remained stone faced as she sipped her after-dinner scotch.

"You're up to something, I know it." *I thought I could trust her, but after that séance I'm not so sure.*

Agnes yawned. "I'm quite tired, will you help me up so I can retire to my room?"

"Oh, you're such a bag. Okay I'll do it, I'll take you there, but I'm not letting you out of my sight."

"Don't worry, I won't try anything funny."

"That is exactly what I'm worried about." Carol rubbed the back of her head. *Need another bloody Aspirin, that's what I need.*

IT WAS NEARLY TWO A.m. when Carol drove her car to the intersection of Shelbourne and Hillside.

Agnes sat all too quietly beside her.

"Tell me again why you've brought Cider with us?" Carol asked quietly as they sat with the car idling.

"I want to know what she senses or picks up while we're here. Never had a chance to do this before. Seeing inside Cider is like looking into another dimension. So, I reckon we take the other dimension to Cider and see what she sees here. I'm excited, aren't you?"

"Not really, nervous actually. Don't know why, just get this sense things

are going to go horribly wrong."

"That's probably from being in an area where time is in flux. I'm getting that same sense. Has to do with the ley lines intersecting and the magnetic flow. When several lines cross or come together it creates a quiet or null zone. All the better to pick up vibrational energies and perhaps sense what happened to Nathan. My mind and Cider's are being blocked trying to locate him and again at the hanging scene at the Empress. I need to go around that somehow." She hesitated and closed her eyes a moment. "I'm beginning to sense the vortex is opening. Let's get out and start walking down the street."

"Vibrational energies, null zones. The only vibrational sense I'm beginning to get is I've got to go to the washroom. How would you know what the vortex opening would feel like if you've never done this before?"

Agnes held Cider in her elderly arms. The old gal was surprisingly stronger than she looked. Carol had begun to realize all her feeling weak, fainting spells and 'I need a rest break,' were simply ways of getting out of explaining things. *My head still throbs, but the lump is going down. I swear I was clocked. But there was only one person in the room. Agnes? She has no problem holding up the heavy skull.*

"I am not letting you out of my sight. I'm starting to think you hit me with something and now you've led me here for another reason. Didn't you tell me that time is like a straight line, except that every once in a while it curves back on itself?"

"Yes, like a loop and sometimes you get stuck in this loop over and over again, until something is done to end it. Then when it is corrected all moves forward again. Why? Is this what you are sensing? That you've been here before?"

Carol frowned as the area began to shimmer. "Yes, I've dreamt this before, or feel like this has happened to me in the past, er future, er in some cosmic twisted reality. Maybe when I met Francis Rattenbury? And I am beginning to think you walloped me in back of the head."

Agnes laughed. "You are most perceptive. You are after all a detective. Ah, what is that?"

Carol looked up into the windows of the Parkwood Place care facility. She caught an older woman waving at them.

"Who is that?" Carol grabbed her phone to take a picture and zoomed in. "Who the hell is that and why is she waving at me? Is this some kind of vision?" She closed her eyes and blinked as everything began to spin away and the sidewalks and asphalt disappeared. The woman in the window rose and put on her large brimmed red cartwheel hat. "Agnes? How are you up there? What in the ..."

"Thanks for bringing me here. You'll thank me someday."

"What?" Carol snapped the picture and glanced over to look at Agnes, who wasn't there. "Agnes?"

She stood on the street by herself. Carol glanced up at the window. No one was there. Quickly everything shifted back to normal and a car drove by on the normal looking street honking at her for standing nearly in the middle of it.

"Agnes?" Carol rushed back to her car as beneath her feet pavement reappeared. "Agnes!" She shouted.

Nothing responded, only the cool Victoria air as Carol opened the cars door and jumped inside. Carol slammed her hand down on the steering wheel. She rubbed at the back of her head. *It was her that hit me, probably drugged me. Crap! Why do I know I just got set up? I trusted her.*

Chapter Fifteen

Carol drove back to the hotel and immediately went up to Agnes' suite.

She knocked on the door. No answer. *Didn't expect one really, did I?* She slid her card in the handle and opened the door. "Agnes?" No smell of incense filled the air. She walked through the room, everything was made perfectly neat. She looked in the drawers and in the closet. No suitcases, no dated forties clothing. No sign that Agnes had ever stayed there. *What in the?*

Carol went back downstairs to the front desk and checked the registry. There was no one registered in that room and no one in the hotel with the name Agnes Van Lunt.

She was never here? Do only I remember her being here? What has she done, she's bloody altered time and got rid of herself. That can't be, can it?

Had it to do with finding Nathan? How is this going to find him? Or was it to do with her hiding from whoever was after her?

LATER IN THE DAY SHE called Jake. "Hi Jake. Don't forget my turn to take you on a hot-date stake-out. Hatley Castle, tomorrow night."

"Saturday's the wedding."

"I know, but Agnes said the invocation would be the night before."

"Agnes? Who the hell is Agnes?"

"Old spiritualist that stayed at the hotel. You met her during the High

Tea. She read your mind and you took off all huffy."

"Lady, you must be smoking some bad-ass shit. I met you at the High Tea thing once this week, but it was just you and me. Although I do remember seeing some psychic woman in Vegas once, thought she was pretty good. Swear she could read your mind."

Yes, even he doesn't remember her ever being here. What the hell has she done? Is it because of what was chasing in the alley that night?

"Seven o'clock for that hot date, tomorrow night. Don't be late." *The only hot thing he's going to get is a poker shoved up his behind if I had my way.*

CAROL ROUNDED THE CORNER to her room and caught sight of a man dressed like someone from a Humphrey Bogart movie knocking on the door of the room opposite hers. She watched, half paying attention to his dated clothing. *Man, some people really like wearing the same thing for about thirty years or so. Wait a minute. It was him from before, our hotel's resident ghost. Francis Rattenbury. Why is he here?*

The man, not having anyone answer his knock turned and proceeded to knock on the next door.

What the...?

Only this time his body shimmered, and it appeared to split. Another smaller, daintier figure pulled away and looked up at her. *Agnes?* It pulled a card from its jacket pocket and bent over. It appeared to slide something under her door before turning and merging back into the distinguished gentleman who began to walk away.

Man, I must be more tired than I thought. "Francis?" She followed the figure of the man as he walked quickly to the elevator. The elevator door hushed open.

Carol ran up. "Hang on old man." Unresponsive, he stepped into the elevator. She grabbed the door before it slid completely closed. He thrust his face at her through the gap before it slid open this time and gasped.

"Danger awaits those who wonder at the wall."

And then he smiled that insipid grin, just like Agnes did when she was being adored. The lights flickered, the elevator shook. Carol grabbed at the button to open the door and turned back to stare at the man in the elevator as the door slid open. Only there wasn't anyone there. He was gone. On the floor a small Teenage Mutant Ninja Turtle figurine, similar to the ones left at two of the crime scenes, stared up at her. Carol picked it up and stuffed it into her pocket.

What...? The shit around here just keeps getting crazier and crazier. She turned and went back to her room. Opening her door, a postcard fluttered at her feet. Carol bent over and picked it up. It was an old sienna colored picture of a brick building and two people posing in front of it, vaguely familiar. Carol walked into the room and turned on her lights, Her police phone rang as she turned the card over. Carol put down the card to answer the call, which if it came in on this line, she knew would be important.

"There's an abduction of another boy being reported, just happened downtown." Carol didn't respond as she felt the figurine in her pocket and picked up the card. She turned it over.

Written on the backside facing her, *Nathan/Now.*
"Carol you there?"

Carol turned over the postcard and stared at the picture again, the building oddly familiar. The man she just saw at her door just now stood beside another smaller figure of an older woman, posing. Everything washed away as the flood of her unconscious memories flooded in. Colliding against a dark van, a woman's body flying through the air. Her hand clutching something, an old key. The building in the photograph, it was the old front of the Windsor Hotel.

"Carol? Carol? Are you there?"
"Let me guess the abduction happened in the Quadra Street area."

"Near the playground. How did you know?" The voice from dispatch brought her back.

"Yes. Don't tell me why but I think I know where the abductor is heading. I'm heading for the old Windsor Hotel." She clicked off the phone, grabbed her keys and ran down the stairs. She was supposed to meet Jake for dinner, he'd have to wait. She texted him as she ran down the stairs, 'been delayed, will hook up as soon as a local police matter is resolved.' I hope I'm not too late. *What did Agnes call that? Retrocognition?* She ran to her car and checked the trunk to make sure her gun was there and her police light.

The Windsor was only a couple of blocks away. She put on the flashing silent police light on her dash, not turning it on and tore up the exit ramp, her guts telling her time was critical here.

ROUNDING THE CORNER of the Empress Carol called on her cell phone. "Dispatch, possible crime scene at rear of Windsor hotel."

Not wanting to alert anyone in the hotel earlier, she flicked on the light and slammed on the throttle. An old lady texting on her phone nearly crapped herself looking up from her car as Carol went around her. *Lucky lady I ain't time for this, or I'd bust your ass.*

Carol slowed on silent approach, as she came around the back of the hotel, a van, familiar from her memories, sat parked there and beside it a small Ford car. Trying to open a door at the rear of the hotel stood an older lady, focused in her headlights.

Carol slammed on her brakes. *God nearly hit her, so I've changed something, she doesn't die. Agnes, it's like trying to put the pieces together from a jigsaw puzzle without the box lid.* She got out and was about to yell, 'police, hands up' as another patrol car came flying around the corner. Blinded by Carol's lights the elder woman ran back towards the van.

"Shit!" Carol watched as she went flying off the hood of the other police car. Her body flung into the air, arms and legs askew like a rag doll. Sirens blaring as another car came around the other side. *Not the same as I remember it, but the same effect. Weird. Is that what Agnes called a time paradox, where events or time changes but the outcome stays the same?*

Carol checked her pulse, there was barely any. "My boys. My boys will miss me," she gasped as her eyes closed and her head fell away. By the way the body went totally limp, Carol knew she was gone. She checked anyways as an officer from one of the cruisers came running out. No pulse.

"I recognize her. That's Gladys Townsend, the hotel's owner."
Carol thought she recognized the woman's face from the local papers.

"Boys. She mentioned her boys."
"My mother worked there just before it closed. No, she was never married and had no kids of her own. But I do remember she said several times how she'd fawn over young boys whenever people would bring them in."

Carol's mind raced. A voice inside her head seemed to speak. Her voice.

Basement. Key.

The trunk.
"Where's the van?"

They hurried to it. Another patrol car had arrived. "Get the doors open."

There unconscious and mouth taped with duct tape lay a body. Carol shined the light on the face of the sleeping boy. She felt his pulse, weak, but alive. It wasn't Nathan, but another. Crap, the one just reported abducted I'll bet. *But the card read Nathan, here.*

"Wake him up, need to confirm who he is before the parents go ape shit."

Okay, not Nathan. Basement? Key? She was trying to get into the back door to the basement. The vision of a key in her hand fell across her mind. *Where's the key I saw in my mind before?*

Carol frisked her pockets, nothing. She caught something white poking out from under one of the black leather gloves she had on. Carol pulled the glove down, a rough bandage swab, still partly blooded soaked stared at her. *Okay, definitely the lady I shot at in Fan Tan Alley with Agnes.* Around her neck dangled a thin chain. She pulled it out, a single old key. She unclipped it from her neck, also on the chain was a five-sided pendant. The face of a creature with large horns on its head. *Not your long sought after loved one then?*

"Where you going?"

"The basement. Don't ask me how I know but it opens something in the basement."

Carol grabbed her flashlight and ran to the door, there scrawled in all of the graffiti she caught what looked like a being with hair aflame. *Odd drawing. The creature from the Avatar trail when I went hiking with Tony.* Her heart thumped.

She knew the lady hadn't time to lock the door. She clicked on her flashlight and began searching around. It was a dingy basement hallway with a couple of empty rooms, but no door that the key could fit. She spied several old boxes stacked up against a wall. Carol walked back into the empty room, the back wall seemed to be several feet shorter than the back wall in the hallway. Looking down, back at the dust, there was scratches and signs the boxes had been moved recently. Carol pulled them aside, there behind them was a small three-foot-high doorway. Carol kissed the key and tried it in the hole, it fit and turned.

Carol took a deep breath, half expecting foul or noxious fumes and shone her light inside the small twelve by twelve room. Shadowy figures appeared to sit in chairs. To her right a light switch. She clicked it on and was surprised when light flooded the room. *I thought the hotel had been closed for years.* She blinked in shocked horror.

The whole room had been painted with murals of a child's bedroom. Toy airplanes hung from strings, posters of movies, Toy Story, Star Wars, Indiana Jones plastered the walls, all painted in bright blues and reds. Toys sat up against the far wall, dump trucks, hot wheel cars, G I Joes.

But it was the five chairs arranged in a semi-circle facing each other in the center that caught her breath. Four of the chairs held bodies of young boys. One empty obviously meant for the last boy in her trunk. Three of the bodies, desiccated and dried, had been dead a long time.

One of the bodies let out a slight moan. "Nathan," she cried and reached over to touch his neck. The lad's eyes opened.

"Auntie," he whispered before he slumped over.

"Nathan!" Carol wanted to hug him but knew better than to disturb him. Her hand ran over his face, he was so cold. She grabbed her phone and called for medical aid. She felt his pulse, he was alive, but barely. She'd probably drugged him somehow, toxicology would determine how. Of the other two, one was cold. Carol recognized the face of one of the victim's abducted this week, the Pendray boy. He was still warm, but his vitals were barely noticeable. She wanted to cut both their bounds loose, but worried disturbing them could end their lives. Leave that to the experts. She took quick pictures of the other two. One had been dead for decades, the other not so long, but judging by the degree of dehydration, years as well.

What sick mind would do this and set this up? Had the lady drugged them, perhaps injected them with embalming fluid in order to preserve them? Judging by the coolness of the room, it was like a morgue in here and normally the bodies wouldn't rot, just dry out. The medics rushed in one at a time.

"Those two are alive, but barely. They've been drugged somehow, probably Rohypnol if I was to guess." That still leaves two others unaccounted for in the four abducted in the last two weeks. But Carol had a pretty good idea where they'd be tonight.

Carol then clicked on her private cell phone as she walked into the back alley getting out of the way of the paramedics and the forensic team rushing in. "Barb, get in your car and meet me at Victoria General. I've found

Nathan. Yes, he's alive, rough shape. No, ask later, get over there. I'm on the way as well. You're welcome. Thank me later, Victoria General." The phone went dead, she knew Barb was already heading out the door. Her thanks was more of a deep grieving sob. *Oh thank God, don't know what would have happened to her if we found him dead.*

So, I've got at least two boys still missing. Okay, now to find this wall of wonder, before it's too late for those two. At least Nathan has been rescued. She glanced at her phone, less than twenty hours to find and save the others. But first, she threw on her police light and followed the ambulance as it tore off for Victoria General, to meet her sister.

Tears blurred her vison as she drove. *Agnes you crazy, nutty old broad. I don't know how you pulled this off, think it cost you your life, but thanks.*

She swerved around another person texting on their phone in their car. *That's two I could have busted tonight, why do people think laws only apply to other people?*

The blue fairy watched from a corner of the room as the police took pictures of the room.

> *See, she seeks justification.*
> *She helped him.*
> *She cares.*
> Pain wracked its soul.
> *We must go.*
> *Will she care about us?*
> *Unknown.*
> *But we will seek her again.*

⚬

CAROL WATCHED THE BUSY coming and goings from outside the hospital, having a smoke. The sign above her read, **No Smoking On The Property**. *I'll pay the fine, try and arrest me.* She stuck around just long enough to know that Nathan would be okay, they had subscribed something to nullify the effects of the drugs Gladys gave him and were giving him a massive blood transfusion. He began to respond quickly. Barbara must have thanked her a thousand times and shed sixteen Kleenex boxes of tears.

Winds were rising from an approaching storm she could see in the distance from the hillside the hospital stood on. British Columbia's winters while mild sometimes were violent along the coast with Japanese currents bringing in major rains and winds. She kicked at the discarded cigarette butts. The air stank with disturbed salty odors coming off the ocean and chaos in the unsettled air.

I don't get it? Why? She stared at the screen of her phone. *Agnes didn't come here for the ghosts. She came to be taken to the vortex. So why have me take her there? She could have done that on her own?*

An American Bald Eagle cried out over head as it struggled to bank in the winds or testing its ability to ride nature's turbulence.

She's ended a time loop of some sort, because only I remember her. She's ended a time loop about me. She said she came here to find an answer to the Jordon Gibson case, which I guess she did. But in the end, she helped me, and I don't know how she did it.

Set up? Carol watched as the eagle cried again as it surrendered to the increasing buffeting and settled onto a tall cedar behind her. *Yup, most definitely I was set up.*

I get it, that doesn't matter. So now I've got to help find these two boys, before it's too late. What matters in the end is that she helped me. Wherever you are Agnes and Cider, Thanks.

The eagle in the tree screeched as it launched itself back into the air.

And you mother nature can go to hell!

⋙⋘   ⋙⋘

CAROL OPENED THE DOOR to Senior Rizzuto's room, it had still been cordoned off from the public. She ran through the forensic reports as she closed the door behind her.

Something in here doesn't make sense. I think Agnes knew that but didn't tell me. The test results showed that the fibers of the rope were indeed a hundred years old, made from American cotton and no surprise there wasn't any DNA to be found on it. *But not any older, so if our ghost was exacting revenge and he died in 1862, the noose is still too young. And the post mortem shows that he didn't die from hanging but from asphyxiation. It suggests that instead someone slipped the noose around his neck and choked him to death.*

She looked at the markings on the ground of where his body lay. The cabinet with its spilled contents. *Okay, he put up a fight before dying, but that means there was someone else in the room. Someone that Mr. Rizzuto would have let in. Or someone that managed to break the code or use a spare key to enter.*

In either case the perpetrator left, closed the door and managed to lock the anchor from the outside. Carol walked up to the entrance door. Her eyes caught the sideboard and she remembered the pack of dental floss laying incongruously on it. Surely people would use the floss in the bathroom? So why was the pack here, next to the door? Unless... She rang the forensics boss.

"Hi George. Need you to get back to the crime scene. I need you to swab the door lock and anchor for any residue that seems out of place. Also, I'm wondering if there was any dental floss found at the scene. Yeah, I remember the open pack, but I mean any lengths, used or otherwise. There were? Okay, was it used? Please check it out, see if there is any saliva or DNA. Yeah, I know, but if you find what I think you will a puzzle will be solved. Thanks." *Now to go over my notes in my room.*

CAROL SAT BEFORE HER laptop. "So, I've Agnes, mad Italians and Satanic rituals. Only she knows, or rather knew, something I don't and won't or wouldn't tell me. Now she's disappeared these tenses are all screwed up. Why?"

She googled haunted sights of Victoria. Dozens of webpages came up. *Wow, she's right, there's a lot of locations here.* She spent the next couple of hours scrolling through page after page.

Carol grabbed a tourist map of Victoria, tossed it on the wall of her office and began to mark with a pen all the known hauntings. She began to triangulate all the data she could on ghosts, hauntings. Yes, Agnes was right most travel in straight lines, like in England on the old churches, and other monuments. So, if this is correct then there should be something strange. Or maybe there's something to see that sticks out. She stared at Hatley Castle.

It stood across the bay to the east all by itself. She drew a line towards it then drew another from several known ghost sightings, St Ann's Academy, Victoria Golf Course, the bay and others. *No, surprise that this is where our Eastern guests are holding their ceremony, it is here the two Ley Lines intersect.*

Carol perused the blog sights. *Several people talked about a Hall of Wonder. What did that spirit at Avatar Grove say? 'Stare at the wall and wonder.' Or something like that.*

Further along from the more northern Ley Line she caught a picture someone took of a door that was an entrance to the sewer systems. Like the aerosol sprayings she caught on the side of rail cars whenever stuck waiting for the train to go by. *Such wasted talent.*

Reports were that this Hall of Wonder is downtown. Some people reported it below the purple lead lined glass covers of some of the downtown streets. In the old days the storage of most buildings was built out below the street level and they added the glass to have basically free lighting to the rooms below. The panels over the years turned purple due to the manganese used in the manufacturing process before 1915. *Only those were installed around 1900 or so, so I don't think this Hall of Wonder is under one of those panels.*

Hang on. I've seen that scrawling or something familiar.

At the Bard and Banker pub in the washroom. And at the back of the Windsor Hotel in my vision. She stared closer at the scribbles painted with aerosol can then printed the picture from her computer.

Take away the rude swear words, there's something here. Carol grabbed an orange Sharpie and highlighted the image. It was like a being on fire. *That was on the door at the Windsor Hotel.*

Carol clicked off the page. Before shutting down her computer she checked her postings on a few threads and blogs from earlier, nothing concrete. She reposted asking about anything regarding the wall or hall of wonder and if anyone knew where this was or what it was about. *There's something going on here, maybe hooked to this weird wall.* She glanced at her watch, realizing she had forgotten to have lunch.

Hmm. Perhaps I should visit the Pendray house for some of their special tea and scones. I think Agnes has got me hooked on lemon cheesecakes, I'll see if theirs are as good as the Fairmont's. Agnes had said she wanted me to visit the place and since she's not with us anymore, bless her soul, I think I shall take up her advice.

⊷ ⊶

GORGEOUS WORK. Carol stared at the blue and red stained-glass panels set above and into the front entrance of the Pendray House or, as it was currently known, the Gatsby Manor, on the property of the Huntingdon Manor Hotel.

Shadows shifted across the walls as she enjoyed the tea and scones. *What?* There was only one other couple in a smaller adjoining room at the time.

"Can I ask something? I hear this place is haunted and especially room five. Upstairs," she asked the waitress when she brought her the desserts.

"The honeymoon suite. Yes, it is. We get a lot of requests for that room, booked solid on Halloween for years ahead." She looked about to make sure management wasn't about. "I shouldn't tell you this, but just yesterday I was in this dining room all alone and noticed the lights were off. I flicked them on and when I did a picture fell off the wall. I put it back up and went to leave. When I came back a minute later, the other waitress had entered the room and I noticed that she had reached up to turn the lights on. I asked why did you do that when I had just turned them on? She looked at me weirdly, and said the lights were off when she came into the room. I told her I'd just turned them on."

Carol watched what was now two shadows move about the room as the lady talked; it was obvious the waitress couldn't see them. Her nose twitched.

"Okay." She flipped her badge. "I'm on police duty. Can I see inside that room?" The shadows moved through the room and up the stairs. She watched as another waitress shivered as they went past. "We're not supposed to. But who am I to obstruct the law? The guests have left for the day and room service is in the middle of cleaning it, so I can let you in for a bit."

"Gimme a moment alone," Carol said as she entered the room and closed the door behind her.

Shadows moved along the edges of the room.

"I can see you hiding, William and Ernest Pendray."

The two men began to solidify in front of her. "We are not hiding from you."

"No, it's just that I see you and know what happened to you."

They sneered at her and grit their teeth attempting to frighten her.

"Give up boys, I'm not afraid. I know the Lekwungen killed you in revenge for what another did on the property of their village of the dead.

There is a curse that needs to be broken if you are to rest in peace."

"We know of them, we know nothing of a curse. They dwell, we believe, below in Tunnels of Wonder. Find the one they cursed and then perhaps we will be released."

Well, that confirmed mostly what I already knew. Now to find this Hall of Wonder.

"Thanks." Carol left them seething. She stared at the cleaning lady as she walked up to her. She looked Mexican or Philippino. "You religious?" she asked looking at her rosary beads around her neck.

"Yes."

"Best hang on to those and do a little praying before you go in. The ghosts are quite restless today." *And I think I stirred them up.*

As Carol paid her bill and was about to leave a scream tore through the building. The cleaning lady came running down the stairs. "I queet this crazy place," she screeched and flung her apron down.

"Yup, definitely haunted." Carol smiled as she left. "And great tea."

Have a pleasant rest of the afternoon."

Although, I think we do serve better scones in all fairness.

⸎ ⸎

WHEN SHE GOT BACK CAROL checked her email. There had been one from George confirming DNA on the floss, but no hits. He thought it strange there was no saliva, however, just epithelial residue – skin cells. There had also been a waxy substance on the door anchor which matched the floss. *So, my hunch was right, shame there's no hits.* She checked the blog sites and had a few responses to the requests. Most were pretty unusual or simply said things like they'd heard about it and the secret tunnels below Victoria. But one caught her eye, from someone with the handle 'Danglepuss'. *Of all things, maybe not so young and pimply-faced after all.* He replied, "I've been there many times and have seen many weird things and people there. Along with a few spirit beings."

Carol noticed he was online. "I am very interested in going there. Are you on?"

He replied, "I can take you there, but want to meet you first. I won't take a stranger there. Need to meet you."

She decided to lay herself on the line as he sounded pretty honest. "Okay, give me a location near there, preferably a Timmies, and I'll buy, I need to get there tonight."

"There's one at the Hillside Mall. Bring two flashlights and rubber boots. I'll be wearing a

'Many Moods of Darth Vader' black tee-shirt. You've got my curiosity up. Why?"

"Same as you, I'm investing several disappearances and running out of time. The Hillside, next to Shelbourne Street. That is where the ..." "Vortex is." They both wrote at the same time.

There was a delay.
"It is. Is this regarding the abducted boys? You a cop?"
"Yes, on both. Undercover."

"Cool. I'm in."

"I'm a brunette, will have a checkered red top on."

—◆—   —◆—

CAROL LOOKED UP FROM her phone as a guy sat down across from her. He looked like he worked out, not the bespectacled dweeb she expected. In fact, he had this solid, handsome look she admired.

"You Justifier?"

"You must be Danglepuss?" She caught his tee shirt.

He nodded.

"What I got something in my nose or something?" He swiped at his nose. "You're staring at me awfully funny."

"No, I was just expecting someone more, well, if I'm to be more honest, more..."

"Geeky looking?"

"Well, yes, I didn't expect a good-looking man."

"Well, agreed. I didn't really expect a hot lady. So, you're a cop?"

Carol nodded.

"You packing heat?"

Carol nodded again and a gleam brightened his eyes.

"That excites you then?"

"Yeah, I'm liking what I'm seeing and hearing already. So, what brings you to the Wall of Wonder, not Hall of Wonder?"

"I'm here to connect with the Lekwungen." Carol told him briefly about meeting Charlie and her adventures with him."

"Wow, just thought it was me that ran into crazy, what's the term?" "Woo-woo," they both spurted out.

"Okay, I have run into some strange beings down there. I think I've

met the ones you want to meet. Not overly friendly that bunch. You're some gutsy broad. Single?" Carol smiled.

"Same. Myself, I do like to work out in the gym. I'm an Electrical Engineer, was a licensed automotive technician, love to hot rod cars and a Star Wars fan, as you can tell by my shirt. I like to go out to comic book conventions and any conventions involving Science Fiction or fantasy buffs. But my real hobby is anything to do esoteric or involving ghosts. Yes, as you tell me there are a lot of ghosts and spiritual happenings here. Due partly to ..."

"The Ley Lines," they both said and laughed.

Carol really noticed it for the first time over his buffed chest. It was eight identical pictures of Darth Vadar, at the top it read, 'The Many Moods of Darth'. Under each one, a word. "Happy, sad, laughing, crying, depressed, mad, angry, sarcastic." Carol laughed. "Like the shirt, someone with my kind of humor." *I've gotta start watching more sci fi.*

Carol looked at her watch, she had to meet Jake in less than three hours. "Look, I'm not trying to be rude, but I'm running out of time. I'm really enjoying your company and could chat all night. I need some answers to the two boys that were abducted recently, and I've got to meet someone soon."

"Same, and besides we need to get down there before dark. It's around the dusk that the shit really happens."

"Okay, let's go."

⟣⟡⟢

CAROL SHONE HER LIGHT down the dark corridor. Water splashed as she walked past the entrance with the typical warning scrawled in spray paint and a rather elaborate painting entitled Power Struggle, with an all-seeing eye creature holding a sword over a helpless man, a river of oil flowed beside them. *Very quasi-commie, no more than I expected. I hope this guy is for real and not some whack job. She glanced up at his face. Danglepuss, a handsome whack job, she didn't even know his real name.* They'd passed several other works of graffiti, including a few of men, hair aflame and for the last half an hour trundled down several tunnels that were cold, dank, wet and rank. Mainly rank, but to be expected in a sewer system.

He guided her along; it was obvious he'd been here many times. Why, she knew she'd find out one day, but not today. *Why does a man come down here time after time? To find serenity?*

Peace in his soul? Or a lost one? Crazy drugged out stoner?
"You're probably wondering why I come down here."

"I was actually." *Oh, crap don't tell me I've met another bloody mind reader pyscho person.*

"I've come down here below the Garden City seeking my dad for the first time. Not alone, with a few others, on a laugh. But the reports were that weird things happened down here. I didn't think I'd find him and in a way I did. I've never done drugs. Always thought I might try it but what I saw here convinced me never to. Still some here find bliss and solace. I guess I'd like to seek the same. But not like what happened to him."

Carol stopped for a second and looked up at him. Moisture seemed to streak his face. "Thanks for that moment of real honesty." She reached up and touched his hand. Danglepuss grasped hers.

"What you want to see is the vial room. That is where the bizarre stuff really happens."

"How bizarre?"

"You'll see. Addicts hang out in there. It's the energy. If my GPS is correct, we're virtually now under the vortex that runs above the street."

She had to ask, her intuition going off. "You found your dad there, didn't you?"

"Yes, he died there. I had to carry him out. Made me determined never to become like him. Now the vial room is ahead on the left. Check out the walls. And then you'll wonder how this is possible."

Carol thought for a moment. *That's what the Lekwungen said at Avatar trail.* As soon as they entered, she felt the coldness and more. Shadowy figures moved everywhere in the gloom. Several candles were alight. Then she caught what Danglepuss said. Along the walls jammed into the mortar were hundreds of needles that glistened in the dim light cast by the flickering flames.

"Not sure how it happened, someone must have begun to stab them into the old mortar, probably not wanting to step on the needles. I call it the Sanctuary of the Lost. We're just in time, watch."

There were three people laying up against concrete slabs. One girl looked out of it. The other two young men had just begun to inject themselves. As they did the shadows began to move and several spirits pulled from the darkness and began to circle. "I was freaked the first time I saw this, but now I come here often to watch. Undrugged people, like us, they aren't interested in. The addicts, now that's a different story."

"I can see why, we're on one of the Ley Lines, I felt the change in the energy the second we walked into this room." Her nose was twitching like mad.

One of the men opened his mouth to scream, Carol moved to rush forward. Danglepuss grabbed her. "Don't, there's nothing you can do."

As he screamed quietly blue flaming spirits moved over his mouth and began to inhale. Carol watched vapors being pulled from the tormented man into themselves. "When you toke up down here, you release yourself from this realm and I'm guessing you're feeding these spirits. In return the stoners say they get the best, most incredible highs of their lives. Many report being taken to other worlds, other times. Something to do with the Ley Lines and maybe the vortex I suppose."

One of the two went limp as one of the spirits flowed into the man, merging into one. He fell away. "A few, like my dad, die; not many. They all say it's worth the rush."

Carol caught lights flickering from the wall where the vials were jammed into as she looked up. "What?" She walked up closer, several of the vials had lights moving in them and as she came closer, she could make out faces. "How is this possible?"

"I knew you'd be able to see them. Few can, to most they are just needles jammed into the wall."

"In my adventures with Charlie I met a being I called Sprity and she left me with some ability. I often see things others can't, especially since I came to Victoria."

"That one there is my dad." He pointed to one vial. "I haven't the guts to take it out of the wall. I watched someone do that to one and the spirit inside died. These ghosts here live on a symbiotic relationship. I think the people kept them alive or make them stronger and in return they give the addicts a greater high than they've ever felt. Some though if they die and one manages to get a needle into them in time keep them alive in the vial."

"Doubt I ever could bring him back, but I have connections that might be able to. When this is over, I'll see what I can do."

"Thanks. And I've seen a few ghosts enter the bodies and walk out of here. Don't know if they can stay in them forever. Some kind of soul transference, I think."

Carol shook her head, for a younger man, he seemed very calm, solid and grounded. *A lot calmer than I'd be if I was down here on my own watching my dad pass away.* "I've seen something like this before in Vancouver, this was my first Charlie case. It was not quite the same, but very familiar. I can also explain this later, but right now I need to find explanations to something and I think the beings that I need to contact are here." Carol stepped back from the wall. She didn't know why and didn't normally share any of her past strange cases; in fact, she thought Agnes has been the only one outside the Force that had much idea, but there was something about him that she deeply trusted.

She stepped forward into the center of the room. "I have come seeking those of the Lekwungen, I have met you before. You have asked me to come to this place. I am here now."

He moved to stand behind her as if to protect her if needed. "This is crazy, but I'm your backup man if anything goes awry."

A surge from the dark tunnels before them. Screams and chants shuddered up into the room, a sudden whoosh surrounded them, and the room filled with a blue shimmering light. The candles, flames exploded upwards, increasing in size tenfold. Sweat formed on her brow as the room warmed up.

The girl laying out cold sat up, her hair smoldering in blue flame, her eyes when she opened them surged with orange flames and as she opened her mouth sparks flew out, as if wind blew across logs were burning on a fireplace.

"Don't run, I've seen these only once before, surprised you knew about them. If you turn to run, they will attack and burn you. One of the guys I was with got second degree burns."

Screams tore from the woman as she fought herself, tearing at her face, the being inside obviously in torment. It was like her soul was being fried. Then she stopped and lifting from the ground gravitated towards the two. "Who calls, we of the Lekwungen." Sparks spat from her mouth as she floated in front of Carol.

"I know how you got here, I am sorry for how my kind destroyed your village. But one of your kind, a shaman, helped create a curse through one of ours, a judge."

"We seek justice and you." The fire being moved closer until Carol could feel the heat radiating from it. "You are a justifier. We sought you earlier. Those that are here, with you will not be tolerated. They bring a being most foul, we will not let him enter here." *Don't tell me they'd start a supernatural gang war?*

"I cannot defeat this demon alone, I need help. You will help us." Carol tried not to flinch as embers fluttered between them. The smell of old burnt wood and plant material flooded over her. Danglepuss put his hand on her shoulder as if to give moral support.

"I ask one thing first, did one of you hang a man from the room of the hotel I am staying at located at the end of the bay that was filled in many years ago?"

"Deception, it was one of his own followers. But there will be others and we won't stop ourselves. We ask again." Its eyes exploded in angry red flames. "There is one we seek that will end this, bring him to us."

"Yes, I can do that. I will help you."

The girl crumpled to the concrete, the fires swirled about and poured down the tunnels, the candles flickered and returned to their former sizes.

Coldness began to seep back into the room.

Danglepuss bent over and checked the fallen girl's pulse. "She's dead."

"Okay, so not even a thanks. It is time to leave."

Danglepuss grabbed her arm, "That was truly freaky."

Carol glanced at her watch, "I need to get moving, my time is running out."

Minutes later they emerged into the street under a darkening sky. She had about half an hour to meet Jake. "Thanks for that, it helped a lot. I've gotta run, urgent police business. Don't worry about the girl, I'll send in a team to retrieve her."

Danglepuss smiled softly at her. "Lady, this has been one fucking spooky date. Don't suppose I could join you?" She nodded no.

"I'd like to meet you again, on a more normal type of dinner date." "Takes one bizarro to appreciate another." They both laughed.

"So, it has. I'll contact you on the net via the thread and set something up." "Deal." He leaned in and kissed her lightly on the cheek.

He pulled away and began to slowly walk up the hill with that natural confident swagger of his. "Yup, one freaky date, really enjoyed it though," he turned and called back to her.

"Yeah, me too." Then it struck her. "Hey, what's your real name if you don't mind me asking?"

"Brad. Brad Johnson. And again thanks, it was a great night."

And mine is barely starting. "Carol Ainsworth." She began to walk very fast back to her car in the nearby parking lot.

So, it was, so it was. What did that insane shaman always tell me, expect the unexpected?

Yup, didn't expect that one iota and no glasses and no pimples.

IN THE VIAL ROOM THE blue fairy being pulled itself from the wall. It had watched the entire event, knowing it could not interfere.

They the others, the whole Lekwungen, would not approve of us. That we know for sure now.

Yes, I also sense they would try to destroy this joining. They are not ones to try and understand.

She is the one, they know this, we know this.
We shall follow, there must be a way to contact her.
Through the male?
That will not help.
How?
We shall find a way, otherwise this being will perish.
This being would sooner perish, than live the rest of its life in this way.
It is agreed.

Chapter Sixteen

Jake scanned the area with his infrareds in the dark.

"There are several guards and they're armed. The walls of the castle itself are too high to climb, so I think we're stuffed."

"Follow me. In my research of Victoria and its past there were several articles on Hatley Castle, how Mr. Dunsmuir was an avowed spiritualist and hence why he built the castle in this spot. It is here that two Ley Lines merge and that is in connection to the earth energy centers as well. A place of what one person said was null energy." *You might not remember her, but I do; Agnes. I might have to ask Danglepuss if he knew of anyone that knew her or if he was in contact with anyone claiming to have travelled in time.*

They walked in the woods around to the west side. "Now he also based a castle design with in mind what all castles must have if they are about to be overcome."

"An escape route?"
"Yes, a tunnel."
"And you're sure of this how?"

"I saw the original blueprints. On the west side there is a tunnel under the grounds that go out about three hundred meters, sorry about a thousand feet or so, you Americans have got to get with the modern world and learn metric. Now the Ley lines come in from the west and if I'm right he'd have built the tunnel to run in between them."

They were well out of view of the castle and the men patrolling when Jake put the glasses back on and looked around. "Nothing, these will only work if the tunnel entrance is either warmer or cooler than the area around it. This is a large area, in the dark, by the time we find it, the ceremony you claim to be happening tonight, will be over."

Carol glanced around at the trees in the area. She grabbed a nearby willow tree branch and broke it off. "This will do."

"What the hell are you doing?"

"I'm making a dowsing rod or as you Yanks call it, a witching willow."

"This is ludicrous, are you mad? We are going to burst into a heavily armed castle via some mumbo jumbo piece of wood. I mean don't they have to be blessed by Tibetan monks or something?"

"My shaman friend Charlie Stillwater showed me how to make one and use it one day for fun. The ends have to curve up and you hold in in the palms of your hands, palm up. Also practised a little the other day after reading it up on the internet."

"Skirt, you are seriously messed up, but I'll go along with this for now until I come up with a better plan." Jake followed behind her as her walked along. "And look I'll apologize for the incident on the boat. I wouldn't want this to go down in my records."

"Apology accepted and I won't report it either. But try a stunt like that again and I will report it. That's if you have any testicles when I'm done with you."

"Thanks, I really shouldn't have done that."

"Okay, enough. Just keep an eye out for anyone patrolling and let me do my thing. One of the Ley Lines runs across Victoria on a horizontal plane. The other runs down from the north to the west through part of downtown and connects here to the other."

"Lady, you're nuts. No one has even proved if these exist."

"Then explain why all of the oldest religious sites in Europe are built on straight lines. Several of which converge at Stonehenge and several at the pyramids of Giza."

"Really? I'm beginning to think you're one smart cookie; weird but smart."

After walking around long moments, nothing seemed to make the rod move. "Damn."

She looked up and a weird little elfish creature with blue flaming hair waved her to come towards it. She knew Jake couldn't see it. The little fairy from the hiking trail. *What's it doing here?*

She walked towards it, the rod began to twitch. "Here's one, the male and female earth energies are detectable by a dowsing rod, we're in luck." She followed the rod as it continued to twitch back a few feet, walking back and forth. "This one seems to run fairly straight. Which means the other is to the north."

Jake stood humbled, "I'll be damned. I was about to give up."

Yeah, me too, thanks blue fairy. "I have reason to believe that an entrance to some sort of spirit realm lies buried on this property. This is the real reason the mob are here; not for the wedding, but to bless the new venture by making a pact with Satan. Hereby ensuring their success."

Just then the rod twitched down again. Carol smiled. "Okay we follow this down to where it meets the other."

She stepped gingerly along walking back and forth as the dowsing rod kept moving. It indeed was moving down towards the other one when Cole noticed something in the dark.

"See that, that raised area there."

They moved towards what looked like a round rocky covering. It resembled a concrete manhole cover, just sticking out of the ground by a few inches, but it was made from local rocks cemented together.

"We found it. I'll be damned."

"We? Excuse me, make sure you get this right in your report. I found it; with this." Carol wanted to wallop him over the head with it.

He gripped the heavy lid and it a hard tug. "Damn! Weighs probably a hundred pounds or more."

"Sure you can lift it?"

"Lady I can bench-press over two twenty." He grunted and slid the cover over until it lay beside the entrance.

"Okay, ladies first." He tilted a flashlight down the entrance. "Seems to go down about twelve feet and veer towards the castle."

Carol pulled her phone free as he peered down the hole and hit send before Jake could see. She sent an alert beacon back to headquarters, just in case being below ground interfered with her phone. She didn't trust Jake, too much didn't add up. She stuffed it away and grabbed her light and down they both went through the dark tunnel, which was surprisingly dry and not damp like the Hall of Wonder.

A dim light ahead told them that they were approaching the other end. Quickly they came to an iron gate. Both had already shut off their lights. Carol glanced down the corridor. Chanting could be heard echoing down the hallway. She recognized some of the words being used, another language, which she guessed was the Enokian Agnes had mentioned earlier. "The ceremony has started."

Carol lifted the clasp and they went inside. The chanting seemed to come from the right. Where there was what appeared to be an open area. Jake glanced around, tried one of a couple of doors and tapped her on the shoulder. He motioned her inside after he looked in. "No one here."

They entered the dark room. Carol could make out chains hanging from the walls and a table with leather straps on it. It looked like a torture chamber of some sort. On the far wall next to the open area on the other side she spotted slits and flickering lights. Carol eased over, careful not to stumble into anything. Chanting was echoing through the stone walls from the room next door. Through the slits she saw over two dozen people all dressed in hooded black robes, so that no one was recognizable. All were standing around a large pentagram in red on the floor. Beside it two cages, containing two boys. "Got them. We can have them charged with abduction." She grabbed her phone and was about to send a text.

"What are you doing?"

"Calling in reinforcements, this ends here and now."

Jake grabbed a rag from his inside chest pocket and quickly clamped his hand over her nose and mouth and pinned her arms with his free arm. "Sorry lady, this does end here and now, only not how you imagined. I can't have you blowing my cover or putting a halt to this ceremony we set up so long to make work."

"We?" She struggled but he was bigger and stronger. Her phone cluttered to the ground as she tried to get her hands free. Carol only had moments before she'd have to inhale.

A door in behind them creaked open. The sound of approaching footsteps as the lights flickered dimly on.

"Oh, how nice. I see you've brought me a new play toy." A familiar harsh female voice spoke as the crack of a whip broke the air.

Carol inhaled at the realization she wasn't in a torture chamber, but in a bondage chamber and passed out again as Rebecca smiled at her.

"We meet again."

Chapter Seventeen

Carol's head thumped wildly as she tried to focus on the room that spun before her. The aftereffects of the chloroform. The hangover-like sensations pounding away would take maybe hours to subside. She tried to move and she realized her hands were tied together behind her and as she looked down, her ankles as well.

The snap of a whip cracking shattered the bounds of her throbbing head. Carol winced in agony. "What in the hell?"

A familiar voice she didn't think she'd ever hear again broke the air. "Welcome back, Ms. Moore. Or should I say Luigi's new plaything, Carol Ainsworth."

Crap I'd been set up. Again. Turning to Jake, Carol said, "Luigi? Luigi Rizzuto? The eldest brother?" *Gotta think, how am I getting out of this?*

Jake nodded in agreement, a sly smile came to his lips.

"Here I bloody thought you were an FBI agent, Cole Brady."

"Hey, a guy's got to make a living these days. Let's just say I trade some favors for a lot of cash."

"In your hotel room when she supposedly had tied you up. You weren't held against your will. You told me when we first met, you liked feisty woman. I think the term should have been dominating women. You were killing off the competition on the boat, you're working for the mob, and the FBI?"

He nodded again, strangely submissive. Carol knew who was in charge.

"Correct. He was just servicing his mistress, weren't you?" *Double frigging agent.*

"You murdered your father, didn't you? What, you gain entry to his room, long-lost heir coming back to make up? Something like that? That's why he let you in. He went to the mini-bar to get a drink to celebrate and you hit him from behind, then strangled him? That noose you killed him with, I found out Victoria would indeed import them up from San Francisco, but according to the tests it was about forty years too young. Once you killed him you locked the door and closed the anchor by way of, say, a piece of dental floss so it looked like an impossible murder? You son of a bitch, you set this all up. And me."

"Quite the detective, aren't you? I took the weapon and disposed of it. I knew I'd left the floss behind but really didn't think you were clever enough to make the connection. Oh well, we live and learn. At least I will."

"A sniveling embarrassment to him, hence why you aren't recognized as the senior son, but Lorenzo was instead. You'd rather play submissive boy toy to Mrs. Big Tits here than be his proud male son."

He is the cursed one, not Lorenzo. Jake stepped towards Carol and backhanded her. "Lady, a coward I am not. Our society doesn't favor the woman in charge. But now that my father is dead, I will become the capo of the clan, acting through Lorenzo. That is one of the things that will be celebrated tomorrow with the joining of the clans. Our successful actions on that ship will show that our clan is strong and ready to begin operations, partly under my command, through my undercover government connections."

She hadn't realized the depths of the mob's involvement in American government meddling. *He lets Lorenzo run the show, be the figure head, while he feeds them information from government sources. A true son of a bitch.*

"I saw you two the other night, getting quite cozy in the lifeboat. He told me how deliciously you were." Rebecca swam into view, she bent over and grabbed Carol hard by her cheek with one hand. She was dressed in black leather panties, with a cinched tight black laced corset, that accentuated her hips. Knee high leather boots on six-inch stilettos left just the thighs exposed. A short open leather top threatened to spill her large breasts out any moment as she thrust them forward. Hot red lipstick shone evilly in the dim light.

"How?"

"Drones. We had a drone setup and it didn't take him much convincing to enlighten us with his tale, did it, my slave." Becca ran her hand down the front of the oddly quiet Jake. She could see him stirring under his pants as she rudely fondled him. Carol struggled to sit up right, the room spun slightly. A glance told her that this time there were no breaking bonds or knots, she'd used plastic tie straps to secure her. Carol thought hard for a moment. "There wasn't a bomb on that boat was there?"

"Nope, I set that up. We had to take out that shipment of drugs to the Asian gangs." There was a report Carol heard yesterday of another ship that had been boarded and found with all the crew dead, its cargo holds empty. A suspected drug shipment sidetracked to the mob. "That luxury ship had been rigged up to either deceive authorities or to take out shipments for the Asian gang's which would have dealers and customers switching alliances to the mob."

"So, you're saying we weren't in danger of getting shot."

"Yeah. We were supposed to just hide in the lifeboat until the killings were done and then get out after I blew it up. Although I did enjoy groping you, too bad you weren't a little more inclined to have some fun together."

"Sick mother, trying to take me against my will. I'm glad women have began to stand up against guys like you."

"You liked it and in the end you're just a woman I had been instructed to get close to in order to learn some vital information for both the FBI and my fellow Rizzutos," he smirked slyly.

Becca, bored by chat that wasn't about her, interrupted. "Now as I recall the last time we got together I never got my rocks off because of you. If he hasn't told you, I'm not the kind of woman that likes being frustrated. So, I guess it will be your job to finish me off." She caressed the long handled whip as she talked, like she was still rubbing Luigi's hardness.

"Lady," Carol croaked trying to find her voice. "I don't do broads."

"Oh, when I'm done with you, you'll want to get me off. Trust me, before the devil has his way with you."

"What?" She fought to focus. She'd read about some of the deprived requirements of the ceremonies.

"Oh, you see he needs some human blood sacrifices, but what really binds his services to us is some delicious female slave to sink into, and guess who just joined the party?"

"Now my job is to get the dinner warmed up for him, if you know what I mean. Although I was hoping you were a little more adventurous, that's a shame because it really turns on some men watching two women pleasuring each other. As for me, if you haven't figured it out yet, I do. There's nothing like a bit of softness mixed with my testosterone, makes for a great night in a threesome. I think he'd like to see you on your knees, pleasuring me with the disrespectful mouth of yours."

Jake interrupted, "Carol, I'm so sad you found out. I really liked you.

But I guess you'd find out sooner or later and I'd have to kill you."

"You're such a bastard." She said trying to fight the haze that threatened to put her out. Wetness oozed from her lip. *I'm bleeding.*

"And you are going to be dead. But you know what? You're probably

the one of the best I ever had." He smiled with a smugness that made Carol want to knee him right between the gonads or grab those testicles again and crush them hard again.

"Probably? Hell, I get more excitement from my battery-operated boyfriend." His eyes opened in fury and he grabbed her by the throat.

"Easy Luigi, you do not see that she is baiting you?" Rebecca put her hand on his shoulder. "If you kill her here, then the ceremony will not finish. No, let me have my fun and then we give her to the Almighty One and he can finish her off while we watch."

Carol struggled to break free, but it was no use, she felt her fingers growing cold. The whip sang out again, but this time it kissed her back as Becca moved behind her.

"Yes, I think I'll enjoy watching this instead of breaking her neck," he growled.

Carol bit her lip as searing pain stung her. "Fuck."

Becca grabbed the front of Carol's shirt and tore it apart, buttons flying.

"What are you nuts?"

She pulled out a long-handled knife from the wall where it hung. Carol's eyes opened. "Don't worry, I'm not going to cut you. Inflict some pain, yes. I'm saving your blood for him." She cut the straps of her bra.

"You know you could just unclip me, that's a thirty-dollar bra." Carol was trying to rationalize with this woman that was crazier than a hoot owl at a barn dance.

"Could, but this is such more fun. Now, once I've your clothes off, anytime you're ready to pleasure your mistress just let me know. Because unlike you, I enjoy inflicting pain and receiving it. Quite exciting." She rubbed her crotch. A few quick moves had Carol down to just her panties as Becca cut away the fatigues.

"You, lady, are one fucked up chick."

"Correct, that's what Luigi loves about me. And you are going to lick me and well, until I'm satisfied. Or else the pain just gets worse. Would you like a little sample?"

Becca snapped the whip a couple of times across Carol's stomach and her breasts. She grunted in pain.

"Shit. That hurts, bitch," Carol gasped. *I won't give her the satisfaction of making me scream.*

"Ever wonder why so many people enjoy the Fifty Shades books and movies?" she asked, her wet tongue licked at Carol's ear as she talked.

"Not my scene."

"Well, I'm giving you a free lesson today, usually charge a fortune to frustrated men and women to do this."

"You get people to pay for hurting them?"

"Yeah, but don't worry. I can hurt you or make the pain, well shall I say, very sensual.

You'll be liking it in a moment."

She snapped the whip softly several times across Carol's legs and stomach. "Stay on your knees or I'll use some wax?"

"Wax? Go to hell."

"Have it your way and most apt choice of phrases. Because it is you that will be travelling there, shortly. But first, that rude disrespectful tongue will bring me much pleasure."

"I'll have you charged."
The whip flicked out several more times over her back in response.

She gasped in agony. Weighing the odds, as much as she didn't want to give Becca any oral satisfaction, the idea of hot wax dripped on her seemed less appealing. The whip sang softly across her inner thighs. Oddly heat began to build within.

"Enjoying that yet?" Becca dropped the long-handled whip and grabbed a short one. The woman moved behind her and shoved Carol forward. With one knee on her back to keep her still she flicked the whip across the back of her upper thighs and then on the cheeks of her ass.

"Get stuffed."
"Give me more time and I'll even get you turned on."

Even if I did, I'd not admit it to her and give her the satisfaction. Carol felt the heat along her thighs. *Damn, the pain is going somewhere I didn't want it to. The bitch knows her stuff.*

"I've done this many times and I can get anyone aroused and keep them on the edge forever.

Until they beg me for release."

"Cunt." It was rare she ever thought of using that word, but this woman deserved it. The heat was indeed building inside. *Never, would I have thought in a million years that this could be a turn-on. No wonder so many people bought the damn books.*

"Really, well I can make it hurt then." She snapped the whip across her back. Carol jerked in agony. She could feel the welts erupting as Becca tortured her with her whip.

Just then a large gong rang out.

"Fuck. They're ready for us," Jake said as he stared at a hole in the wall to the next room.

"Damn, that's twice you've frustrated me. I guess it will just have to be up to the man servant to finish me off after this is all over."

"Okay, tell them the main course is coming." Becca and Jake placed her on a mobile platform. "You're lucky, I was just beginning to get into this." Becca kissed Carol on the lips and licked her cheek. "Damn, would have enjoyed you. But I can't delay my Master any longer." Carol spat at her. The redhead backhanded her.

They tossed a long white robe over her body.

Becca stepped back and flicked a switch in the wall. Two large sections of the walls began to slide back. The lights in the room faded out until only blackness remained.

From beside her Carol she caught a waft of cold air and shadows moving. *What? There's someone or something in here with us.*

We will help as agreed, but bring the last of his linage to us or you will burn in hell with that foul creature and there is no further help due from us. There is another that will help, don't move until the moment is right or all is undone. We are one with the flames. The words whispered in her head.

Cold fingers tugged at her bonds, a sudden heat flared, and the plastic ties melted away like dripping wax and blood rushed back to her fingers.

Francis? No, the Lekwungen? She wanted more than anything to leap off the turntable she was mounted on. Carol spied her clothes beside her, the gun and its holster lay on top. It would be so tempting to leap off this device and put a bullet between both their eyes.

The moment, wait. You must wait. Whispered in her ears.

She remembered what Agnes told her about the ceremony.

Chapter Eighteen

About two dozen people filled the room eerie in their long black robes, hoods over their heads. A heavy breathing reverberated in the large chamber and a foul scent. From the center of the penta-gram a hideous figure rose, The Devil Incarnate. At the corner of each point of the pentagram a pot of coals burned on a four-foot-high pedestal and on the front one a crystal skull rested. *It can't be, is it?*

From what she had read, the devil was most vulnerable when he transversed from his realm to this one. In the pentagram he could be trapped, only once he was fully here.

"Thanks for that. I'll take over now." Becca strode regally into the room. Her whip coiled on her hip. She had donned a red flowing cape, the sign of the pentagram on it in black, her stilettos making an eerie clicking noise as she walked in.

Shit, that figures she was the master of ceremonies. Made sense. Bitch, wasn't kidding when she said she'd get even.

Becca bowed before the grotesque figure in the center and began to chant.

Ilas micalzolo obelre doa casare Aidagh era aftame qus ah Moza, maoffasa. Noca, hoatha Saitan!

We welcome you to this realm most powerful being. One of the burning flame! You are called to this kingdom: Move and appear before the mysteries of your creation! I am the same as you, a humble servant!

The true worshipper of the holiest King of Hell!

"Now, bring us the first of three gifts we offer, the gift of pleasure, followed by the gifts of blood."

Someone in the crowd gasped as Carol was rolled before the altar and her white covering pulled aside. Carol couldn't tell who it was behind the mask or who it came from. She shivered from the cool air on her nearly naked body.

The foul being in the pentagram growled. Carol gasped at the size of his phallic member as it dangled obscenely near his knees. It moved one cloven hoof forward materializing, now fully here, red lights from lands below flooding upward.

"Bombs away," yelled someone in the crowd as they lurched forward, grabbed Cider and flung it behind the hideous creature. It screamed in rage as a crystal skull filled the center of the pentagram and jammed itself into place. The red lights from below blocked.

"Carol, you know what to do," yelled Agnes. "He can't retreat, cut off his forward progress."

What to do? The moment. One with the flames. Fire flickered with a blue haze in the burners. *The Lekwungen.* Carol flung herself at one of the alters and knocked it over. The creature turned to lunge slowly at her still disorientated from its journey through the ether, she knocked another aside. Blue creatures erupted from the sparks and shards of coal and began to tear at the devil.

Rebecca screamed her rage and moved to stop Carol as the room filled with screams of beasts being tortured. The devil incarnate writhing in agony as the Lekwungen tore their rage into him.

Carol grabbed another pot of burning coals and threw them at Becca. Coals went flying, sizzling across the air. Landing all over her.

"Crazy bitch." Rebecca screamed, pulling her whip loose as she shook her head, her hair singed and melted away, smoke oozed from it. "You're going to pay for that."

"Takes one to know one."

A shot rang out. Her shoulder exploded in agony. Carol dropped the last hot pan. Charcoal exploding as it hit the ground. Jake took aim again, "Good bye, skirt. No one does that to my mistress." Another shot took her high in the chest. Blood spurted behind her. Carol crumpled to the ground as Jake took aim again. Her vision dimmed.

Flames from the pots flickered to life as figures emerged. Beings of fire, some licked at the wall hangings, they exploded in flames. Others ran after the mob of people, robes began to go up in flames. Pandemonium reigned.

Smoke billowed to the stone ceiling.

The Lekwungen.

Agnes leaped towards Jake and pushed him and Becca towards the raging beast trapped within the points of the pentagram, screaming its anger. It knew if it stepped off the pentagram it was trapped in this realm.

The beast grabbed them both by the throat.

A flash of fire as the blue beings followed Agnes and everything from within vanished.

She clutched at a rosary bead and the figure of Christ on the cross. The devil's hand burned at the touch and it dropped Agnes as the Lekwungen surged towards it and surrounded the pentagram. The beast grabbed Jake by the throat and in one smooth flick of its hand, a loud snap rang out. He flung the man from the circle as the mysterious blue winged Fairy being appeared. It stared at Agnes as she struggled to her feet and the bleeding Carol as she lay on the ground, blood pouring from her chest.

"You have no idea what you've done. For this you will have to pay," Becca said as she pulled her whip free.

The fairy flew into Becca and pushed her into the pentagram, screaming.

"No!" she screamed as the evil creature grabbed her. Saliva dripped from its mouth as it tried to fight off the Lekwungen raging all around it. Several exploded as it flung her around like a rag doll, swatting them away.

Then, its need for pleasure overruled everything else. It tore Becca's leather from her, the arousal taking over.

"Oh, looks like the main course is off, I think he'll enjoy the alternative instead," Agnes yelled to Carol as she rushed to her aid trying to stem the flow of blood.

The redhead screamed as the devil pulled her to him and sank his insidiously long tongue down her throat.

Using the creature's distraction, Agnes dove into the pentagram, grabbed Cider and continued rolling out of the way. Unable to support either end the circle collapsed into a black vacuum trapping the two within.

Only Agnes, the Lekwungen, and the still figures of Carol and Jake remained in the room as sirens began to echo outside. Rebecca's screams faded away as both her and the devil faded into some corner of hell to be trapped for all time.

Carol gasped, blood streaming from her chest and her mouth as Agnes came back to her and covered her nearly naked body with her robe. She tried to stem the flow of blood.

"This one is the last first-born male of the Rizzuto line, the one you seek," Agnes pointed to Jake. From the walls several smoking blue forms surge forth and grab his shadowy essence trying to leave the room. A background scream silently filled her ears as the fire ghosts grab his shadowy frame and pulled him back to the dank walls. *It is done. They echoed to her before disappearing. We may rest now, and we are released.*

Agnes cried out as Carol moaned. "I can't stop the bleeding. She's dying, you need to help her."

We cannot, we are already dead. The Lekwungen said, their voices echoing into the room as they began to flow upwards into the earth.

"You bastards. You can't leave her here like this. Hang on, Carol, hang on." Carol's body went limp. Blood oozing into the white sheet.

Carol cried out as nine white beings descended, called to her soul about to pass into their realm. The nuns in large flowing gowns and began to circle, forming the sign of the cross over themselves, praying.

The blue being began to follow the others upwards. Several turned and glared at it. "Stay away from us," they sneered.

The fairy sank to its knees, tearing began to flow down its face. *We are unwanted.*

"Have you no compassion in your heart. She freed you." Carol gasped fighting to keep alive.

"Angels are coming for me."

"No lady, keep fighting. They ain't going to take you today."

Agnes felt a cool blue hand on her shoulder as it pushed her aside. *Can we help, unsure?*

To not help, goes against us, our soul, our core. Why we were created.

She freed us, so we will die trying.

We are no better than them. And even they don't want us, they have left us behind.

We are free to go. But to not try, what good are we?

No better than them.

Agnes could see the being struggling inside itself overhearing its thoughts.

"Please, you must help her."

We, however are not Lekwungen, nor human but elemental like her. We shall try. The blue fairy creature sat on its knees before Carol. *She cared. She alone out of all of the others, loved us.*

No, we are released.
Agnes watched amazed as the creature continued arguing with itself.

We can go above, to the hill of butterflies. To dance in sun with them.
No, if we go we will be still alone forever.
We will stay and save the one that released us, or die trying.
The fairy bent over as the nuns continued praying louder than ever.

Ignoring them, the blue fairy leaned into Carol's mouth and kissed her. Sucking out a stream of hazy matter into itself it coughed twice spewing out shards of blue sparks which fluttered about the room like moths before each one popped.

Agnes watched the flow of blood stop. She grabbed the sheet and pulled it aside. Only a faint jagged throbbing blue scar remained where the bullet entered her chest.

The fairy slumped fighting to keep awake as it spat out two bullets.
The cycle calls we must heal. We are so weak.
Not yet. We are not yet done.

It blew its blue life essence into Carol and collapsed beside her. A blue halo surrounded Carol for a moment and she convulsed for a second before her eyes opened and she lurched upward as if shocked back to life. She felt her chest and wrapped the blood stained robe around herself. "You saved me."

We know. The blue being wrapped itself with its wings, before slowly surrounding itself in a blue cocoon.

Coughing, Carol whispered to it, "Thank you. I'll forever owe you for doing this for me.

Wait, I don't even know your name." *Neither do we?*

Carol thought a moment, remembering the bizarre sight across from the hotel when the butterflies lifted from the totem and she thought she was being watched. "Floats like a Butterfly."

So, we are called. We are not alone now.

A sigh came from the cocoon as it deepened in color and solidified.

The angels, no longer needed, flooded upwards into the ceiling.

Agnes watched them disappear before helping Carol up. "Well, can't say I've ever seen a blue fairy, nor live angels before. I'll cross that off my bucket list."

"And I can't ever say I've ever been so glad another woman kissed me."

"Safe to say you've got a tick off your bucket list as well."

They both laughed as they stood up, holding each other. Carol still very weak struggled to stand.

"Is she?" Carol asked, pointing to the cocoon.

"No, I think when they go to sleep or need to rebuild, they go into a cocoon to regenerate," Agnes replied.

"How do you know that? Let me guess you read its mind." Agnes smirked.

"And speaking of regenerating, where the hell did you come from? I thought you were gone."

"Me too, let's just say that was one hell of a trip. I gotta do that again if these old bones can take it." She picked up Cider and dusted her off, as the thud of heavy boots echoed down the corridors towards them. "Sorry ol' gal, didn't mean to get your backside toasty."

"Thanks for coming back and saving me," Carol said. "But how the hell did you pull that stunt off, crazy old broad."

"Well, I could murder a cup of tea and some of those finger sandwiches, tell you then."

Agnes watched as the police began to handcuff several of the Bellettis and Rizzutos milling about in the hallway. One of swat team opened the cages to release the two terrified boys and another came up to her and drew its handcuffs. "She's with me and the cocoon."

"You are?" He stared at her and went to grab his handcuffs like he was about to arrest her with the rest of the mafia suspects.

"Officer Ainsworth, of Vancouver PD, number 12655, fifth squad." Carol reached to flash her badge before realizing she was naked under the robe. "Oh, do I look like I have ID on me?" She opened her robe, his eyes bugged out.

"If you follow me, my clothes and badge are in the next room." She wrapped the robe around herself.

"Too bad about Jake, he was quite the hunk." Agnes winked.

Carol laughed. "You'll never change, will you? I hope I have half the spunk when I get to be your age. If I manage to live that long. Did you know he was a Mafia member?"

"No, that was covered by the devil and his spells. Oh, I've seen your future, and you do live that long. Although I think our Italian friends will not have quite the kind of wedding reception or hangover they expected."

Carol responded, "I think the only sound they'll be hearing tomorrow is the clink of jail cell doors and not wedding bells."

Agnes looked over at Jake's prone body. "And it looks like Victoria has just added another ghost to its collection."

Epilogue

Agnes explained to Carol all that she knew as they sipped at their tea.

"I had already learned from Cider that you wouldn't find Nathan when I was investigating the Jordon Gibson case. Gladys used the vortex to abduct him and Nathan and by doing so she inadvertently created a time loop. Something to do with time and relativity in dimension to space. Bit like that Doctor What's-his-name keeps on about."

"Doctor What? Don't you mean Doctor Who?"
"Thought you didn't watch science fiction?"

"I don't." *Although I might have found a reason to start.* "But everyone knows of Doctor Who."

"Anyway. All I know is that sometimes-bigger events are trapped inside one area of time than should be. So basically, time feeds back on itself, unable to get out. Hence why I couldn't get a grip on what had happened in that room and to Nathan. As they say on the show; it's bigger on the inside. So, I had to see your future in order to get ideas without you knowing about it." Agnes sipped back at her tea with one pinkie raised, like a high society woman, again dressed to the nines in her quaint yet distinguished frocked skirt and red brimmed cart wheel hat.

"You did this in order to save Nathan? Thank you. But how did you know this would work?"

"Well, I didn't the first dozen times."

"Dozen?"

"It's a time loop. Don't get it right and it starts all over again."

"This is confusing and really bizarre. I don't really get it."

"Ever watch the movie, Groundhog Day with Bill Murray? Every time he went to sleep, he woke up back to the same point in time, in essence repeating the day all over again. So, he has a lot of fun seducing a woman, creating a lot of trouble and having some fun. Finally, he knew what he had to do in order to end the cycle, because like you, you remembered me being here and no one else."

"I gotta watch more sci fi. I met someone who's a fan in all of this."

"I know." Agnes smiled like she knew a secret. "I figured out how to leave the clues I needed in order to break the cycle."

Carol frowned. "The size six shoe print in the dirt outside Nathan's window, the toys from 1990 and the flashbacks of me running over Gladys."

"Yes, that was due to the future echo time loop and with Francis' help in your dreams and at the Satanic Rituals."

"The figures aflame?"

"Can't take credit for that. I reckon it was the Lekwungen themselves."

"As for myself, who do I look in the future, old, fat and wrinkly? Or some drop dead mature woman, married with two point five kids?"

Agnes wiped at her lips. "I can't say much otherwise it would change the timeline. Well except, well done job, C.I. Ainsworth."

Just then Carol's private phone rang, no name, blank screen. "Probably bloody advertisers." She set it down, allowing it to go to voice mail. Oddly it kept ringing.

"What the? It's supposed to go to voice message after three rings. Excuse me, Agnes."

Carol rather annoyed picked up her phone, "Hello who is this?"
"Carol? Is that you?"

Stunned, it took a moment to realize. "Charlie Stillwaters? What are you doing calling me?" She stared at Agnes in shocked amusement. "Congrats. Your own series now, eh? I heard you were fighting Woo-woo critters without me. Thought I'd give you a call just to poke my head in there and get a scene-stealer like they do in the movies."

Carol blinked in disbelief several times as Agnes calmly sipped her tea with a little smirk on her lips. "How, the hell?"

"Ah you know the whole 'fundamental interconnectedness of all things' thing, I get news flashes via the underground vibes that travel through the roots. I thought I'd take a break from playing poker with my Buddhist monk buddy, Carman the squirrel and George the Sasquatch."

"How'd you reach me and get this phone to not go to voice mail. Couldn't you just send a text?"

"Text? On this new-fangled phone of mine? Not sure I can do that with the rotary dial."

"Rotary phone? That's analog. How'd you get it to work on a digital system?"

"Ah, bit tricky, but doable. Pulled a couple of weird smudging spells, let the pesky raccoons have a go at it with their hockey sticks and then dropped it a couple of times. Seemed to do the trick."

"Raccoons? What do raccoons know about phones and electricity? Or playing hockey come, to think of it?"

"Apparently a lot that they aren't letting on about with those opposable little thumbs of theirs. So just thought I'd congratulate you on the job well done and for starting the new spin-off series. Perhaps I'll cross over into it one of these days. And if you need a hand, just give me a ring. Gotta go, I think I just saw George catch Carman trying to slide a card out from under his sleeve. This is going to get ugly." Something crashed in the background and the sound of a body hit the ground. "Yeah, real ugly. Gotta go."

Carol shook her head in bewilderment. "He didn't even leave a number,"

she stared at her blank screen. "Doubt he needs to, dear." Agnes sipped at her tea.

"Oh yeah, that's sound like Charlie."

Carol caught the shimmering male figure enter the tearoom. "Shh, watch this."

The two watched as Matthew Begbie walked up to Margaret sitting there sadly and put his arm out. The woman looked up, intense surprise and a smile that hadn't decorated her face in decades spread ear to ear. The two, arm-in-arm, walked from the tearoom.

Agnes looked at Carol. "How?"

"Let's just say he owed me a favor after we released him from the curse. Part of that curse mentioned that he'd never marry. I put two and two together and paid Begbie a visit at the beach house yesterday. Asked if he'd do me a favor and ask Margaret out on a date. I'm afraid the

Garden City will have lost two of its prominent ghosts."
"What about our weird fairy friend that saved your life? Is she okay?"

"Yes, as you know I allowed the boys in blue to let me deal with her. I sent out a mental request to Sprity. She came to my aid and was more than happy to have a young protégé to look after. Kinda like a daughter, I suppose. So Floats with Butterflies is in good hands."

Agnes looked at her, "weird name."

"Lovely, but weird being. I'm getting used to being around the abnormal." She stared at Agnes and they both laughed.

"I get the feeling this creature has been formed from the joining of Lekwungen and the druggies in the sewers. Now, I've gotta go soon. I've got a date tonight with a rather handsome ghost hunter."

She'd emailed Brad earlier and he was very excited to meet her again.
"Danglepuss?" Agnes smiled and shook her head at her. "I know now

why you were called a Justifier. You seek justice even in matters beyond those of criminal endeavors. Now shall we murder the rest of these sandwiches and scones?" "Especially the scones. They are to die for." The two laughed.

CAROL STOOD IN THE Shelbourne vortex as the city collapsed all around her and only a dirt road remained. "Agnes told me about how you helped her. She suggested I come here to find you and say thanks."

Francis Rattenbury removed his black top hat and bowed in front of her. "I am but a humble servant of higher forces. My pleasure." He stepped back through the vortex. Carol watched him slowly shrink and fade away. The road quickly solidified and electric city lights blinked back into existence. *Well that was an interesting meeting, can't say I've ever had a thank you from a ghost before.*

Carol turned her back and walked back towards her car as the vortex began to fade away.

A Brightness flashed behind her. "What the..."

Francis stood there staring wide eyed clutching at his hat in both hands as a car zipped by.

"I thought you were gone."

"I did too. We've got a problem."

Where's the vortex and how is he here? "What kind of a problem?"
"Simply put, something's afoot."

Afterword

Other Novels by Frank Talaber
Stillwater Runs Deep Series

Book One: Raven's Lament

(based on a true incident)

A madman cuts down a rare tree in protest of logging, releasing something he didn't intend to. Reporter Brooke Grant investigates the story, finds the love of his life, only to lose her to said being. Enlisting the aid of a deranged shaman he has to save his love and stop the world from being changed forever.

Book Two: The Lure

EVER GO OUT DRINKING and don't remember what you did? What if there was a bar where spirits use your body for whatever they want until you sober up? What if the city's mayor has been murdered, his family missing, no clues and a witch has been released from her centuries old imprisonment? A deranged shaman shows up leaving clues and vanishes. So begins police detective, Carol Ainsworth's first big case.

Book Three: The Awakening

HOW ANGRY WOULD A MYTHICAL god be if he found himself beginning to awake inside a mortal after centuries? A deranged shaman breaks his way into jail to stop all hell from breaking free while police detective Carol Ainsworth has to bring justice to a forest being's murdered mother.

(**Characters from the *Stillwater* Series mentioned in this novel are noted below**)

Raven's Lament – Book One

Charlie Stillwater: Mad Haida Shaman. Has command over several animal spirits who will come to his aid when needed. Zany sense of humour and still in love with the Montreal Expos despite the many years it has been since they left him. Our first meeting sees him battling with the Haida God Raven, who, when released from his incarceration by the cutting down of the Golden Spruce tree, decides he does not like what has become of his world and people and decides to change it all back.

Martin Crow: Raven's human form. As with all ravens, he is always ravenous so it is not surprising that on his first meeting with Charlie he insists he buy lunch.

The Lure – Book Two

Charlie Stillwater: Charlie is again battling another spirit released into our world, this time a witch who was transformed into a rock for previous misdeeds and left to rot in Stanley Park.

Carol Ainsworth: Newly promoted detective, her first assignment is investigating the death of Vancouver's Mayor, who's been brutally slain in Stanley Park. Guess who she meets here?

Martin Crow: Brief appearance in a bookstore to spook Carol and slander Charlie.

The Awakening – Book Three

Charlie Stillwater: Bluffs his way into position of Elder at Prince Rupert's penitentiary as psychic shockwaves have warned him trouble is coming and this, for some reason, is the place to be.

Carol Ainsworth: Virtually press-ganged by Charlie into assisting, she works under-cover as a prison guard in the female section.

Martin Crow: Much the same as in The Lure only this time in the grocery store. Guess Raven's turned into a bit of a stalker.

Gyhldeptis: Haida spirit of the forest. Seeking justice for someone close to her, she enlists Carol's help, knowing she is a Justifier.

REVIEWS Of The Joining

I hate you! My wife, who is off on medical leave, won't get out of the bathroom. Can't put your book down. LOL.

Bruce W.

The ghosts of Victoria, BC are restless. The Joining is a riveting read for crime fiction lovers and those fascinated by tales of hauntings. Talaber expertly draws you into a multi-leveled world of local history, crime, and the supernatural, where a blue fairy, comprised of two sorrowful creatures, is more powerful than it knows. A perfect read for those foggy West Coast nights.

Melanie Cossey, A Peculiar Curiosity

I bought four of his novels, all right up my alley, urban Fantasy and Paranormal thrillers. But as we were leaving my girlfriend opened up the copy of The Joining, I had purchased and said, "Stop! You gotta go back I have to buy this book." Frank had hooked her in the first three pages. Well Done.

Joyce Nicholls

I've read and reread his previous series, Stillwaters Run Deep, several times. Frank's writing is original and compelling. You run into characters and situations totally unexpected. Keeps you on the edge of your seat and your heart.

Greta Olsson

Oh my goodness!! Frank Talaber, I cannot even begin to describe how much I love your book The Joining. I am in the middle of reading it right now and I am LOVING this book! Honestly this is one of the best books I have ever read and I am so excited to read more books by you. I love that The Joining is set in Victoria. I live on the mainland and I recognize names of some places in this book and I was honestly so ecstatic to be reading a book that takes place in BC. You are an amazing writer I have no idea how you came up for the concept of this book but it is fantastic. Also, are the legends featured in this book actually real legends?

Ava Hobbs

Authors Note: To answer Ava's Question

Yes, the ghosts of Victoria mentioned in this novel are indeed real. I believe in incorporating as much realism as possible. So, if you go there one day and stand in those places you'll get a real feel of the events, the streets and the beauty of the history of Victoria.

Further Answers To Those Wondering If There's Ghosts In Victoria And Why

Walking into the stunning lobby of the Fairmont Empress in Victoria, BC, Canada, with its amazing multi-faceted crystal chandelier, you'd never know that, among the thousands of tourists, walk several ghosts.

Its designer, Francis Rattenbury, who died a very lonely death in England after being bludgeoned to death by the very young lover of his second wife is reported to be one. As a bold young architect he moved to Canada and won his first blind entry into designing the BC parliament buildings by signing it, 'local Canadian architect'. Then built the five-star hotel that everyone views as they come into Victoria, The Fairmont Empress.

Another is Margaret from Calgary, an elegantly dressed older woman, taking afternoon tea, always searching for her would-be beau. On the outlook for the man that admired her large-brimmed hats. She passed away in her room, having lived there for months on end in the winter. The room later became the un-rentable room as lights would flicker and TV channels would change.

Working on the redesign of the hotel when the Fairmont chain bought it two construction workers quit when they spotted a man hanging from the rafters. In fact, a man did hang himself in that room decades earlier in the fifties.

There are reports of maids being spotted long after their deaths, still servicing the rooms. A woman who knocks on the suites' doors trying to find her room. Guests who try to help her are surprised when she leads them to the elevators and vanishes.

Bastion Square, in central Victoria. The site of the original cemetery, was covered over and built on. None of the nearly thirteen hundred bodies were moved, only the headstones, some of which were found in an old storehouse. "You left the bodies and you only moved the headstones". Okay, I pinched that from a very famous movie (PS. I've talked to some of the store owners and yes they have crazy stories of things that have happened). Wonder if things fly about in nearby buildings!

The ground of the original cemetery under Bastion Square gets water soaked in the rainy spring and often coffins, which are sealed tight, would come shooting out of the ground.

They hired guys with long steel poles to smash the coffins in on the sides to let them in the water after the mourners left, for a couple of years before moving the cemetery to Ross Bay.

In the late 1800's Jacob Sehl came to Victoria from Germany. He bought the land at the end of the inner bay and began to build his furniture factory there. Clearing the land, the workers complained of boxes falling out of the trees, along with bones and bodies inside them. Not being very respectful of native traditions, at that time, they either burnt or tossed everything into the ocean. The Lekwungen chief was outraged, claiming they've disturbed the dead and the spirits were now trapped here, as they believed the dead spirits still live and had set up an entire village for them to dwell in. The Lekwungens moved away from the area, fearing for what might happen. A few years later, Jacob's house caught on fire and oddly enough at that same time a mile away, his factory did as well. Mrs. Sehl claimed she saw beings, hair aflame stoking the fires. She died a few months later of insanity."

The Lekwungens were correct in stating the dead ones would be trapped here. By destroying the dead remains of their bodies, their souls can't leave this realm and continue on their journey's growth.

William Pendray then bought the land, several years later. So, on the land now known as Deadman's Point, where the village paying homage to the Lekwungen deceased once stood. He decided to build his own factory on it.

He installed a very advanced sprinkler system, at least for its time, in the factory, obviously being somewhat cautious regarding what happened to the previous owner. He went to inspect the factory one day shortly after opening and a large chunk of the sprinkler pipe overhead broke away falling thirty feet, crushing his head.

His only son, Ernest, came racing up to the factory the hearing of this on his horse drawn carriage when the horse jolted to a stop and Ernest was flung off the carriage onto the ground in front of the horse. The horse bolted right over the prone man crushing his head. Their ghosts are the ones believed to still inhabit Pendray house at the sight of Huntington Manor Hotel next to Laurel Point, as it is now called.

Perhaps that, and the fact that ley lines are reported to cross the area, is the reason that Victoria is the most haunted city in North America.

And Above All Else

To my wife Jenny; who does all of my corrections, grammar and proper punctuation before the rest of the world, and any editor, gets to see it, along with putting up with all of my sh*t. This novel and all of my others wouldn't be possible without all of her work.

PS. And she still loves me unconditionally (also she just edited this over my shoulder!).

If you really enjoyed this Novel,
Please, feel free to leave a review

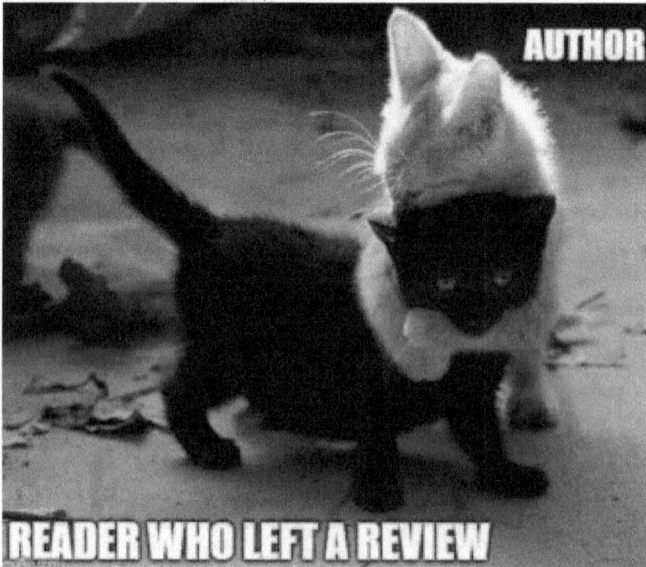

The author will highly appreciate it
Thank You!
AFTERWORD
Other Novels by Frank Talaber
Stillwater Runs Deep Series

BOOK ONE: RAVEN'S LAMENT
(based on a true incident)

A MADMAN CUTS DOWN a rare tree in protest of logging, releasing something he didn't intend to. Reporter Brooke Grant investigates the story, finds the love of his life, only to lose her to said being. Enlisting the aid of a deranged shaman he has to save his love and stop the world from being changed forever.

REVIEWS

YOU BASTARD!! I PURCHASED Raven's Lament from you. I don't like your genre or your style of writing. All this woo woo stuff and moving underground through the root systems, it's not for me, I thought. Until I read the first chapter and couldn't put it down. I had to keep reading to find out how you would bring the story together. Then I bought another four books! You bastard! I met you at another event last week and bought another four books. Now, I can't wait for your next books to come out. You have hooked me! Did I mention you're a bastard?!

Barry Harris

This novel has the ring of an epic "Lord of the Rings" journey -this is one journey that I'll always remember!

Stephanie A. Bridgeman/ The Glow Faeries

This is one of these books that you don't want to lay down until it's finished. Great stuff!

Tara Swanson

"After being stranded twenty kilometers from the nearest road at the tip of Rose Spit, Haida Gwaii, and having to push Frank's spanking new SUV a few kilometers along the beach before the tide came in and we ran out of booze, my first reaction on being asked to write a back cover blurb was, "over my dead body." Some people will do anything to get an endorsement."

Susan Musgrave/Cargo of Orchids/Given

On the west Coast, a journalist investigates a killing linked to destruction of old growth forest on First Nations land, and finds a spirit war as well as a real-work environmental struggle. He also finds love and meaning. It's a lovely, timely story line, and the outcome is arrived at in a surprising confluence of plot and subplot which makes the book ultimately charming and moving.

Candas Jane Dorsey

WHISTLER INDEPENDENT BOOK AWARDS Fiction Evaluation

Easy to follow and immerse oneself into this well-told story.

The pace unfolds so naturally, I forgot that I was reading - which is essential to achieving this result.

Loved the narrative voice that brought Characters to life through vivid descriptions and unforced dialogue.

Time and place are masterfully captured through poetic and beautiful imagery.

The writing style is wonderful, a celebration of words, both visual and imaginative.

This story has depth, the themes are heartfelt and lingered long after I finished reading it.

The pulse of energy - otherworldly, Raven's Lament is a classic in waiting with dream-like narration. I loved every inch of it.

[Thanks Frank & good luck!]

Molly Harrison

WiBA Coordination

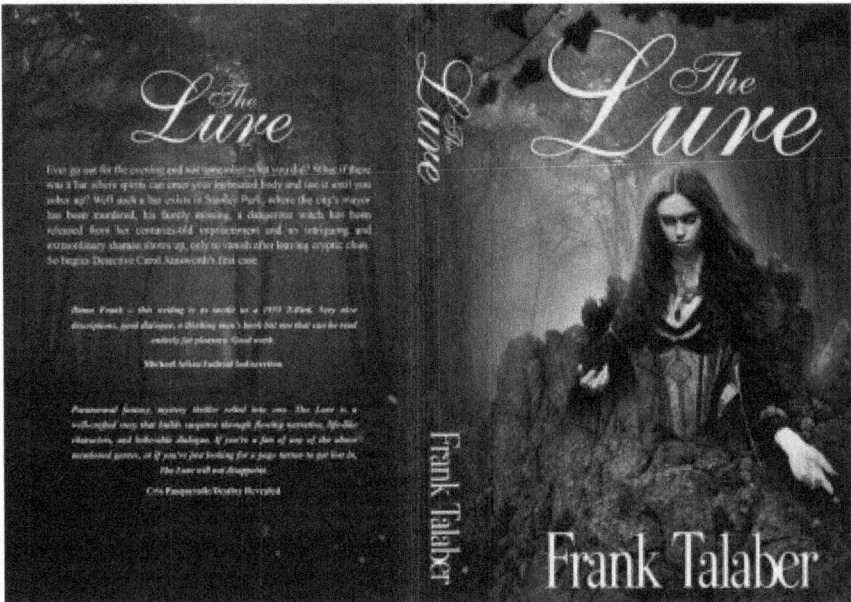

BOOK TWO: THE LURE

EVER GO OUT DRINKING and don't remember what you did? What if there was a bar where spirits use your body for whatever they want until you sober up? What if the city's mayor has been murdered, his family missing, no clues and a witch has been released from her centuries old imprisonment? A deranged shaman shows up leaving clues and vanishes.

So begins police detective, Carol Ainsworth's first big case.

REVIEWS

Your book kept my attention riveted from beginning to end. I liked the way you presented the female character being in control of the outcome and the fact the story was based on local settings. i.e. Victoria, B.C. Canada Riveting Work .....

Linda Low

A refreshing change from the usual and all too familiar cast of deities and spirits. Talaber pulls his characters from the vast and untapped riches of aboriginal myth and legend, bringing to life their intricate stories largely unfamiliar to wider audiences. He intertwines their ancient tales with the dark, gritty and dangerous under belly of contemporary urban life. The whole makes for an interesting and compelling read with an ending that's impossible to predict.

Robert Winslow

Damn Frank—this writing is as tactile as a 1955 T-Bird. Very nice descriptions, good dialogue, a thinking man's book but one that can be read entirely for pleasure. Good work.

Michael Arkin/Judicial Indiscretion

Paranormal fantasy, mystery thriller rolled into one. The Lure is a well-crafted story that builds suspense through flowing narrative, life-like characters, and believable dialogue. If you're a fan of any of the above mentioned genres, or if you're just looking for a page turner to get lost in, The Lure will not disappoint.

Cris Pasqueralle/Destiny Revealed

A gritty book flavored with primitive urges and mysticism. As I followed Carol's foray into the realm of shamanism, I realized that it took a special touch to pull off a complicated plot the way you did. Your prose was concise, powerfully descriptive, the dialogue lively, and your photographic mastery of the fixtures and streets in Vancouver's hub, in clear evidence.

Kenneth Edward Lim/The North Korean

Carol, the head detective, has to solve several murder cases: with many twists and turns. There's Shamans, Animal Spirits, and "The Lure" thrown in for good measure. No wonder, Carol wanted to resign! Yes, this novel is a roller-coaster ride, with the author cleverly hinting along the way, ending with a roller coaster ride! Read this book. It is different. It's as if Elmore Leonard has risen as a shaman, to guide others to write about Indian lore.

Nancy Bridgeman

Your book was a rollercoaster ride thorough my emotions which, when I got off, left me stunned and breathless.

Your portrayal of sociopaths and the criminal mind in the pursuit of the sexually **willing** was so disturbing I had nightmares and had to set the novel aside for days. But the writing was so compelling I had to finish it, and I'm glad I persevered.

I literally cheered "go get them!" when Charlie used his protectors to deal rather uniquely with the antagonists. I was enlightened to the Native spiritual culture which pleased me for which I now have a greater understanding and respect.

Carol G.

I want the author to take me to their world. I love the adrenaline rush I get from reading a book that scares the crap out of me. You know, the ones that have you screaming to the characters in your head or out loud. It tells me that the author did his or her job by getting me emotionally involved. I give up on books if I don't feel something. This book isn't one of those.

April Wolfgong

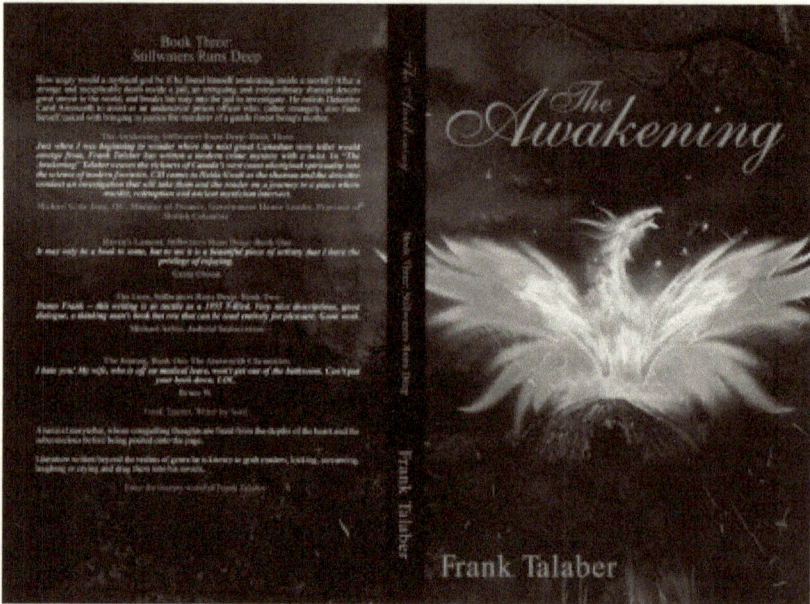

BOOK THREE: THE AWAKENING

ITS GHOSTBUSTERS TEAMED up with a female Mickey Spillane who has a Native Shaman sidekick nuttier than a squirrels winter stash as a side kick.

Agatha Christie, roll over in your grave, new sleuths on the prowl. A deranged shaman breaks his way into jail to stop all hell from breaking free while police detective Carol Ainsworth has to bring justice to a forest being's murdered mother. How angry would a mythical god be if he found himself beginning to awake inside a mortal after centuries? The duo are determined to find out who killed the previous native elder before all lightning and thunder breaks loose. They encounter deranged inmates, mystical beings, ancient serpents, wood sprites and someone who should have been

dead long ago.

Not your usual crime/mystery!

Not your usual criminal investigators!

You thought Jack Nicholson was mad in The Shining...

Wait until you meet Charlie Stillwaters in the Sweat lodge.

REVIEWS

There are many aspects true to First Nation's beliefs. For example the transformation of animals and anomalies within our realm. Frank Talaber's writing is clear and concise, leaving no grey areas. But his true talent as a writer is not only a sense of time, history and capturing First Nation's humor, but going from the real to the surreal and the supernatural. A gift he plies very well.

Tom Patterson Nuu-Cha-Nulth Artist and Master Carver

Just when I was beginning to wonder where the next great Canadian storyteller would emerge from, Frank Talaber has written a modern crime mystery with a twist. In "The Awakening" Talaber weaves the richness of Canada's west coast aboriginal spirituality into the science of modern forensics. CSI comes to Haida Gwaii as the shaman and the detective conduct an investigation that will take them and the reader on a journey to a place where murder, redemption and ancient mysticism intersect.

Michael G. de Jong, QC, Minister of Finance,
Government House Leader, Province of British Columbia

REVIEWS Of The Joining

I hate you! My wife, who is off on medical leave, won't get out of the bathroom. Can't put your book down. LOL.

Bruce W.

The ghosts of Victoria, BC are restless. The Joining is a riveting read for crime fiction lovers and those fascinated by tales of hauntings. Talaber expertly draws you into a multi-leveled world of local history, crime, and the supernatural, where a blue fairy, comprised of two sorrowful creatures, is more powerful than it knows. A perfect read for those foggy West Coast nights.

Melanie Cossey, A Peculiar Curiosity

I bought four of his novels, all right up my alley, urban Fantasy and Paranormal thrillers. But as we were leaving my girlfriend opened up the copy of The Joining, I had purchased and said, "Stop! You gotta go back I have to buy this book." Frank had hooked her in the first three pages. Well Done.
Joyce Nicholls

I've read and reread his previous series, Stillwaters Run Deep, several times. Frank's writing is original and compelling. You run into characters and situations totally unexpected. Keeps you on the edge of your seat and your heart.

Greta Olsson

Oh my goodness!! Frank Talaber, I cannot even begin to describe how much I love your book The Joining. I am in the middle of reading it right now and I am LOVING this book! Honestly this is one of the best books I have ever read and I am so excited to read more books by you. I love that The Joining is set in Victoria. I live on the mainland and I recognize names of some places in this book and I was honestly so ecstatic to be reading a book that takes place in BC. You are an amazing writer I have no idea how you came up for the concept of this book but it is fantastic. Also, are the legends featured in this book actually real legends?
Ava Hobbs

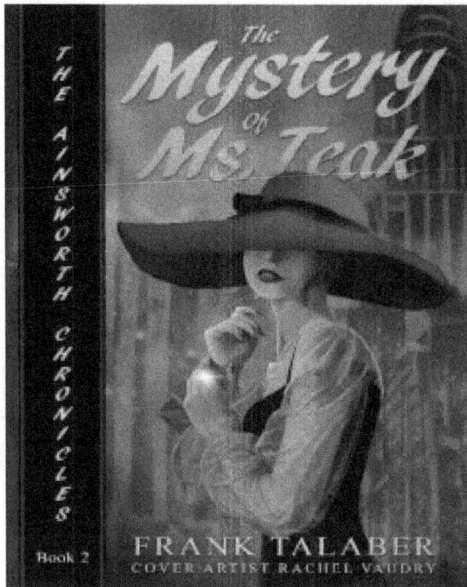

THE AINSWORTH CHRONICLES, BOOK TWO: THE MYSTERY OF MS. TEAK

Agnes at her craziest best. Only what secret does she have to hide from herself and the one she thought dead? How does one psychic stop another from hunting her down, especially when the other hires the services of a mystical being long thought perished!

WHAT IF IN ORDER TO save a young boy's life Agnes, our esteemed psychic, had to alter timelines?

As for Carol, she has her hands full with pissed-off Russians, the reborn builder of much of Victorian Victoria (yes, *the* Sir Francis Rattenbury), a young girl claiming to be our aforementioned psychic, and, to top it all off, there's something very wrong with Nathan, her nephew that they saved from death. And as for our psychic, Ms. Teak? She ain't helping much, is she! But in traditional English fashion High Tea is *of course* still being served.

REVIEWS

Do not read this book! Seriously, do not read this book - unless you are prepared to deal with a rift on your personal timeline. You will find that this book causes you to postpone activities that you would otherwise be doing.

You will be transported into a world of history and mystery, crime and grime, Spirits and other worldly time travel, with the delectable Detective Carol Ainsworth.

An amazing tale, which I thoroughly enjoyed.

Paddy Kopieczek

Fasten your seatbelt as Frank Talaber takes you on a multidimensional trek through time where history comes alive to reveal buried secrets and tortured souls. From the stately tea salons of old Victoria to the haunting desolation of British Columbia's rugged West coast waters, The Mystery of Ms. Teak will both entertain and invite you to confront the demons that live within us all.

Michael de Jong

I hate you, I can't put this book down. Every page gets more interesting, suspicious, wondering what is going to happen next. I sit down to only read one more chapter but end up having to read two more, because I need to know what happened in the past. Each chapter keeps you wanting more and now I hate it even more since I can't get to it before Long weekend coming up. I just read the last six chapters, clinging to every word, every sentence thinking I know what is going to happen next. Oh no, you take me in a completely different direction. Great book.

Sandy Strebe

Cover Not Yet Released

The Ainsworth Chronicles, Book Three: Into The Dark Side

Carol Ainsworth dives deeper into darkness as she tracks a cunning serial killer disguising murders as drug overdoses. Alongside her shaman ally Charlie Stillwaters, who faces off once more with the enigmatic Raven, the team must confront a disturbed vigilante targeting drug dealers. This dark and gritty psychological thriller explores the depths of human despair—and the supernatural forces watching from the shadows.

Seeds Of Ascension Book One: Spirits Awakening

IN A NORMAL RELATIONSHIP a man gets married and has the time of his life on a memorable honeymoon in Hawaii. A small dilemma begins for Roger Harrison when normality ceases existing with the discovery of metallic alien metal planted in his body.

Roger is thrust onto a path he never dreamed his life would ever take as one of the chosen few to start something that philosophers and spiritualists have discussed for centuries; the Ascension of humanity.

Only this isn't how the human race's next level of evolution was supposed to happen, and nor did Roger think he was the guy that would pull it off.

Toss in a guardian angel, alien hunters and Roger soon begins to realize his life's perfection ends with the understanding that memories are the illusion to which reality is draped and all is rarely as it seems in the journeys of a soul's growth. Especially when he doesn't even know how to spell chakra, let alone deal with having to master the seven levels in order to attain ascension.

Nor can time, as he knows it, be measured in heartbeats or lifespans and a heavy price must be exacted in order to stand in the gateway between memory and knowing, reality and illusion.

Especially when that effort means stopping those who would doom humanity's next phase of evolution.

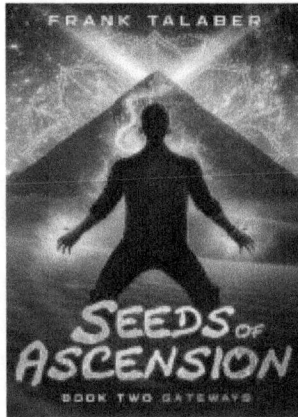

Seeds Of Ascension Book Two: Gateways

Roger discovers his guardian angel is not only real,
but an alien that needs his help,
in order for humanity to reach ascension
with the rest of the universe.
This thrusts him into unlocking the portals needed
to reach this goal.
That and him discovering the true essence
of what he is to become,
by learning about the spiritual chakras within him
and having to pass these tests.

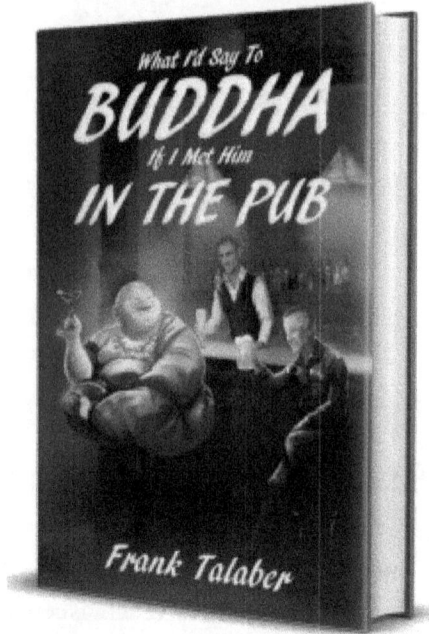

Short Story Anthology Volume One:
What I'd Say To Buddha If I Met Him In The Pub
(Includes Sylvia's Sun-catchers, voted #1 by the readers in
Rejected Manuscripts Anthology)
ENTER THE LITERARY world of Frank Talaber, Canada's
Foremost Off-Beat Author

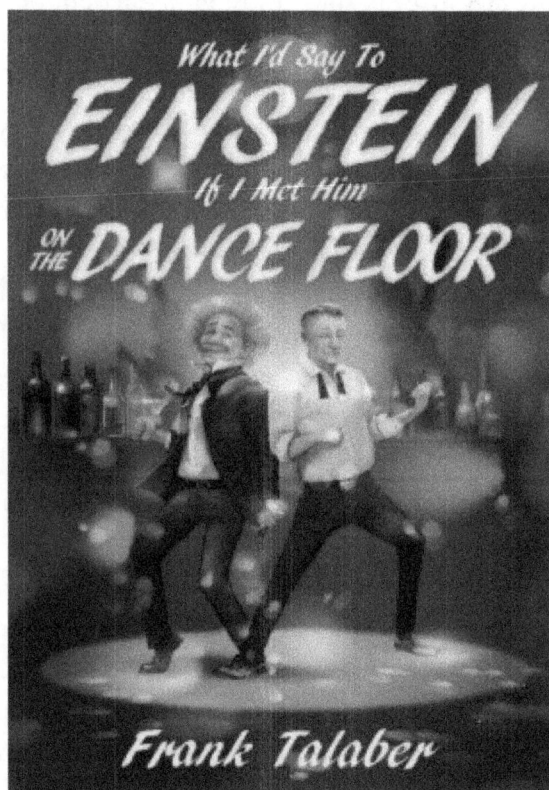

Short Story Anthology Volume Two:
What I'd Say To Einstein If I met Him On The Dance Floor
(Includes Sylvia's Sun-catchers, voted #1 by the readers in
Rejected Manuscripts Anthology)
Enter the literary world of Frank Talaber, Canada's Foremost
Off-Beat Author

FRANK'S BIO

THE AUTHOR HAS BEEN told, 'Most guys can't do romance, let alone write it. Nor want to.' Hence the pseudonym, Felicity Talisman in his more romantic writing ventures which are listed below this bio.

Born on the wild Canadian prairies but tired of the winter months in Edmonton, Frank immigrated to the more temperate cedar forests of coastal British Columbia. Yes, they get snow in Chilliwack during the winter months, and on that odd occasion Frank is forced to search out the snow shovel, dust off the cobwebs and have a go. At the snow, not the cobwebs.

His run-of-the-mill day job of auto technician/service advisor seems at odds with being an inspired, off-the-wall, author, but his zest for life, the environment, and the little muses that won't let his pencil stay still, spring from his mother's Hungarian ancestry. It's the Gypsy blood, he says, which pounds through his veins with wild abandon, driving him to the realms of fantasy.

This is the muse inside, the essence of Frank Talaber.

People who have read Frank's books describe him as a natural storyteller who writes like his soul is on fire and his pencil is his voice. They go further to say that they find his books grabbingly intense and hilarious at times, screaming everyday life from such a realistic viewpoint you're drawn into his world, hook, lime and plum bob, unable to stop; almost cursing that they can't set the book down, page after page. Frank takes great pride in the realism of his work, painstakingly visiting most of the locations, (obviously, only the "real-life" ones!) and he is so thorough that many readers have remarked that they can hear, taste, visualize, smell and feel the essence of the place. "It really is like being there" one remarked. There isn't a greater compliment to be made.

His tagline is Canada's Foremost Off-beat Author (also the name of his YouTube channel; check it out for his witty and informative videos) who writes in urban fantasy, science fiction, crime, spiritual, romance, erotica and comedy genres. Well, anything that comes to him, basically! Except westerns. Although he does like to ride Gangnam style; does that count?

To date he has over fifty articles/short stories, sixty blog posts, over ten interviews and fifteen novels written or published.

One novel, The Joining, top three finalist in the Canadian Book Club Awards in 2020, out of nearly two hundred entries.

And to be honest, I love to write novels, like a rock star that loves to thrill an audience and get that response that I've moved them, made them laugh, cry, scream and dream. But overall entertain them in a way they have never been entertained before unable to put the book down.

Literature written almost beyond genres, whose compelling thoughts are freed from the depths of the heart and subconscious before being poured onto the page. Or, as he often says, "you don't have to be mad to be a writer, but it sure helps".

Novels Under the Pseudonym Felicity Talisman

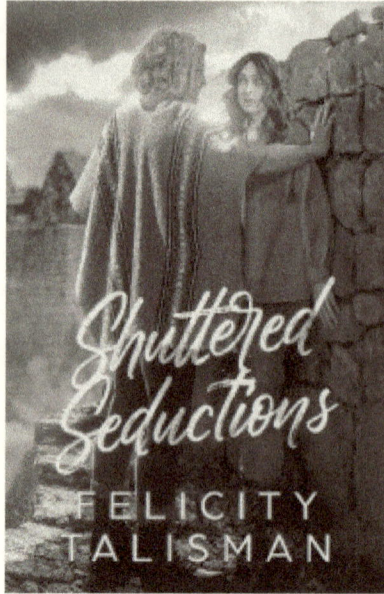

Shuttered Seductions Romance Novel

She only wanted Not to fall in love with him.
He only wanted to steal her company. Roy only wanted to
seduce Julia-Rae and convince her to sell him her company.
Julia-Rae wanted to shut him out of her heart like
every other man that ever got close. Only what do you do
when you fall in madly in love with the enemy
and the enemy with you. Will the dark secrets they hold
tear them apart or bring them closer together?

Autumn's Summer

WRITTEN IN HIS WIFE'S hand a beautiful leather-bound diary is delivered a year after her passing which contains many secrets. Showing how his lonely empty-nester wife's life changed profoundly after a purely-by-chance meeting in, of all places, a mundane, corner grocery store. She embarks on a voyage of discovery with the spiritualist, Summer, to find new meaning to her life, that, once commenced, transports her to realms and dimensions she never knew existed.

A contemporary literary romance novel mixed with a suspense-filled mystery thriller. The writer combines magical realism and paranormal urban fantasy on a profoundly spiritual level unlike any novel you have ever, or will ever, read.

Reviews

I thought I'd have a quick peek at Autumn's Summer and then finish the book I was currently reading! I was entranced and spellbound from that moment, my current read neglected! Couldn't put it down, read it in one day. Yes, the love scenes were intense, passion blossoms in many forms! I enjoyed this immensely!

Shelley W.

Run, don't walk to your nearest bookseller and pick up a copy of Felicity Talisman's Autumn's Summer. I didn't know what to expect from the book, but I was immediately drawn into the world the author has created. It has everything a reader could want, real characters in a fantasy world while bridging the gap between fantasy and reality.

Great job by this Canadian author!

Greenhill

What's A Lady Got To Do To Fulfill Her Life

TWO HEART-WRENCHING tragedies in the same week served as a stark reminder of the brevity of life. It was time for Leanne to free herself from the humdrum world of real estate and fulfill her heart's desire. The need to achieve her dream became even more poignant when she discovered her mother had carried the same dream of wanting to paint, but self-doubt had prevented her from even trying.

Leanne embarked on a road-trip to Banff, a town nestled in the heart of the magnificent Rocky Mountains, surrounded by the most perfect of nature's beauty. Since this was where her parents had fallen in love, it felt crucial to achieve their shared dream there. However, unbeknownst to Leanne, her run-of-the-mill road-trip turns into anything but and her journey to fulfillment becomes even stranger than fiction.

Don't miss out!

Visit the website below and you can sign up to receive emails whenever Frank Talaber publishes a new book. There's no charge and no obligation.

https://books2read.com/r/B-A-FCHU-QVRZB

BOOKS 2 READ

Connecting independent readers to independent writers.

About the Author

Frank Talaber was born in Beaverlodge, Alberta, where the claim to fame is a fox with flashing eyes in the only pub, yeah, big place, that's why his family left when he was knee high to a grasshopper and moved to Edmonton, Alberta. Eventually he got tired of ten months of winter and two of bad slush and moved to Chilliwack, BC. Great place, Cedar trees, can cut the grass nine months of the year and, oh it does snow here once or twice. Just enough to have to find out what happened to the bloody snow shovel and have to use it. GRRR.

He's spent most of his life either fixing cars or managing automotive shops and is a licensed automotive technician. However it's the little muses that keep twigging on his pencil won't let his writing pad stay blank.

He's had several short stories published, short-listed in contests over the years and a few automotive articles published in RV magazines, including one story that was entered into an anthology of over 300 entries, voted #1 by the readers. He has several novels published, which include the genres of urban fantasy, thriller, crime and romance. He also has written in science fiction, spiritual, erotica and comedy genres as well. This novel, The Joining, was entered into the 2020 Canadian Book Club Awards and made a top three finalist.

When asked once, "where does this creativity spring from?" He answered, "It's the Gypsy blood from my mother's Hungarian ancestry."

Literary madness that drives his wife crazy when he leaves their bed in the middle of the night to pound out some sort of prosaic induced brilliance. "Here we go again, the next War and Peace, Aka 21st century," she moans, only to realize it's either gibberish or there's no lead in his pencil and he's scribbled on sixteen blank pages in the dark.

When asked about Frank Talaber's Writing Style? He usually responds with: Mix Dan Millman (Way of The Peaceful Warrior) with Charles De

Lint (Moonheart) and throw in a mad scattering of Tom Robbins (Even Cowgirls Get The Blues).

PS: He's better looking than Stephen King (Carrie, The Stand, It, The Shining) and his romantic stuff will have you gasping quicker than Robert James Waller (Bridges Of Madison County).Or as is often said: You don't have to be mad to be a writer, but it sure helps.

Read more at https://franktalaberpublishedauthor.wordpress.com.

www.ingramcontent.com/pod-product-compliance
Lightning Source LLC
Jackson TN
JSHW020430200725
87812JS00002B/4